A RIVAL FOR RIVINGDON

THE LORDS OF BUCKNALL CLUB #3

J.A. ROCK

LISA HENRY

A Rival for Rivingdon

Copyright © 2021 by J.A. Rock and Lisa Henry.

All rights reserved.

No part of this book may be reproduced in any form or by any electronic or mechanical means, including information storage and retrieval systems, without written permission from the author, except for the use of brief quotations in a book review.

This is a work of fiction. Names, characters, businesses, places, events and incidents are either the products of the author's imagination or used in a fictitious manner. Any resemblance to any actual persons, living or dead, or actual events is purely coincidental.

Cover Art by Mitxeran.

ACKNOWLEDGMENTS

With thanks Bridget, who is invaluable.

ABOUT A RIVAL FOR RIVINGDON

He must marry well, to secure his fortune.

The Honourable Loftus Rivingdon is poised to make his debut into Society. He's beautiful, charming, and quite the catch of the Season. If only he could find the right *hat*. With the zealous assistance of his doting mother, Loftus has one ambition only: to meet and marry a wealthy peer. And Loftus knows just the peer—the dauntingly handsome, infinitely fashionable Viscount Soulden. Good thing there's nothing standing in his way.

He must *also* marry well, to secure his fortune.

The Honourable Morgan Notley is poised to make his debut into Society. He's beautiful, charming, and quite the catch of the Season. And he has just found the *perfect* hat. With the zealous assistance of his doting mother, Morgan has one ambition only: to meet and marry a wealthy peer. And Morgan knows just the peer—the dauntingly handsome, infinitely fashionable Viscount Soulden. Good thing there's nothing standing in his w—

Damn it all to hell.

Their ambitions collide.

When Loftus and Morgan both set their sights on Soulden, the rivalry of the Season begins. Their mutual hatred escalates into spite, sabotage, and scandal, as all of Society eagerly waits to see which diamond of the first water will prevail. Except the course of true loathing, just like true love, never did run smooth. The harder they try to destroy each other, the closer they come to uncovering each other's deepest vulnerabilities—and the more difficult it becomes to deny the burning attraction between them.

A Rival for Rivingdon *is the third book in the Lords of Bucknall Club series, where the Regency meets m/m romance. The Lords of Bucknall Club can be read in any order.*

CONTENTS

Chapter 1	1
Chapter 2	12
Chapter 3	19
Chapter 4	30
Chapter 5	42
Chapter 6	57
Chapter 7	81
Chapter 8	91
Chapter 9	101
Chapter 10	121
Chapter 11	137
Chapter 12	153
Chapter 13	164
Chapter 14	172
Chapter 15	183
Chapter 16	211
Afterword	221
About J.A. Rock	223
About Lisa Henry	225
Also by J.A. Rock and Lisa Henry	227
Also by J.A. Rock	229
Also by Lisa Henry	231

In 1783, the Marriage Act Amendment was introduced in England to allow marriages between same-sex couples. This was done to strengthen the law of primogeniture and to encourage childless unions in younger sons and daughters of the peerage, as an excess of lesser heirs might prove burdensome to a thinly spread inheritance.

CHAPTER 1

March 26, 1818. One week until the Season begins.

*L*oftus Rivingdon, third and youngest son of Baron Rivingdon, stood before his tailor's mirror and slowly lifted an ivory silk hat, trimmed with apple-green ribbon, in both hands. He placed it carefully atop his head and studied himself.

Behind him in the mirror, his mother, Lady Emmeline Rivingdon, watched, her hands clasped in anticipation. "Oh Loftus—" she began in a breathless whisper.

"I hate it," Loftus declared loudly.

Lady Rivingdon gasped. "Loftus! But you look simply stunning."

"This ribbon does not match my eyes!" Loftus whirled to face his mother. "I was promised a ribbon that would match my eyes!"

M. Verreau—"Clothier to the Nobility – Elegance to the Discerning Gentleman"—placed his hands on his hips. "That is the closest colour I could find." He spoke with a light French accent, and did not appear at all fazed by this crisis, which angered Loftus further. He wanted the fellow thoroughly fazed.

Loftus ripped the hat from his head and hurled it to the floor, then turned to the mirror once again. "I look terrible." He tugged his waistcoat. "I have no waist—look at this! Mother, these stays are not doing their job."

"You are thin as a spindle," M. Verreau said. "I do not know what you are worried about."

"Tighten them," Loftus ordered, hastily unbuttoning his waistcoat and tossing it to join the canary yellow coat he had removed earlier. He yanked the tails of his shirt from his trousers, then raised the shirt to reveal the short stays around his waist.

"Loftus!" His mother tittered and said, unconvincingly, "Manners." She glanced at Verreau. "My apologies. He's been a little highly-strung of late, anticipating the start of the Season."

"Yes, I recall from his fitting," the tailor said flatly. "Mr. Rivingdon, your stays are already tied more tightly than is at all good for the laces."

Loftus shot the man a glare as his mother began untying his stays.

"Here now, my Loftus," she said, pulling the laces as tight as she could. She grunted with the effort, and Loftus hissed in a breath, bracing himself against the wall as she yanked.

"Tighter, Mother," he insisted through gritted teeth.

"You need a smaller size." Verreau did not even raise his voice to be heard over the groaning and hissing. "As I have few gentlemen seeking stays, I am not sure I have anything smaller. But I can have something made. It will take roughly two weeks."

Loftus opened his mouth to denounce the fellow and his entire business. He knew Verreau prided himself on his innovative establishment, which sought to procure practically any garment or accessory a gentleman might require, from coats, to handkerchiefs, to pins, to hats. Why, there was a time not so many moments ago when Loftus had been quite impressed with the fellow. But two weeks was unacceptable! Two weeks from now was one week after Lord Balfour's ball—the opening event of the Season. He could hardly attend looking bloated as a cow!

But all that came out was a whimper as his lower ribs nearly cracked with his mother's efforts.

Just then, the bell on the door tinkled, and Loftus watched through the mirror as two figures intruded upon their privacy. A short, impossibly slim man stood by the door. He had thick, glossy chestnut curls and large, dark eyes that—if he'd had any idea how to use them to proper effect, which he clearly didn't—might have looked doelike and alluringly vulnerable. As it was, his face appeared shrewd, calculating. Loftus felt a surge of furious jealousy all the same, studying the reflection of his own deep-set eyes—no wonder the tailor had not noted their proper colour! They ought to be larger, their lashes darker. His lashes were practically white, and his silver-blond hair suddenly looked lank. Would he look better with thick, dark hair, like this stranger's? *Of course not*, he reassured himself. *You are a diamond of the first water. The society pages have said so.*

The stranger was accompanied by a woman who looked to be his older sister. She wore a dress of palest yellow and a matching shawl beaded in pink, topped off with a satin hat sprouting ostrich feathers. Her hair was as dark as her brother's, but worn in tight, shiny ringlets. She carried a glittering reticule, and poking out of it was the head of the smallest dog Loftus had ever seen, a little black-and-tan thing with the fur at the top of its head tied in a bow that matched the woman's dress. All of them—woman, man, and dog—stared at Loftus as his mother knotted the laces. "There!" Lady Rivingdon said in satisfaction, tugging Loftus's shirt down over the stays. "Is that better?"

Loftus could make no answer. He could also draw no breath. He turned slowly toward the front of the shop, his ribs grinding as he did. It was humiliating to have been seen by strangers in a state of half dress and with his mother lacing his stays. But he made no move to grab his waistcoat or coat. M. Verreau stepped away and greeted the new customers, and his mother seemed to realise she and Loftus were no longer alone in the shop. "Oh my!" Her voice, normally high-pitched and with a slightly scratchy quality, reached a note that only the dog in the reticule could properly hear on "my."

The new fellow wore a waistcoat of the deepest, most brilliant blue Loftus had ever seen. His coat was dark grey, the buttons ivory. His hat was satin and trimmed with a series of small, curled ribbons, his cream coloured cravat starched so aggressively that it looked rather as though it had been cast in plaster of Paris. He gripped a silver-handled cane. His face was small and smooth as a child's, but he carried himself like a gentleman.

Loftus loathed him at once.

"Mama," the man said, turning his head slightly toward the woman—not his sister, then!—while keeping his enormous eyes on Loftus. "I thought we were to have the shop to ourselves?" His voice was soft, low, and a bit raspy, caution in it as though he were trying not to startle wild animals. "You know I do not want anyone to see the styles I am choosing and copy them."

Oh-ho! Did this little weasel truly think himself such a paragon that anyone in the *world* would wish to copy his style? How pathetic!

"Apologies," the tailor said to them. "My previous appointment has gone over the allotted time."

Loftus clenched his jaw, yanking his shirt straight. "Mother, do you hear this? Is Monsieur Verreau suggesting that we are less important than—"

"I am suggesting," Verreau said firmly, "that your appointment was to finish at noon. And we are well past that."

Loftus's mother, who had been standing as if in a stupor, now swelled up. She spoke to the dark-haired woman, her high-pitched voice struggling for any semblance of dispassion. "Lady Notley."

"Lady Rivingdon," Lady Notley replied, her nostrils flaring.

"I don't believe you know my youngest son, Mr. Loftus Rivingdon. Loftus, this is Lady Cornelia Notley."

"How lovely to meet you, Mr. Rivingdon." The woman dipped her head toward Loftus. Her voice was nearly the same low, soft rasp as her son's. She did not sound as though she found their meeting lovely at all. "This is my younger son, Mr. Morgan Notley."

Loftus's mother offered Mr. Notley a stilted acknowledgement and then assured the Notleys that she and Loftus were just preparing to leave in search of a tailor who knew what he was about. "Get dressed, Loftus dear," she said, her cold gaze still on Lady Notley. Loftus turned, seething, to locate his waistcoat.

"Oh, Mama," Mr. Morgan Notley said. "Look at that hat on the floor, there. I should like that one."

"Anything you wish, dear," his mother replied.

Loftus burned with rage. He whirled back to face Notley. "You may not have it," he snapped. "I was just about to purchase it!"

Notley's cupid's bow of a mouth made a tiny O. "That is your hat? Forgive me, sir." He could not have sounded less sincere, and Loftus wanted very much to pummel him with his own silver-handled cane and then say, "Forgive me, sir," in that same unctuous tone.

Notley went on, "It is only that...its colour seems like it would draw out the yellow in your complexion in an unflattering way. Especially when paired with that very *bright* coat. And its ribbon does not even complement your eyes."

Loftus bit down on a furious retort. When in the hell had Mr. Morgan Notley had occasion to note the colour of his eyes?

"It looked well on me, I'll have you know." Loftus was aware that his voice was taking on the pitch of his mother's. "But this pitiful excuse for a tailor said that was the closest colour he could find for the ribbon. And it is much too light!"

"Loftus," his mother urged nervously. To Lady Notley she said, "My son has been rather excitable of late. He is to make his debut this Season, and we expect a great many suitors. What with *The Morning Chronicle* praising him so extensively."

"Ah, my son is debuting as well. And I rather think he has even more cause to be excitable than yours, as the Prince Regent himself has already said he looks forward to seeing Morgan at Lord Balfour's ball."

"Yes, with the amount of attention Loftus has already received, I would not be surprised if he has married a title by the time the Season is even underway."

Lady Notley's dog barked.

"Let's go, Mother," Loftus muttered, buttoning his coat and then yanking it straight.

"So you *do* wish to purchase the hat?" M. Verreau asked.

"No!" Loftus snapped. "I never wish to see such a hideous hat again." He was going to go elsewhere and buy a hat with trimmings that matched his eyes perfectly, and when Mr. Morgan Notley saw him at Lord Balfour's ball, Notley would be the one sick with envy.

"Well, I should say you wouldn't purchase it." Morgan Notley strode forward with a confidence that hardly matched his small frame and soft voice. "Let me see." His face was suddenly inches from Loftus's, and Loftus froze with the shock of their proximity. Notley's skin was truly as smooth as a babe's, so pale that Loftus could see thin blue veins at his temples. And the lashes on those large eyes seemed to brush his cheeks when he blinked. His gaze searched Loftus's with such intensity and concentration that Loftus was momentarily confused. Until Notley announced, "It is not simply that the shade is too light. It is the wrong hue altogether. You need something deeper, with more blue in it. The green of your eyes is more forest than pear."

He stepped back, and Loftus realised he had not breathed the entire time Notley had been studying his eyes. He exhaled, and for a moment he and Notley stared at each other without speaking. A strange sensation twisted Loftus's stomach. Then he clenched his jaw again. "Worry about your own hats, and please, spare me your misguided opinions," he said tightly. "You clearly know nothing of fashion. Your buttons are garish." He brushed past the Notleys, heading for the door.

Before he could reach it, it opened, and in walked the most beautiful gentleman Loftus had ever seen. He was tall and lovely, with a figure so well-made that Loftus imagined the proportions of a Greek statue underneath his clothing. Well, perhaps not *all* his proportions, as Loftus's studies of both himself and, furtively, his brothers and schoolmates, had made him believe that the sculptors of antiquity hadn't been very generous when it came to certain parts of the anatomy. But he was sure that this gentleman had the chest and shoulders and thighs of a Greek statue. He certainly had the visage: heavily-lidded eyes, a noble nose, a strong jawline, and lips that looked both plush and enticing. His dark curls, when he took off his hat, were brushed forward onto his forehead in quite the epitome of fashion, and his clothes—tall boots made of shiny, supple leather, impeccable eggshell pantaloons, a cravat that bloomed from the collar of his Prussian blue tailcoat, and a visible sliver of a dove-grey waistcoat underneath—fit him perfectly.

"Viscount Soulden!" M. Verreau exclaimed. "What a delight, my lord!"

Loftus gasped. A viscount!

From the other side of the shop, Morgan Notley turned his head to stare at Lord Soulden like an owl that had just spotted a mouse.

"Good day, Monsieur Verreau," Soulden said. "I apologise for bursting in like this, but I find myself in sudden need of a new coat."

"But of course!" M. Verreau said, fluttering around the viscount like a butterfly. "It would be my pleasure, my lord!"

It would be anyone's pleasure, Loftus thought breathlessly, to run their hands over Lord Soulden in a state of half undress. Almost unconsciously, he took a step towards the viscount.

And his mother, perhaps seeing the way his thoughts were leading him, snatched up the hat, caught him firmly by the arm, and tugged him outside into the street. The door swung shut behind them.

Leaving—Loftus gasped in outrage at the awful realisation—Lord Soulden with Morgan Notley.

~

In the afternoon, Morgan Notley attended Warrington House in St. James's Square. He still felt a little breathless after his encounter in the tailor's shop. He had never before understood what all that swooning business was in the book he read in secret at night, but after seeing Lord Soulden today, he was beginning to understand that dizzying sensation of being so entirely overwhelmed that one's body simply collapsed. Morgan was only on Chapter Two of *The Maiden Diaries*, and from what he'd heard he had a lot more to anticipate than swooning, but if the rest of the sensations were half as thrilling, he very much looked forward to them.

He was admitted to the house by a footman and left his hat and gloves in the man's care. Then he hurried along to the small but cosy library.

"Uncle Francis!" he exclaimed in delight.

Francis, Earl Warrington, started, spilled ink all over his blotter, and swore as he dabbed it up with his handkerchief. "Ah, Morgan," he said. "The...the children are out, I think." He brightened. "Though Clarence is about somewhere, I expect."

Morgan laughed and sat himself down at his uncle's desk. How silly to think that Morgan might want to speak with Cousin Clarence. Clarence was three. "I like visiting with you, Uncle Francis."

Earl Warrington blinked down at the puddle of ink now seeping through his handkerchief. "Is it...is it about buttons again?"

Morgan gasped. "Do you know, the most abominably rude fellow told me today that my buttons were garish. *Garish!*"

"Oh dear," Earl Warrington said softly.

"As though I should even listen to a word he said! He couldn't even choose a ribbon that matched his eyes!"

"Ah."

"You don't think my buttons are garish, do you?" Morgan asked. "They're ivory."

"They're very nice."

"Thank you, Uncle Francis!" Morgan hadn't realised how tense he'd been with worry until his uncle's reassurance, and he sighed and relaxed, leaning back in his chair. "It's only a week until the first ball of the Season, and it's of vital importance that I don't begin to doubt myself now. Everyone is saying that I am the catch of the Season, you know."

"Yes." Earl Warrington's eyelid twitched. "I believe you have mentioned it before."

"You know, Warry ought to come with me next time I go shopping. He pays so little attention to his wardrobe, and is always reading *books*. And Becca–" He cut himself off. Becca was *twenty-three*, and not married yet, which was scandalous. Not scandalous in a thrilling and fun way, but in the sort of way where people were beginning to whisper that there was something *wrong*. It was the type of thing that could taint an entire family's reputation, so it was Morgan's dearest wish that someone—anyone—asked her to marry them this Season. "Well, I'm sure that this year Becca will find a suitor! She's still quite pretty, after all."

"She's twenty-three, Morgan, not eighty-three."

"Oh, yes," Morgan agreed hastily, making a mental note to report back to his mother that she was right: Uncle Francis was far too indulgent of Becca's eccentricities—like not actively seeking a spouse at every opportunity. Morgan's mother was Uncle Francis's sister, and she quietly despaired of him. Morgan could see why. Uncle Francis didn't seem to care that Becca was still unwed, and he was barely even interested in buttons or ribbon! Still, Morgan loved him for all his faults. "Will you be going to Balfour's ball, sir?"

"I expect so." Uncle Francis sighed, as if it were a great imposition. "Have you learned all your dance steps yet?"

Morgan gasped. "Certainly! I have been practicing my whole life for my debut into Society!"

"Of course you have."

"I expect everyone shall want to dance with me." Morgan chewed his lip for a moment. "Uncle Francis, do you know Lord Soulden?"

Uncle Francis sighed, and stared at the ceiling for a moment. "Soulden? Oh, yes. That'd be Philip Winthrop, heir to the Earl of Grantham. I think young Hartwell knows him quite well from that club he goes to."

"Bucknall's?" Morgan asked sharply.

"That's the one. Hartwell's a decent fellow. He's sponsoring Warry to join the club, actually."

The cogs in Morgan's brain whirred. "If Warry joins, then he could sponsor *me*."

"Why d'you want to join Bucknall's?" Uncle Francis asked. "Hasn't your father got you into White's yet?"

"Yes, of course. But Soulden doesn't go to White's."

"Ah." Uncle Francis sighed.

Morgan sat up straighter. "And do you know Mr. Loftus Rivingdon?"

"Rivingdon," Uncle Francis mused. "Well, I know Baron Rivingdon. I expect Loftus is one of his sons, is he? I don't know him though."

"No, he hasn't made his debut yet," Morgan said. "He's dreadful. He's the one who said my buttons were garish."

Uncle Francis pinched the bridge of his nose.

"I expect he and I shall be rivals. I already detest him."

"Of course you do."

"My buttons are *not* garish!"

Uncle Francis blinked at him. "Of course they're not."

Morgan fingered his buttons worriedly, and bit his bottom lip. "You don't think they're too plain, do you?"

"What? No." Whatever else Uncle Francis might have been about to say was interrupted by someone rudely shoving the door open and stomping inside. It was Clarence, trailing his leading strings like a horse trailed its reins after tossing its rider. "Ah! Clarence, my fellow!"

Clarence beamed at Morgan and then reached out to him and tried to grip the edge of his tailcoat with his perpetually sticky fingers. Morgan leapt to his feet in horror, backing away from the little menace.

"I think I shall see if Aunt Caroline is in!" he exclaimed, hurrying from the room.

"Good boy," he thought he heard Uncle Francis murmur fervently behind him. "Excellently done, Clarence!"

Well, that couldn't have been right, since Clarence had rudely interrupted their conversation. But Morgan thrust that thought behind him and set off into the house to locate his aunt, who, even though she didn't care at all as much about ribbons and buttons as a woman of her status ought to, was sure to have something wonderfully cutting to say about Loftus Rivingdon's nose.

CHAPTER 2

Loftus winced as his mother tugged the bristles of the brush through his hair, catching a tangle. He knew better than to complain. He caught his mother's face in the mirror and her pursed lips warned him of the mood she was in. She wasn't angry at him, he knew—Loftus was her favourite child, without question—but she *was* angry, and he suspected it was for exactly the same reason he was.

Morgan Notley.

Morgan Notley and his unfairly glossy dark hair, and his perfect Cupid's bow of a mouth, his waist that was so beautifully slender, and the glorious fit of his snug trousers.

This Season was supposed to be Loftus's Season. Mama had been training him for it his entire life. He was supposed to dazzle, with both his beauty and his wit, and snare himself a rich and titled husband or wife, and marry well. Although, anyone could marry well. Loftus was expected to marry *spectacularly*. The problem was that he was the third son of a baron, and a baron was the lowest rank of the peerage. Mama wanted Loftus to marry better than she had, and they were both afraid his pedigree might not be enough to do it, especially nowadays when so many members of the *ton* were looking greedily towards the sons and daughters of wealthy men of commerce to marry. Loftus had a pedigree, but he certainly didn't have twenty thousand pounds a year like Miss Genevieve Sherwood, whose father was something to do with cotton mills, had. In a just and proper world, Loftus shouldn't have had to compete with the children of *tradesmen*, but the world, as Mama liked to remind him, was neither just nor proper.

Hence the existence of Mr. Morgan Notley.

It was bad enough that Loftus had to compete with commoners whose wealth eclipsed his own. But Mama had told him that his beauty was singular, that he would stand out like a porcelain figurine surrounded by plain corn dollies. Yet Morgan Notley was beautiful too, wasn't he? And he was the son of a viscount, damn him, not a mere baron. It was sickeningly unfair.

Loftus gazed at his new hat sitting on a stand on his dresser. He could scarcely imagine wearing it in public after the comments Notley had made. He leaned against the curved back of the chaise longue, his legs tucked up beside him, trying not to wince as his mother scraped the brush roughly against his scalp.

"The Prince Regent has expressed eagerness to meet him. Who on earth would be eager to meet him, Mother? Who? He's awful."

She did not ask of whom he spoke. She knew. "I know, darling. I can't imagine Prinny would be much impressed upon meeting him, but he does have the sort of eyes that might fool anyone—even royalty!—at first encounter."

"That's what I'm afraid of. His eyes are very large."

"Too large, I would argue."

"Yes, too large."

"I pity whoever has the misfortune to marry him. Sometimes, as in your case, Loftus, outer beauty speaks of a soul to match. And sometimes, it is a trap."

"As in Notley's case?"

"As in Notley's case," his mother confirmed.

"What should I do? You see, I have already decided I shall marry Lord Soulden—"

"Lord Soulden!" His mother gave a brief, sharp squeak.

He hesitated. "You do not think him a good choice?"

"I think him an excellent choice. Oh, a *most* excellent choice."

There was a 'but,' Loftus could sense it. And yet his mother did not continue. Loftus's stomach stirred uneasily. "You do not think I can charm him?"

"Oh *course* you can charm him. And you will!" Her voice took on that dog-whistle note whenever she was not being wholly truthful. Such a coldness he felt in himself then. Why had his mother spent so long assuring him that he was the *most* beautiful, the *most* charming man in all of London, if she did not think him capable of winning the viscount's favour?

She scraped his scalp quite harshly with the bristles, and he hissed.

"But you saw how Mr. Notley looked at him," he said.

"I saw how the viscount seemed to look right through Mr. Notley as though he were not even there. While his gaze lingered on *you*."

"You don't mean that." Loftus was feeling very fragile indeed. He thought of a butterfly he'd once seen, clinging weakly to the trunk of a tree—its butter-yellow wings paled by the sun and giving occasional, half-hearted flicks of movement. He understood that creature's pain.

"I would not lie to you, darling." His mother sounded wounded.

"Perhaps he only looked at me because of my bulging waist."

"My dear, you are but a slip of a thing."

"Mr. Notley is a slip of a thing. He said I have yellow in my complexion, do you remember? I am as pale as china, am I not?"

"Of course," his mother murmured, setting the brush aside and coming to sit at the end of the recamier. He had to move his feet, which left him very little room to sprawl languidly. Sprawling languidly was one of his favourite activities. That and pushing his dish of pudding aside after two bites and saying, *"I couldn't possibly."* "He was only trying to bring you low because he knows his own inferiority. It was an act of jealousy, no more."

"But what if the Prince Regent *does* like him?" He didn't add that he himself had been momentarily transfixed by Mr. Notley's beauty, and by the confidence with which Notley had assessed his eye colour. What if Notley told the Prince Regent what colour ribbon would best match his coat, and Prinny was charmed and took Notley on as his personal wardrobe consultant?

No. If Notley possessed that sort of audacity, Prinny would no doubt be offended by it, and perhaps would order Notley hanged. Now there was a satisfying thought.

His mother put a hand on his ankle. He tried to shake her off petulantly, but he had not even the energy for petulance, and so was forced to let her hand remain. "You shall shine more brightly this Season than the Morgan Notleys of this world could even imagine. You are the very light of my life—beautiful inside and out."

His anxiety quelled slightly at the familiar praise.

"Your father's beauty—now that was a veneer, wasn't it?"

He tensed. He did not always enjoy this part of the script.

He glanced at her small hand clasped over the cuff of his narrow, high-waisted trousers, which were just the style Brummell had brought into fashion.

He didn't answer.

"I fell for that beauty, and he has proven false every day since we were wed. Oh, I'd have written off my own life as a lost cause long ago were it not for you, darling. I know how proud you'll make me this year."

Loftus's throat tightened. He did not much care for his father's company, for the man could be terribly cruel, and his poor decisions had run the family into the ground. But his mother spoke *so* often about her unhappy marriage. Sometimes he rather wished she wouldn't. Loftus had learned the lesson well: marrying for love got you nowhere. Marrying a title—now wouldn't *that* turn the tide of his family's fortune?

He hated to think of his mother's disappointment should he fail. But he would not fail.

He might not have found the perfect hat just yet, but he had excellent trousers, and he was beautiful inside and out, and—

Lord Soulden wore pantaloons. That thought was on him suddenly. Perhaps Soulden thought pantaloons superior to trousers. Perhaps Soulden was so busy living a gentleman's life— which Loftus imagined including a lot of shooting and steeple-chasing and talking loudly about Napoleon—that he did not yet know how superior trousers were. Perhaps, at Lord Balfour's ball, Soulden and Loftus would have occasion to speak, and Loftus would enlighten him. Perhaps Soulden would be so grateful that he would invite Loftus to accompany him to Bucknall's afterward, and when Loftus admitted he did not have a sponsor yet, Soulden would assure him it was as good as taken care of, and they would drink port together and talk loudly of Napoleon.

His mother patted his ankle again, bringing him back to reality. "But just in *case*..." she said, and his stomach twisted once more. For she sometimes would do this: speak of how perfect he was in every way, express the utmost confidence that he would achieve whatever he set his mind to, and then say, "But just in case..."

"*Oh darling, I am certain you will keep your lovely figure over the winter and arrive in London as svelte as ever. But just in case...*" And she'd presented him with the stays that now gripped his midsection so tightly he felt queasy.

"Just in case what?" he mumbled.

"Just in case Mr. Notley should use his false beauty to his advantage, it never hurts, dear, to think about ways you might *ensure* you take centre stage when the Season begins."

"Ensure? You mean...buy another hat?"

"Well, no, dear, not precisely. Sometimes, in order for us to shine, we must first dull what shines around us."

"Buy some new neckcloths," he said confidently.

"I think we can go farther than that."

"Get a nicer...horse?" His grey gelding was a fine animal, but getting a bit long in the tooth. He'd asked for a new one last year and been told they could not manage the expense. But perhaps his mother had changed her mind?

"Loftus." She let out a long breath. "Imagine how difficult it would be for Morgan Notley to command the Prince Regent's attention were he to, say, twist an ankle. Or bruise his ribs."

Loftus frowned. "But mother, how would he do that?"

"I don't know, dear. Minor misfortunes befall people all the time. I should think it would be quite easy to trip during a promenade, or to be thrown, were one's horse to spook."

Loftus was growing more confused by the second. "But Mr. Notley is grace itself." He had not meant for that to come out. Mr. Notley was a blight on society. A beautiful blight with excellent taste in waistcoats, but a blight nonetheless.

She laughed lightly. "Ah, well, even grace itself might tumble if you kick it in the shin hard enough during a turn about Hyde Park."

Loftus stared at her, not sure whether he was comprehending, but very afraid that he was. "Are you suggesting that I hurt him?"

"No! No, Loftus, of course not. Goodness, no. I am suggesting that you invite him for a walk—or a ride—in the park as a way of solidifying your new acquaintanceship and perhaps apologising for what you said about his buttons."

"They *were* garish."

"Be that as it may, you were not your usual charming self to him. And so, to smooth things over, you might visit the park in his company."

"And hope that he twists an ankle? I do not think he will."

"Many things can happen when two gentlemen, made boisterous by the esprit of youth, take the air together. A walking stick might be carelessly thrust into one's path. An elbow might accidentally jab ribs. One gentleman might clap the other on the back so heartily it sends the fellow sprawling...one simply never knows."

"So you...*are* suggesting I hurt him?"

His mother made a sound that implied she was nearing the end of her patience, and her speech grew clipped. "I am suggesting, my sweet, that you invite him out with you, and if you happen to knock into him quite forcefully as you point out a pair of stunningly matched bays or trip him with your walking stick out of sheer clumsiness, and the resulting injury makes it difficult for him to dance, then yes it would be a tragedy, but perhaps one with a silver lining."

"Oh." His mother wished him to do physical harm to Morgan Notley. He did not know why the idea sent such a flutter of panic through him. Had he not moments ago fantasised about seeing the fellow hanged? It was just that the idea of having to get his own hands dirty was so unpleasant.

But he thought again of Morgan Notley's over-large eyes and his slim waist and impeccable coat with buttons that Loftus could not stop thinking about. They were not garish, they were perfect. Elegant but not showy. Morgan Notley was perfect, and if Loftus did not do something to mar that perfection, just a little bit, then Morgan Notley would steal Lord Soulden from him. And there would go Loftus's title, the family fortune, and his mother's affection for him.

He swallowed hard. "I shall invite him for a walk tomorrow to make amends." He attempted to wink, but he'd never quite got the hang of closing one eye at a time, and so he ended up simply blinking.

His mother's smile shone bright, and he felt a soul-deep relief knowing he'd pleased her. "My dear Loftus, I think that is an *excellent* idea."

CHAPTER 3

The sun was already high in the sky when Morgan drifted down the stairs in a cloud of orange blossom scented toilet water. He could hear Mama in the drawing room, although he could not make out any of her words from the bottom of the stairs, only the hiss of the more sibilant sounds of her speech. It reminded him of the susurration of the waves at the beach at their home in Norfolk, and for a moment Morgan felt a hollow sensation in his stomach that seemed a little like homesickness. He drew a deep breath and vanquished the feeling. It was silly to think of the family estate outside of Sheringham with anything but a kind of gentle nostalgia, and certainly not with *longing*. Morgan was about to make his debut into Society. By the end of the Season he intended to be the spouse of a wealthy and titled lord or lady. He was primed to accept only the finest things that the world could offer him, and he would *not* pine for the Norfolk seashore when he was so close to being the envy of every other debutante this Season. He wasn't just beautiful, he was *perfect*, and he only had to turn the head of Lord Soulden to win his heart. Mama had promised him.

Morgan heard laughter from the drawing room, more a horse-like whinny than any sound a human ought to make, and recognised it as belonging to Lady Darnley. She had a horse-like face to match her laugh, and Morgan felt frail enough this morning after his night of disturbed sleep—his buttons were *not* garish!—and his momentary encounter with homesickness that he couldn't bear the thought of her company. So he avoided the drawing room and went to the parlour instead to see if there was breakfast waiting for him.

Breakfast was indeed waiting. So, unfortunately, was Morgan's brother Cecil, whose nose twitched when Morgan entered the room.

"What's that smell?" Cecil sniffed loudly.

"It's orange blossom toilet water," Morgan said. "It's from Mr. Floris's shop on Jermyn Street."

"You smell like an upturned fruit cart." Cecil laughed.

Morgan sat, arranging his limbs in a pleasing manner, and selected a seed cake to nibble on. "What are you doing here, Cecil? Father doesn't arrive until tomorrow."

"Yes, I know." Cecil looked surprised. "I'm here to see you, you silly thing."

Morgan wrinkled his nose. "Really?"

"Of course." The look of surprise deepened across Cecil's dull, flat face, and Morgan felt a jab of guilt.

He and Cecil had very little in common except their parentage. Cecil, four years older than Morgan, had inherited not only their father's unfortunately bovine features, he'd also inherited his graceless pragmatism, which on more than one occasion had tipped over the edge into downright rudeness. Cecil didn't like books, or plays, or art, or anything even slightly rarefied, and he'd once been beaten at school for saying "Ballocks!" in the middle of the Nativity play, when he'd been dressed as an angel and was supposed to have said "Hark!" instead. The whipping, Morgan privately felt, hadn't much improved him.

"Harriet said I ought to make more of an effort," Cecil continued, unabashed, "so I thought I'd come around and see if you wanted to go to the club with me."

Morgan blinked. "White's, do you mean?"

"No, actually. I'm rather avoiding White's at the moment. Do you remember Finchley from school? The elder one?"

"Yes, I think so. He was quite beastly."

"He was an *arse*," Cecil said, and rolled his eyes. "Still is, which is why I'm avoiding White's. I've been going to Bucknall's instead."

Morgan was almost overcome by a rush of delight. "I had no idea you were a member of Bucknall's!"

It seemed he wouldn't have to ask Hartwell to get him in after all, if his brother could do it instead! And to think Morgan had spent his entire life believing he and Cecil had nothing in common! Why, membership of the Bucknall Club was just the sort of thing that might soften the rather cold feelings between them into something close to fraternal affection. Perhaps Cecil might even listen to Morgan's suggestions about his wardrobe, his coarse manners, and the way he wore his hair. He wasn't a handsome man at all, but a proper haircut could, Morgan supposed, possibly take the edge off his ugliness.

"Yes." Cecil leaned back in his chair, and the buttons on his waistcoat strained against his paunch. "For several months now."

"That would be delightful. How is Mrs. Notley?"

"Harriet? She's as big as a house!" Cecil said, beaming broadly.

"Oh, Cecil, you mustn't say such things!" Morgan exclaimed. "Even if they are true!"

"Well, it is true. She's due any day now." For the first time in the conversation, a faint hint of a shadow crossed his face. "I think she sent me here to keep me from fussing."

Morgan blinked. He couldn't imagine his boorish older brother fussing over anyone. He rather thought it would be like watching an ogre try to use a porcelain tea cup: initially amusing, but ultimately doomed to failure. Still, he could understand Cecil's worry, as so much could go wrong in bringing a baby into the world. And he did seem to genuinely love Harriet, even though she was plain, and had a distracting mole on the bridge of her nose, and her father was horribly middle class and owned a cotton mill in Lancashire.

Mama hadn't been pleased about *that* at all. Cecil's marriage, which Father had arranged, had made her more determined that Morgan would marry well. Mama was the daughter and the sister of an earl. She was the wife of a viscount. She ought not to have to share an occasional dining table with a cotton mill owner from Lancashire.

"I shall have to change if we are going to Bucknall's," he said thoughtfully.

It was Cecil's turn to blink. "What for? You look fine."

"I look fine for spending the day inside the house," Morgan corrected him. "But how on earth do you expect me to walk into Bucknall's wearing a *morning coat*?" He laughed at Cecil's confusion. "Oh, my dearest brother, I must wear a tailcoat. I have the most wonderful new tailcoat from M. Verreau. It's, well, I should hesitate to call it maroon. It's more vermilion. It's quite exquisite. Oh! And I shall need my new Hessian boots."

Cecil stared.

Morgan reached for another seed cake, and then remembered how narrow and willowy Loftus Rivingdon had appeared at Verreau's. He put the seed cake back on the plate regretfully. "Do you know, I have seen a picture of the most marvellous skirted frock coat. M. Verreau says that the Parisians will be wearing them by the end of this Season. I wanted to order one immediately, but Mama is afraid they are a little too shocking. She says that it's important to have the latest fashions, but one must be careful not to step too far ahead, you see, or you may find yourself quite alone, and the subject of ridicule. She says I must wait until I know for certain that they are wearing them in Paris, and then she will support me wholeheartedly in having one made. She frets, which is terribly sweet of her."

Cecil made a grunting sound that Morgan decided passed as

agreement, although it wasn't as enthusiastic as he would have liked. Sometimes he thought that he and Mama were the only people in the world who knew how important the cut of a coat was, or the placement and number and design of the buttons that adorned it. And Morgan shuddered to think how indifferent most people were to clocked stockings. Then he thought of Loftus Rivingdon, and while he obviously detested him with every fibre of his being, Morgan thought that at the very least the fellow knew fashion. He did not know as much as Morgan, if he'd thought to buy an ivory hat with his skin tone *and* dared call Morgan's buttons garish, but he was certainly doing his best, which was more than Morgan could say for almost everyone else of his acquaintance.

Morgan looked at the seed cake again and ignored his grumbling stomach. He smiled brightly. "Well, I shall go and dress, and then we will go to Bucknall's!"

"Yes," Cecil said. He looked at Morgan, and then down at the seed cake, and then at Morgan again. "Are you going to eat that?"

"I am quite full," Morgan lied.

Cecil shrugged, and picked up the seed cake and shoved it in his mouth.

Morgan should have been appalled at his manners, but instead he was grateful for having had the temptation removed. First an invitation to Bucknall's, and now seed cake temptation removal? Cecil was proving a better brother than Morgan had ever known him be, even though it was entirely accidental on his part.

It was, Morgan decided, a sign that even better fortune awaited him!

～

*M*ama caught them just as they were about to leave.

"Morgan, darling!" she exclaimed. "Where are you going?"

"Cecil is taking me to Bucknall's," Morgan replied.

Mama's faint look of disapproval vanished immediately, and her face lit up with delight. "Oh, how wonderful! What an excellent idea of your brother's!"

"I'm right here," Cecil said dourly.

"Yes, Cecil," Mama said, fussing over Morgan's velvet cuffs. And quite rightly too, because he had put his coat on without assistance and disturbed the nap of the velvet. Mama smoothed it back into place. "Oh, darling, you are a vision! But before you go..." She reached into her sleeve and produced an envelope. "You have received a letter. From Mr. Loftus Rivingdon."

Mama's eyes were as wide as an owl's, and Morgan suspected his were too. He took the envelope and opened it, drawing out the letter. He read it and gasped.

"What is it?" Mama asked, clasping her hands at her breast.

"Mr. Rivingdon wonders if I would like to join him this afternoon for a walk," Morgan said. "A *walk*!" He blinked rapidly. "I do not understand. He was very cruel about my buttons."

Mama narrowed her eyes. "Yes, he was."

"I cannot think!" Morgan exclaimed. He fanned himself with the letter. "What does it *mean*?"

Cecil cleared his throat. "Perhaps if he was cruel, he wishes to apologise?"

Mama laughed, the sound short and sharp. "Cecil, don't be ridiculous."

"There is certainly something afoot," Morgan said. "But what can it be?"

"I'm going to get a cab." Cecil started for the door. "Morgan, if you're coming, hurry up."

He stomped outside.

"He gets his manners from your father," Mama said.

"So rude," Morgan agreed. "But, Mama! The letter! What do you make of it?" His mind spun like a whirligig. "Surely it cannot be an overture of a romantic nature?"

Mama gasped. "Certainly not! That would be most improper! Even," she added ominously, "for a son of Emmeline Rivingdon!"

Morgan felt a thrill at Mama's unusual forthcomingness, and at the promise of a history of animosity between Mama and Lady Rivingdon. He had to know everything, at once! Although—he glanced at the door, which the footman was holding open patiently—Bucknall's was waiting, and even sweeter than the thought of running into Lord Soulden again was the thought of running into Lord Soulden and later bragging to Loftus Rivingdon about it on their walk.

"I shall go," he decided.

"You must be properly chaperoned!"

"Of course, Mama!" Morgan knew from his close readings of *The Maiden Diaries* that the only thing preventing him from becoming a victim of shocking yet apparently enjoyable depravity was the presence of an eagle-eyed chaperone, and possibly not even then! Certainly Slyfeel, the villain of *The Maiden Diaries*—or perhaps the hero, Morgan wasn't entirely sure—didn't seem to have much trouble separating naïve virgins from their guardians. "I shall ask Cecil to accompany me, or, if he is busy, perhaps Becca and Warry. I would never meet with him alone!"

Mama pinched his cheeks to bring more colour into them. "I know, darling. You have worked too hard to stumble now."

Morgan nodded and drew a deep breath. "Will you send a reply to Mr. Rivingdon on my account? Tell him I shall be pleased to meet him this afternoon."

Mama stared at him intently. "Do be careful, my darling."

"Of course. Mama, you know I will be." He glanced at the door again. "But I must go!"

He hastened outside to find Cecil already sitting inside a cab. The cab driver paid Morgan no attention and he hurried towards the vehicle where the horse snorted and stamped impatiently.

Morgan climbed up into the cab and flung himself into the seat beside Cecil. He discovered he was still holding Loftus's letter and flapped it to shift the still, warm air around. The cab started with a jolt and a lurch, and Morgan folded the letter as flat as he could and slipped it into his inside pocket. He hoped it wouldn't crumple and ruin the line of his coat.

Morgan's thoughts raced, and he drew deep breaths to calm himself. Whatever Loftus Rivingdon was playing at, Morgan couldn't allow it to distract him now. He didn't dare walk into Bucknall's looking either too flushed or too pale, not when Lord Soulden might see him there. If he was to have the opportunity to catch Soulden's eye before his official debut, he didn't want to ruin the encounter by having a less than perfect complexion. Good Lord. What if he was so anxious that he flushed, and Soulden mistook the flush for lack of composure? No, Morgan had to collect himself before arriving at Bucknall's.

He continued to breathe deeply and evenly, ignoring Cecil's strange looks at the cab rattled along the streets.

The Bucknall Club was on Pall Mall. It was a grand, rather ornate building that wouldn't have looked out of place in Renaissance Florence or Rome. A boy darted forward and opened the cab door as they pulled up, and a footman waited on the wide steps to usher them inside. Cecil stomped through the doors, the heels of his boots clicking on marble. Morgan glided after him, his chin held high and his expression, he hoped, calm and a little distant. He practised that expression a lot. Mama said it was important to appear slightly indifferent; after all, the flowers did not chase the bees. Still, despite his apparent disinterest, Morgan was very much aware of the looks he attracted as he walked through the club. Heads turned when Morgan Notley stepped into a place, and had done since he was a ringleted cherub of a toddler. There was a lot more heat in the gazes he attracted nowadays, and, thankfully, a lot less cooing and cheek pinching.

Morgan walked with Cecil up a grand staircase, his gaze sliding over the columns and statues and artwork that adorned the club. What a balm this place was after the noisy streets outside! It was quiet in here, apart from the occasional burst of distant laughter, and the sounds of muted conversations that drifted out of dark-panelled doorways.

"This is the Blue Room," Cecil said as they approached a door.

Morgan followed him in.

The Blue Room was a beautifully decorated space. The paper hangings, Morgan supposed, gave it its name. Large windows, draped with lush, heavy curtains, let the sunlight in. A fireplace dominated one wall. Bookshelves, the books all bound in dark, rich leather, dominated the wall opposite. All around the room, chairs were clustered around small tables. Men sat and smoked and drank. Morgan glimpsed a game of cards in progress. A gentleman perused a news sheet as he reclined in a comfortable chair, his polished boots resting on a cushioned footstool.

And over by one of the windows—Morgan caught himself before he gasped—sat Lord Soulden with a group of other men. Morgan had recently begun to consider gasping less. There was much to be startled by in the world, but on Cecil's last visit he had joked that Morgan sounded like his maid whenever she attempted stairs, and it was a challenge to forget such a cutting comment.

Soulden was glorious, like a painting of Alexander or some other ancient hero. Had he fought the French at Waterloo? Morgan would need to find out. He certainly would have looked stunning in a red uniform decorated with gold braid and shining brass buttons. He had such aristocratic features—*real* aristocratic features, and not the large ears and lack of chin that unfortunately plagued much of the *ton*.

One of the men in Soulden's group noticed them and rose from his chair. He was the second type of aristocrat, but he had a very friendly smile, so Morgan tried not to hold it against him.

"Notley!" he exclaimed.

Cecil moved forward to shake his hand. "Crauford," he said warmly. How are you?"

"Oh, well, well." Crauford nodded, and his already diminished chin was swallowed entirely by his neckcloth. "And this must be your brother, eh?"

"Yes," Cecil said shortly.

Morgan bowed slightly to Crauford. "It is a delight to make your acquaintance, sir."

Crauford blinked at him. "Good lord. Your manners are exquisite. Almost as exquisite as your—"

Cecil made a sound like a displeased mastiff, and Crauford snapped his mouth shut.

"Join us for a drink, Notley?" he asked. "And Notley Minor, of course."

The thrum of anticipation that ran through Morgan was curtailed by Cecil's gruff, "Not today, Crauford, thank you."

He slung a beefy arm around Morgan's shoulders and steered him to the other side of the room. Morgan sat where Cecil indicated, disappointed.

Cecil dropped into the seat beside his and narrowed his eyes at Soulden and the group of men with him. "Bloody rakes, the lot of them. What a nerve!"

Morgan peered hopefully at Soulden, but the man was deep in conversation and didn't spare him a glance. "We could certainly have had a drink with them, I think."

Cecil huffed, but his glower softened. "They're not a bad bunch," he said at last, "but you're too pretty, and that lot would be over you like ticks on a dog's arse."

Morgan grimaced at that particularly vivid image. "But, Cecil, I'm supposed to be meeting people. It's my debut!" He lowered his voice. "Is Lord Soulden *terrible*?"

"He's a fop," Cecil said. He raised his eyebrows as though the thought had just struck him. "You'd probably like him a lot."

"Yes," Morgan said eagerly, "that's—"

"I don't think Mother would appreciate it very much if I brought you to Bucknall's and let you get pawed." Cecil sat up straighter as a footman approached to take their drinks order. "Ah, yes! Two sherries."

Morgan sighed, leaning back in his chair. He certainly had no intention of being pawed, but if Cecil thought Mama would prefer him sitting in a corner where hardly anyone could see him, he really didn't know her very well at all.

He sipped his sherry when it arrived, stole glances at Lord Soulden, and comforted himself with the idea that even though he hadn't exchanged a single word with the fellow, Loftus Rivingdon didn't know that, did he?

CHAPTER 4

Mr. Notley was such a wisp of a man that Loftus nearly missed spotting him near the north-west enclosure of the park, surrounded as he was by a small group of—friends? Admirers? Loftus immediately wished he'd worn his stays tighter. They were nearly crushing his ribs as things stood, and yet the sight of Morgan Notley made him fret about the figure he cut.

He walked over determinedly, trying not to imagine what Notley would think of him, his figure, or his clothing.

As Loftus drew near, Notley was laughing at something one of the young ladies had said. His laughter died when he spied Loftus, replaced by a tight-lipped smirk Loftus didn't care for at all. "Ah, Mr. Rivingdon." Notley bowed with practised ease, as graceful as the swans that glided across the nearby pond. "Good day."

"Good day, Mr. Notley." Loftus was aware that his own bow was a bit stiff. He was introduced to the gaggle around Notley, but a second later he couldn't recall a single name besides that of Notley's cousin, Lady Rebecca Warrington. He would have to do better at Lord Balfour's ball. His mother had taught him a trick for remembering names that involved coming up with a rhyming word for each one, but he was too distracted by Notley to even attempt that now. This walk had been a terrible idea. His mother's ideas were usually sound, but this… He hated Morgan Notley with an intensity quite equal to his adoration for Lord Soulden. He did not wish to feign interest in the man's company, not even to sabotage him.

Mr. Notley wore pantaloons of palest pink—was it possible that the *ton* really did prefer pantaloons to trousers for daywear? That Brummell had been a fashionable fellow, if a bit understated for Loftus's taste, but then he had got into all that nasty gambling business and had fled to France. Perhaps Loftus should not endeavour to emulate such a man?

He continued his assessment of Morgan Notley's dress. The man's waistcoat was striped pale yellow and white, with little rows of embroidered rosebuds along the white stripes. His sage coloured coat was unbuttoned, and his cravat was tied in the most perfect Mailcoach Loftus had ever seen. Not a wrinkle in it! Notley's walking stick today was of an elegant, light wood with a stag horn handle, and the small hand that gripped it was encased in a spotless white glove. Loftus's own walking stick was black, and he grasped it a little tighter, recalling his mama's suggestions for how he might use it to do harm to Notley's person.

The rest of Notley's group peeled away, waving their goodbyes and leaving Loftus with Notley, Notley's cousin, and one of the other ladies whose name Loftus could not recall.

"Lady Rebecca and her companion Lady Huston shall chaperone us," Notley announced. "Mama fears that a paragon such as I shall be subjected to advances wherever I go."

Loftus barely stopped himself from remarking that Notley had nothing to fear from *him* on that front—he'd as soon have drowned himself in the Serpentine as made an overture toward Notley—and instead swallowed the bitter taste in his mouth. Why had his own mother not insisted on a chaperone? Did she not think he would be subjected to advances wherever he went?

Why *wasn't* he subjected to advances wherever he went?

Lady Rebecca rolled her eyes. "Yes, Morgan. One look at your buttons and everyone in the park will race to undo you."

Lady Huston giggled.

Notley shot his cousin a glare. "Sarcasm does not become you, Lady Rebecca."

"Perhaps not. But it feels so very good."

Loftus lifted his eyebrows. He had heard rumours that Lady Rebecca's manners left something to be desired. She had a charming enough sparkle to her blue eyes, but Loftus knew any lady unmarried at twenty-three must have at least one flaw too terrible to imagine.

Notley addressed his cousin again. "I will thank you ladies to walk several paces behind us, so that Mr. Rivingdon and I may converse on matters concerning gentlemen."

Lady Rebecca curtsied like a servant. "Yes, sir." She twirled her parasol up onto her shoulder, smirked at Lady Huston, and then smiled over-sweetly at Notley. "Do lead the way."

They set off, heading along the Serpentine.

"It was good of you to invite me out," Notley said to Loftus, smoothly but with a note of indifference that made Loftus want to bash him over the head with his stick, no pretense of an accident at all.

"It was good of you to join me." Loftus forced a smile. "It is a surprisingly warm day. I wonder that you didn't fear to sweat in that lovely coat."

Morgan's laugh tinkled like a lady's. "Oh, it is kind of you to wonder. But I do not sweat. My mama is the same way."

"Ah. How fortunate."

"Yes, it is."

They continued on. Morgan held himself very straight, but his posture did not look stiff or forced, and he seemed to glide rather than walk. How did he manage it?

"I feel we may have got off on the wrong foot yesterday," Loftus said.

"Oh, yes." Notley laughed again. "You did call my buttons garish."

"I suppose I was only..." Loftus did not know what to say; he ought to have planned this better. Flustered, he went with the truth. "I suppose I felt a bit stung that you made such an accurate assessment of my hat and my eye colour. I apologise for my rudeness."

Notley's impossibly large eyes widened further. "Why, think nothing of it, dear chap. It can be devastating to realise that one's sense of style is not quite so precise as one might like to think."

Loftus gritted his teeth for a long moment before forcing his jaw to relax. "Yes, well. I thought this walk would help clear the air between us."

"Indeed. It is a lovely day, as you mentioned."

Behind them, the ladies talked softly to one another. Loftus cleared his throat. "I was not sure whether to suggest walking or riding. I thought—"

"Oh!" Notley exclaimed, interrupting him. He gave another of those high, tinkling laughs. "I would certainly not have expected an invitation from you to ride." He glanced at Loftus a bit pityingly. "Why, my mama has told me that your mount is something of a screw. She recalls when your mama bought the animal, *quite* a long time ago. My own horse is very young and spirited; I'm sure it would be difficult for your old fellow to keep up. Won't your parents buy you another one?"

Loftus couldn't believe he'd ever thought it might be difficult to do bodily harm to Morgan Notley on this excursion. It would be as simple as blinking. "I am rather fond of my current mount. Otherwise, naturally, I should have a new one."

"Oh, how charming. What's his name? I do love when people have droll names for their animals."

"Hercules." Loftus spoke tightly, realising at once that such a name on so old a horse would undoubtedly invite teasing.

Notley managed to clap his hands together without losing his walking stick. "Isn't that delightful. Mine is called Wellington. After the Duke of."

"Ah." Loftus glanced over his shoulder at the ladies, who were watching a pair of curricles race along the border of the gardens. He took a deep breath. "Look there!" he exclaimed, lifting his stick and swishing it in a wild arc toward Mr. Morgan Notley's head.

Notley ducked and stumbled, his hat toppling to the grass, then popped up again. He stared wildly at Loftus. "Good Lord, man!" He bent to pick up his hat, then once again popped up, rather like a badger. "What on earth—"

"I'm so sorry!" Loftus said—for he *was* sorry that he had missed Notley's skull. "I was rather astonished watching those curricles there. They were racing, I believe!"

Morgan didn't even look toward the curricles. He just gaped at Loftus. Eventually he shoved his hat back on. "I say. Perhaps you ought to take up cricket."

"Please, do say you accept my apology. Is your hat all right?"

"Quite all right. Think no more of it." But there was an edge to Notley's tone now.

Lady Rebecca called from behind them, "Be careful, you two! I'm merely a chaperone, not a surgeon."

Loftus was growing agitated. He could not think what else to make conversation about, and if he attempted another swipe at Notley so soon after the first, it would look suspicious.

Fortunately, Notley spoke. "I'm quite looking forward to Lord Balfour's ball, you know."

"As am I." At least on that they could agree.

"Do you know, I've spent so long wondering who will be the first to take my hand and lead me to the dance floor. But I think I have a better idea now of who it will be."

"That's wonderful." Loftus could not have cared less who Notley danced with. "I have several possibilities myself. I shall just have to wait and see who claims me first."

"Yes," Morgan went on as if he hadn't spoken. "I had the loveliest chance encounter with Lord *Soulden* this morning. I rather think he will make it a point to ask me."

Loftus did not even think about it. He simply stepped closer to Notley, lifted his walking stick, and brought its end down firmly on the top of Notley's Hessian boot.

Perhaps more firmly than he had meant to, because Notley howled like a banshee and took the injured foot in his free hand, hopping up and down in a way that would have been quite comical were it not for the stares they were beginning to attract.

"Oh dear!" Loftus exclaimed. Seeing that Notley was about to topple over, he surprised himself by reaching out to steady the man. "Good Lord, I'm terribly sorry. I'm so clumsy."

Notley hopped and panted for a few seconds more, then leaned on his walking stick and slowly lowered his foot to the ground. His eyes narrowed as he nodded at Loftus's stick. "You should not be allowed one of those, my friend. You're a menace with it."

"I don't know what's the matter with me," Loftus said. And truly, he didn't. This was all wrong. The Season was less than a week away, and this was not how things were supposed to begin for him. His breathing became harsh and shallow. His stays were too tight, much too tight. Suddenly he could not draw breath at all; the air was warm and muggy, and the edges of his vision began to go black. "I shall perhaps walk a few paces away from you," he offered faintly.

"Yes, that would be fine," Notley fairly snapped.

"Mr. Rivingdon!" Lady Rebecca called, an edge of suspicion in her voice as well. "I am expected to return my cousin in one piece."

Loftus felt himself flush, and he could not quite turn to face her. "I'm very sorry for the harm I've done your cousin, Lady Rebecca." His voice sounded weak even to his own ears. He could use a glass of something cold. How was it that Notley was not even breaking a sweat?

They continued their circuit, a stony silence between them now.

And then Notley said, "Oh! That man on horseback there. Is that not Lord Stratford, who they say lives outside the city—in a cottage, like a servant? How tragic, for he is rather handsome. And what a sweet goer he's got, look at that!" And then his shoulder slammed into Loftus's, sending Loftus sprawling on the ground.

He gazed up at Notley, chest tight. The stays dug even harder into his ribs, and he realised to his chagrin that he could not get off the ground without help. Humiliation flooded him. He made one half-hearted attempt to rise but sank down again, not wanting to think about what the grass might be doing to his trousers.

"Oh, I say. I seem to have caught your clumsiness as well," Notley declared. But he was staring down at Loftus with the slightest smirk curving the small bow of his lips. "Perhaps we had better cut this walk short, lest we both end up maimed." He put out his hand. "Come on, there's a good fellow."

Loftus breathed through his clenched teeth and reluctantly extended his hand. It seemed that something sparked in him when his gloved hand met Notley's. Then Notley was hauling him up with some force, so that Loftus's ear was suddenly level with Notley's lips. Notley whispered savagely, "Bring that walking stick anywhere near me again, and I will put your eyes out with it. Am I understood?"

Loftus was too furious and humiliated to do anything but pant. Notley eased him back, making a pretense of brushing something off Loftus's coat. "There you are, old chap. No harm done, I hope."

The world swam around Loftus, and that blackness tickled the edges of his vision again. But to his relief, he did not collapse. He staggered away from Notley. "Thank you for joining me," he wheezed, wishing he could infuse the words with the coldness he desired. "I suppose I will see you at Lord Balfour's ball."

"Yes," Notley said calmly. "Unless you decide between then and now that you pose less risk to Society by staying home. If you can make such a muddle of walking, I shudder to think what damage you might do on the dance floor." He smiled, a smile that did not touch his eyes. "I only tease of course. Good day, Mr. Rivingdon."

Loftus caught bits of the man's hushed conversation with his cousin and her friend, who seemed concerned as to whether or not Loftus was well. But the trio departed swiftly, and Loftus stood there, watching the people pass by, wondering how many of them had witnessed his terrible sprawl. How many of them were now noticing the grass stains on his trousers. He seethed, balling his hands at his sides. Morgan Notley had humiliated him. Loftus could not let such an act go unpunished. As soon as he got home— Lord, he could not stop gasping; he must get these stays off—he would begin to plot what cutting thing he would say to Notley at Lord Balfour's ball.

"Are you all right?" a voice asked, so softly Loftus almost didn't hear it.

Loftus turned unsteadily and looked up to see the fellow on horseback whom Morgan had pointed out. Stratford, he had said.

He was a nice enough looking fellow, his figure improved by how well he sat his horse. Solid build, with dark hair of an unusual colour. More of a charcoal grey than brown, with a few flecks of silver in it, though he looked rather young. He had a kind, oval face, something a bit wistful in it, as though he were imagining that he was somewhere else entirely. He seemed to have trouble looking Loftus directly in the eye. His horse was a fine, tall beast, so dark a brown it was almost black. A little white snip on its nose. Loftus suddenly missed Hercules.

"I'm fine," Loftus said shortly.

"You are quite pale." Goodness, did the man always speak like this, in a voice barely above a whisper?

"I'm afraid the heat of the day does not agree with me." Loftus attempted once again to get his breathing under control. "I should like to be home." His voice quavered slightly, and he was even more deeply ashamed of himself than before. His mother always said his one fault was that he became easily overwrought. And that his waist was a bit thick. And that his countenance sometimes appeared sullen.

"Shall I find you a cab?" the gentleman asked.

"No!" Loftus snapped. "I wish to be left alone."

"I feel that way much of the time," the man said with a hint of a sympathetic smile. "Good afternoon then. Be well." He went off at a trot, and Loftus squeezed his eyes briefly shut, feeling more alone than ever. "He did not even introduce himself," Loftus whispered, despising Stratford's poor manners. Was there no decency in the world anymore?

He exhaled, wishing he had never set eyes on Morgan Notley. Wishing that Morgan Notley had never been born. Wishing that he did not now feel such a churning dread at the prospect of Lord Balfour's ball.

~

Loftus was faint with nerves by the time he stumbled through the door of M. Verreau's shop on Jermyn Street.

He was close to home, but he couldn't bear the idea of facing Mother and having to recount the details of his humiliating defeat at Morgan Notley's hands. Well, at his shoulder. And so, to soothe the sting of humiliation, he sought comfort in the familiar—coats and ribbons and hats and cuffs and lace and buttons and shirts and neckties.

"M. Verreau!" he wheezed as the man stepped out from behind the counter. "I must have some lace-trimmed handkerchiefs at once!"

The tailor's eyes narrowed behind his spectacles. "At once?"

"Yes, at once!" Loftus's breath shuddered out of him. "Or a hat ribbon, or a pair of stockings. I have had the most terrible day!" And then, much to his consternation, he burst into tears.

"Oh," said M. Verreau. "Oh dear."

The tailor placed a gentle hand on Loftus's shoulder and guided him to a chair in the middle of the shop floor. Loftus collapsed miserably onto it.

"A handkerchief, you say?" M. Verreau next said something rapid-fire in French, and a moment later a boy appeared with a stack of flat boxes, and knelt on the floor in front of the chair, offering them up to Loftus as though he were some sort of humble penitent and Loftus was his god.

Loftus sniffled, lifting the lid on the first box. Ivory silk and lace revealed itself to him, and a gentle wave of contentment swelled through him. He took a deep breath, a little less wet than his last, and blinked. His tear-clumped lashes felt heavy. He drew the handkerchief reverently out of the box and dabbed gently at his eyes. Yes, this was a lovely handkerchief, and Loftus adored it, but perhaps there were even lovelier ones to be found in the other boxes? Loftus gave a happy sigh and began to check.

"Ah, the first Season can be... overwhelming," M. Verreau said. "So much to do, so much to worry about, hmm?"

Loftus nodded, grateful for his understanding. "I haven't even been to my first ball yet, and I already have a rival. He's awful! He knocked me over today, in Hyde Park."

M. Verreau's eyes widened. "No!"

Loftus enjoyed the man's outrage and decided not to mention how he'd stabbed Notley in the foot with his walking stick. "I fell on the grass. My shoulder is quite sore."

It wasn't, not really.

"Jean," M. Verreau said, snatching the handkerchief boxes out of the boy's arms, "go and fetch Mr. Rivingdon a cup of tisane. Chamomile!"

The boy scurried away.

"You're too kind," Loftus murmured. "I must look magnificent at Balfour's ball."

"The clothes I made for you are–"

"They're lovely, yes," Loftus said. "They are quite the loveliest in all London, but I need to be singularly beautiful, do you see? How am I to be an incomparable if everyone keeps comparing me to *Notley?*" He spat the name with barely-concealed contempt.

"Ah," said M. Verreau. He pinched the bridge of his nose, jostling his spectacles.

Loftus sat up straighter. "M. Verreau, but of course you know what Mr. Notley is wearing to the ball!"

M. Verreau looked uncomfortable. "I do not think I could share that information with you, Mr. Rivingdon."

Loftus waved away his concerns. "Yes, yes, but you could make me something that he hasn't got, couldn't you? And you would know he hasn't got it. You don't need to tell me what he's wearing, not if all I'm asking is that you make me something different!"

M. Verreau hummed thoughtfully. Then he moved to the counter and returned with a French magazine. He opened it, displaying a picture to Loftus. The man, with a fashionably pinched-in waist, was wearing a coat. A magnificent coat. Loftus had never seen a coat with tails quite like this one. The tails were almost a skirt.

"It is a skirted frock coat," M. Verreau said. "It will be all the fashion here by the end of the Season. Mr. Notley was quite taken with it, but his mother would not let him buy one."

"It's beautiful," Loftus said, though he couldn't have said if he was more in love with the coat itself or simply the idea that Notley didn't have one. All he knew was that a coat like that, combined with his modest collection of new handkerchiefs, had taken most of the sting out of his encounter with the awful Morgan Notley. He may have lost the battle, which was a bitter thing to concede, but he had by no means lost the war. And a coat like this would not only make Notley seethe with jealousy, it would undoubtedly impress and captivate Lord Soulden too. "I must have one!"

M. Verreau's eyes sparkled, and he smiled. "Oh, how wonderful, Mr. Rivindgon." He hesitated. "The thing is…it will be very difficult for me to complete this in such a short time. The ball is just a few days away!"

Loftus's stomach plummeted. He could not lose the glorious prospect of this coat—not when he'd just got his hopes up. "I will pay any price. Whatever you think fair compensation for the urgency of the matter."

A smile split M. Verreau's face. "Parfait, Mr. Rivingdon! Parfait!"

CHAPTER 5

The Balfour Ball

Morgan's heart pounded harder with each jolt of the carriage that made its way toward Lord Balfour's home. How many years had he waited for this night? He couldn't say precisely, only that ever since he could remember, he'd been looking forward to his first Season. He'd understood from an early age just how many doors a beauty like his might open. His mother had made private mockery of the gentlemen who wished to be admired for their shooting, their riding, their knowledge of politics, their sparring matches at Gentleman Jackson's. Morgan, she asserted, would be admired for his beauty. *"You will have many suitors,"* she'd told him. *"But you must find one who will treat you as the prince you are."*

Lord Soulden would, Morgan was sure of it. Soulden was a man who appreciated fine things. A man who understood beauty.

He was positively giddy with anticipation! He only wished he understood how giddiness could feel so much like nausea.

Mama would be in attendance tonight, but he had not come with her. He wished to appear as a beautiful rose surrounded by butterflies, and though he loved Mama dearly, she was no butterfly. He had instead arrived with three cousins, and was grateful that Rebecca was not among his party. While he might have enjoyed her conversation well enough, it would not do to make his entrance in the company of an ape leader like Becca.

And then suddenly, they were pulling into a half-circle drive in front of a large but strangely cold-looking house. Why, Lord Balfour could do with a statue or two, or perhaps a fountain. His topiaries were trimmed almost savagely, but not into any sort of clever or impressive shapes. Best not to dwell on the gardens, however. This was it! Good Lord, this was really it. Morgan alighted from the carriage with his usual easy grace, hoping there were eyes on him as he did. He adjusted his hat and set the tip of his stick upon the ground. And then he walked with his cousins toward the entrance.

The revellers did not immediately stop what they were doing and turn to stare in wonderment at Morgan, which was a bit disappointing. And the ball was not quite what Morgan had expected. For one thing, Lord Balfour's home was rather dark, and—dare Morgan think it?—dreary. Lord Balfour was a peer of the realm, his ball the first official event of the Season. Oughtn't he to have decorated his home more with more care and...*savoir vivre*? Then one of Morgan's cousins pointed out their host, and he understood at once. Balfour wore black without any sort of adornment. His face was disconcertingly smooth and glassy, like the surface of a pond. He looked positively allergic to *vivre* of any sort.

Morgan had agonised over his dress for this evening. With so many newly purchased clothes at his disposal, it was difficult to make a choice. He had eventually settled on a pair of grey silk breeches that had an almost silver sheen and a waistcoat of deep red and black brocade that looked well with his dark hair. He'd thought to wear his favourite coat with ivory buttons painted with small roses. He loved that coat dearly. But the recollection of that horrible Rivingdon fellow calling his buttons garish—and those had merely been the carved ivory buttons, no roses in sight—had soured his feelings toward that particular garment. Instead, he'd worn another smartly cut black coat with silver buttons. Let Rivingdon try to call his buttons garish now.

Except...he wished he'd worn his ivory-and-rose buttons. With silver buttons, he looked just like several dozen other fellows here. He *liked* his painted buttons. They made him feel more himself. He wondered if he might ask his cousins for permission to take their carriage home and change. No, that would not do. He must stand by his choices with confidence. Where was Rivingdon anyhow? He was to make his debut tonight as well, and Morgan sincerely hoped he tripped and fell right in front of the Prince Regent.

He suddenly had little idea what to do with himself. The cousins he'd come with were older and had gone off to dance or chat with friends. He was still hovering at the end of Lord Balfour's entrance hall, looking out at the dance floor, which was not over-crowded just yet. He could go to the punch table, he supposed, and try to look as though he were enjoying himself. Which of course he was. He forced a smile in order to prove it, but nobody even seemed to be looking at him. How was that possible? He had a strong urge to seek out Mama—an urge that was followed at once by a stab of humiliation.

He glanced down at himself. His shoes had been polished until he could practically see his own reflection in them, their rosettes perfectly fluffed. His neckcloth had been wrapped around a stiffener and tied in a Ballroom knot. Mama had told him before he left that he looked perfect. So why didn't he feel as he'd expected to—vibrant, beautiful...*happy*?

He didn't suppose peers of the realm ever grew so tongue-tied as he was right now. Lord Soulden, for instance—why, just in those few moments Morgan had seen him at the tailor's shop, it was clear that Soulden was bursting with confidence. Remembering it caused Morgan's blood to stir, and he knew he must find the man at once and strike up a conversation. He advanced into the ballroom, trying not to appear hesitant. For all that the house was dreary, the laughter of the *ton* was gay and seemed to come from everywhere. He scanned the crowd purposefully, seeking Soulden but keeping one eye out for that horrid Rivingdon as well. Before he could locate either man, one of his cousins approached and whisked him off to be introduced to Lady someone or other.

Morgan used the time making small talk with Lady Morton to regain his composure. It was a relief to discover he was much more beautiful than she, and he felt his confidence slowly return. An old woman tottered by—goodness, she had to be a hundred!—and Lady Morton whispered conspiratorially to Morgan that this was Lady Agatha Watson, a notorious gossip. Morgan frowned after the woman. Perhaps he could use this to his advantage. He found one of his cousins and requested an introduction to Lady Agatha. The old woman was hard of hearing, and it was quite difficult to talk to her, but Morgan braved it. After listening to her opinions on Gunpowder versus Orange Pekoe for what felt like an hour at least, he chanced to speak. "Have you by chance seen Lord Soulden in attendance tonight?"

She cupped a hand to her ear and told him to speak up.

"Lord Soulden," Morgan repeated loudly. "He and I were together the other day at the Bucknall Club." That wasn't a complete lie. He and Soulden *had* both been at Bucknall's—in the same room, no less.

"Lord Sylvan?" She looked confused. "Why, he has been dead for years. Died in that horrible carriage accident some ten years ago. They say the hackney stepped on a tortoise."

"*Soulden*. I mean to dance with him tonight."

The old woman nodded without seeming to comprehend. Morgan bit back a sigh of frustration. He needed her to spread gossip about his potential courtship by Lord Soulden. Once the viscount heard said gossip, he would realise what a good idea such a courtship would be.

"So that's something to talk about, isn't it?" he prompted her.

"That the viscount, who is perfection itself, should take an interest in my humble self?"

Lady Agatha mumbled something unhappily, then tottered off leaving Morgan right back where he'd started. His heart sank.

And suddenly, there was Loftus Rivingdon. Wearing a stunning crystal cravat pin with a centre jewel that *did* match his eyes. The cravat itself was cream satin, and his coat—

Morgan stared, blood rushing to his head.

His coat.

It couldn't be.

His coat was a *skirted frock coat*.

Morgan felt a rage wash over him that was so pure, so blindingly incandescent, that for a moment he could barely breathe with the force of it. It crashed over him like a wave, and then receded leaving him dizzy and shocked.

A *skirted frock coat*.

Morgan held his chin up and closed the distance between him and that—that skirted frock coat-wearing *monster*. By the time he reached Rivingdon, the shaking in his hands had ceased, and his smile, he hoped, did not reveal his inner turmoil.

"Good evening, sir," he said, and bowed.

Rivingdon bowed in return. "Good evening."

"What an *interesting* coat."

"Thank you," Rivingdon said, even though Morgan hadn't said it was nice. He'd only said it was interesting, and lots of things could be interesting—the way the ancient Romans read the auguries in the gizzards of animals, for example. Interesting, yes. Nice? Certainly not. But, to Morgan's horror, the coat was nice. No, it was more than nice. It was *beautiful*, and Morgan seethed with envy.

"Where did you have it made?" he asked through a grimace of a smile.

Rivingdon ran his slender fingers down a masterfully crafted sleeve and blinked innocently at Morgan. "Why, M. Verreau made it for me. Isn't it delightful?"

Morgan hid a gasp under a feigned cough. "M. Verreau? I see."

The fiend, the betrayer, the *Judas*!

Morgan reached out a hand to steady himself, and found that he was holding the edge of the table upon which sat a large punch-bowl. A woman moved away from the table as Morgan clutched it, carrying a glass of punch. Morgan caught the faint scent of brandy and oranges as she, and it, wafted past him.

He was seized by a wonderful, terrible idea. With shaking hands he reached for a glass, and scooped a ladleful of punch into it. He took a sip and then turned back to face Rivingdon.

Rivingdon was watching him with his head tilted at an angle, and a knowing smirk tugging at the corners of his perfect lips. His hair, which was almost silver in the light of the chandeliers, gleamed brightly. And his figure, willowy and elegant, was framed beautifully by that fucking perfect skirted frock coat. Morgan gasped to have thought such a word, and then thought it again, several more times.

"M. Verreau was so kind as to make it for me on rather short notice." Loftus's tone was perfectly polite, but Morgan didn't miss the barbs behind his words. Each one struck him as soundly and as mortally as the arrows that had stabbed Saint Sebastian. "Why," Loftus continued, "I–"

Morgan darted forward and tipped his glass of punch right down Rivingdon's front.

For a moment, Rivingdon didn't move. He stood there, shocked, and Morgan felt a cruel and satisfying sense of triumph settle over him. Then Rivingdon's bottom lip trembled, and his eyes filled with tears as he stared at Morgan.

"Oh, my God," he said. He did not shriek as Morgan had expected. Instead, his voice was low and tremulous, ragged at the edges as he fought his tears, and Morgan realised in rising horror the enormity of what he had done.

"It was an accident," he blurted, although they both knew it was not.

Rivingdon lifted a shaking hand to his drenched cravat, now stained quite an ugly shade of red. "I... I was to meet the Prince Regent." He blinked, and a tear slid down his pale cheek.

"I'm sorry," Morgan said. He wished he could take back the last few minutes. He hated Rivingdon, it was true, and perhaps a part of him had wanted to see him humiliated like this, but still—to attack a man's *clothes*? It was a step too far. Clothes were sacred, and the poor skirted frock coat was an innocent victim.

Rivingdon lifted a hand to his mouth to cover a sob and then, before Morgan could say anything else, he turned on his heel and fled into the crowd.

~

"Nobody so much as looked my way," Morgan announced to Becca the next morning in the Warringtons' drawing room, "for Lady Hartwell made a complete fool of herself by getting too drunk, and there was a *Bow Street Runner* present, did you see? What on earth was he doing there, among fine company? Viscount Soulden didn't even *attend*, so the night was practically a waste from the start. And then that horrid little snake Loftus Rivingdon showed up in a *skirted frock coat*, and did such irreparable damage to my sanity that I *accidentally* splashed punch on his coat, and people snickered about it. I was so embarrassed I could not even think of meeting Prinny…The whole thing was quite horrendous!" he declared. "And now today I find that all anyone can talk of is your brother and his wretched scandal! It's terrible!" He nearly stomped his foot, a behaviour his mother had recently suggested he ought to cease.

Becca's eyes blazed, and he at first assumed she was angry on his behalf, but he soon realised she was angry at *him*. "Morgan, really! There was a grave misunderstanding that resulted in Warry being put in a difficult position. It will work out, I hope. But you might show a little sensitivity."

"Sensitivity?" Morgan was incredulous. Was Becca really suggesting he be sympathetic to *Warry*? "To the man who ruined my debut?"

The man who'd ruined his debut was Loftus Rivingdon, but it suddenly seemed he ought to direct his ire toward Warry as well.

"To your cousin, who had a more trying night than you could possibly imagine."

"What do I care?" Morgan demanded. "You are no help to me at all, Rebecca."

"I find I am more able—and more inclined—to be of help to you when you are not acting like a child," she said firmly.

He sighed, tilting his head back. Then he brought his chin down again and chewed his lip—not hard enough to damage the flawless pink of it, but he *was* rather anxious all of a sudden. "What if the reason people did not look at me was my buttons?"

"Your...buttons," Becca repeated.

"Yes. I wore silver buttons last night, and that is the fault of Loftus Rivingdon as well, for did my uncle tell you the ill-mannered weasel called my buttons garish the other day? Anyway, he made me rather self-conscious about the idea of wearing my painted ivory buttons, and so I wore very bland silver buttons, and while I did dance with several people, including Lord Crauford—did you hear I was introduced to him at the Bucknall Club just recently?—I have nobody I can yet call a suitor." He blew out another breath.

"The Season began not twelve hours ago, cousin. You do not need to be engaged today, or tomorrow, or even this year."

He glanced sideways at her, careful to keep his spine straight even though he longed to slump in despair. "God, I feel so awful! Is this how you feel all the time, knowing no one will have you?"

Her eyebrows lifted, and her face took on an expression that Morgan had seen once before when he'd watched her take aim during archery practise. "Really, Morgan, is there anything at all between your ears but air? If you will excuse me, I must see if there has been any word from Lord Hartwell, or my brother." She rose from her seat and stalked out of the drawing room, leaving Morgan alone.

"Be that way, then!" he snapped, long after she'd disappeared. He suddenly felt a terrible press of guilt and did not understand why. The memory of Loftus's watering eyes and ruined coat remained burned into his mind. Had the fellow not deserved it for attempting to break Morgan's foot?

Ah, but the *coat* hadn't deserved it.

He left the drawing room, storm clouds gathering over him. He would return home at once and see if Mama had any new ideas for how to win Lord Soulden. Ooh! And he would ask her about her history with Lady Rivingdon. The apple hadn't fallen far from the tree, he imagined. He was certain Lady Rivingdon was as beastly as her son, and he would enjoy hearing the details.

He nearly ran into Earl Warrington, who looked like a wild animal caught in the glow of a street lamp. His uncle hurried on with a mumbled, "Oh, Morgan, dear fellow. Do excuse me."

Morgan's ire grew, and he felt tears blur his vision. Which was terrible, for only a feeble-minded thing like Loftus Rivingdon would weep in front of others. Yet it was impossible for his eyes not to sting. Nobody cared. Nobody *saw* him. Nobody—

Earl Warrington stopped just before the staircase and turned slowly back. "Morgan? Are you well?"

"I'm fine!" Morgan snapped. Then, an instant later, shook his head, dashing angrily at his eyes with his fist.

Earl Warrington approached tentatively. "Is it Joseph you're upset about?" The Earl sighed. "I suppose half of London has heard the news by now. Oh, it is bad, I know, Morgan. It is. But Lady Warrington and I have been in conference about it, and I assure you, we will find a way to get Joseph through this. Perhaps not unscathed, but—minimally scathed. Ah, I could wring that Hartwell's neck!"

Morgan's throat tightened. Why was everyone so concerned about *Warry*, when it was Morgan who had experienced a trying night? He sniffled, aware that it made him sound precisely like the child Becca clearly thought him.

"Oh, Morgan." The earl checked his pocket watch and sighed again. "Come and sit in my library for a moment."

Morgan wanted to protest. Wanted to storm out of this wretched house and never return. But he did not want anyone else, even the servants, to see him in this state, and he did find his uncle's library soothing. Morgan had a vast appreciation for books —not for reading them, precisely, but for the beauty of their leather bound covers and elegant print. So he followed the earl into the cosy room of dark wood and sat on the chaise longue near the large oak desk.

His uncle sat behind the desk and leaned back, looking as exhausted as Morgan felt. "Oh, my poor son. He is—well, you know he was a happy child. He could dizzy me with his chatter, but I loved having such a sweet boy. I don't know what has happened these past few months, but he has not been the son I know. And now to learn he has disgraced himself with Lord Hartwell…"

Morgan frowned. This seemed like a very personal matter, and if the earl had given it two seconds' thought, he would have realised it was of little interest to Morgan. Still, he recalled Becca asking if he had anything between his ears but air—no wonder she was not yet married; she was unthinkably coarse—and forced himself to look as though he were paying attention. He *was* curious about the details, distasteful as he was certain to find them. Why, the rumour he'd heard was that Warry had been caught in Lord Balfour's bedroom very nearly unclothed, with Lord Hartwell's arms around him and Balfour himself lying slain beside them both. Morgan shuddered just thinking of it. His cousin did not seem like a murderer, but as Mama always said, you never could tell about a person. Hartwell, on the other hand, seemed perfectly capable of murder, and was most likely the one who had killed Balfour. Morgan would be sorry to see him hang, but now that he had Cecil to sponsor his application to Bucknall's, he supposed he no longer required Hartwell for anything.

"I am sorry for what Warry is going through." The words felt thick and strange on his tongue. It was difficult to be sorry for someone else's misfortune. "It was quite a bad night for many of us. I had thought the opening of the Season would be much more…" He did not know precisely what he'd thought. "Beautiful."

Earl Warrington looked as though "beautiful" and "the Season" were two terms he'd never thought to put together.

"Did you know, Uncle, that with all of the night's ghastliness I was hardly looked at?" It was a difficult thing to admit, but it would have been even more difficult to pass another moment without anyone's sympathy.

"Oh." Earl Warrington looked confused. "Well, I'm sure…I'm sure you were looked at."

"I was not! Or rather, only by those who saw me spill punch all over Mr. Loftus Rivingdon's new skirted frock coat."

"Morgan, how could you do such a thing?" The earl sounded genuinely shocked.

Morgan stared at him open-mouthed. "I did not do it on purpose!"

It was a lie, to be sure, but why had his uncle assumed that Morgan intentionally harmed Rivingdon's coat? Morgan was not that sort of person. It was only that Rivingdon had driven him to the very cusp of madness!

"Oh." The earl's brow wrinkled. "Forgive me, I thought…"

"I feel terrible!" Morgan went on. "I feel—" He tried to think what would sound right here "—guilty, and—and—remorseful, and—" Oh, surely he could come up with another word that would make him sound sympathetic.

He thought again of Rivingdon's eyes filling with tears and was surprised to feel a jolt of genuine pain. How humiliating it must have been for the fellow. Why did Loftus Rivingdon's humiliation bring him so little satisfaction?

"—I feel as though I am in the wrong!" he blurted. And then he sat there, stunned, for he had never uttered such words in his life.

His uncle looked a bit dumbfounded. "Well, Morgan." The older man scratched behind his ear, seeming uncertain. "That is something." He leaned back further, making his chair creak. He was quite thick around the middle, and Morgan wondered that he didn't wear stays. Perhaps when one was old, one lost one's devotion to personal betterment. How tragic. "It is the usual way of things, when you have done something to hurt someone else, to extend an olive branch."

Morgan was uncertain what a piece of tree could have to do with the ins and outs of polite society. Unless Earl Warrington meant some type of walking stick fashioned from the wood of the olive tree? Morgan was about to seek clarification when his uncle went on.

"Apologise? Make amends?"

Apologise? To Loftus Rivingdon? Morgan nearly laughed. Ah, but his uncle did not have the full story. "Yes, you see making amends was what Mr. Rivingdon claimed to want when he invited me to the park not five days hence. Yet it was a trap, and he attempted to break my foot. He is also attempting to steal my intended suitor. So you understand, I cannot possibly offer him a fine walking stick. That is not a gift he deserves."

Earl Warrington looked baffled. "A fine...?" He batted the air. "Never mind. Be that as it may, I have always known you to be—well, to wish to appear—well-mannered. And however this chap Rivingdon has wronged you, you have the chance to prove yourself a true gentleman and apologise for your error, even if he does not do you the same courtesy."

Morgan looked down at his cornflower blue coat with its dull covered buttons, and mumbled.

"What was that?" the earl asked.

"You *do* recall that he called my buttons garish?"

"I do. You have mentioned it so many times, I fear even the oblivion of old age will not let me forget." He said the last part a bit softer, as though he did not entirely intend Morgan to hear.

"I was too out of sorts to even wear my ivory buttons last night. You know the ones with the little painted flowers?"

"I—"

"He has ruined *everything*, Uncle! Everything!"

"Nevertheless, I recommend that you think of something to offer him that will allow you both to put your animosity behind you and enjoy the rest of the Season." The earl drummed his fingers on his desk.

"But Uncle, wouldn't you like to see me marry well, given that Warry is now disgraced and Hartwell sure to hang?"

The earl would cause permanent furrows in his brow if he didn't stop frowning. Morgan only ever furrowed his brow delicately and briefly, to avoid wrinkles. "Hang? I'm really not sure it will come to that."

"Even if he does not, the scandal will be dreadful. Am I not the family's only hope for redemption?"

"Of course I should like to see you marry well, but what has that to do with apologising to the Rivingdon boy?"

"He wants to steal my suitor," Morgan reminded him. His uncle truly was growing senile with age.

"Ah, yes. And who is your—your intended—suitor?"

"Lord Soulden." He was surprised his uncle had not heard this already from Mama. Perhaps he had heard but forgotten? Morgan had been told Uncle Francis was somewhat unwell, but he'd been under the impression it was the man's heart, not his mind, that ailed him.

"Lord S—" The earl paused and gazed somewhere past Morgan's shoulder. "Ah yes, I can see it. Well, if this Rivingdon really is as wretched as you make him out to be, Lord Soulden will surely be impressed by your superior manners."

This had not occurred to Morgan. "You're right, Uncle! I shall show Soulden that I am the superior man, not just in beauty but in character." He stood, his spirits lifting.

"That's the way." His uncle offered him a small smile. "Off with you now, and let me know how things progress. And do not let those poor elephants have died in vain, Morgan. Wear your ivory buttons proudly."

"Thank you, Uncle, I shall! I— What do you mean, elephants?"

The earl frowned again. "You do know that ivory comes from elephants. Yes?"

"Of course. From their great white tusks."

"Right. I was merely saying they shall have died for a good cause if you wear your buttons proudly."

"But why should they have died at all?"

"Morgan, how do you think people acquire the tusks?"

Morgan stood very still for a long moment. "Surely the elephants don't have to *die*." He was beginning to feel sick in the pit of his stomach. "Surely the—the ivory collectors can simply—cut off the tusks—why, it's just like old bone, right? It doesn't hurt them to take it?"

Earl Warrington blinked. "Morgan, I…"

Just then, a knock came on the library door. "Father?" Becca called.

"Come in!" Earl Warrington sounded relieved.

Becca flung the door open. She looked rather flushed. One of many reasons she was unmarried, he supposed. "I've just had word from William. Warry is well. He's on his way home. Father, I beg of you, remember what we discussed this morning and go easy on him. For you see…" she bit her lip as though suppressing a smile. "I believe William intends to offer Warry the protection of marriage."

"Good Lord!" The earl stood.

"Please, nothing is certain yet. William has not proposed. But he has spoken to his parents, and he has asked me to accompany him and Warry and Lord Christmas on a picnic tomorrow. He says he has an important matter to broach with Warry and should like my advice. What else could that mean?"

That was Morgan's cue to leave, for he had amends to make and some serious thinking to do about ivory. It did seem strange that Becca was smiling about Warry becoming engaged to a murderer, but he supposed Hartwell had had a good reason for killing Balfour, such as defending Warry's honour. Morgan was now up to chapter five of *The Maiden Diaries*, and the rake Slyfeel had already slain a vagabond to protect a lady's honour. Morgan supposed it was necessary sometimes.

He said goodbye to Earl Warrington and offered a cold nod to Becca, but neither seemed to notice, so engrossed were they in discussion of Warry's engagement.

Morgan slipped out of the library, eager to collect his gloves and hat and be on his way.

CHAPTER 6

The morning after Lord Balfour's ball, Loftus sprawled languidly on the chaise longue in his bedroom and refused to be moved from it. Mother was in quite the huff about it, but Loftus didn't care. He was distraught. Last night had been a disaster. Why, if it hadn't been for Lord Warrington being found undone in the company of Lord Hartwell, Loftus knew for certain that the entire *ton* would be talking about *him*—and not in the way he had ever envisioned it. His face burned anew as he recalled his shame. Notley had tipped punch on him! On purpose! Loftus had been horrified when it had happened, and he still felt ill with shame now, but a coldness had seeped into his blood while he lay on his sofa, and his need for revenge built slowly and surely until it was the strongest of all his battered emotions. Why, he even thought about seeking out a chemist and enquiring about poisons, for surely even a jury would agree that ridding the world of a monster like Morgan Notley was a great service to society. They wouldn't hang him for it. They would probably cheer as they released him from the dock, and present him with a medal.

Loftus could only summon two consolations from last night: firstly, that Lord Warrington's scandal surpassed his own shame, and secondly that Lord Soulden had not even attended the ball, and therefore he had not seen the sad state of Loftus's coat after that beast Mr. Notley had defiled it. Neither consolation was quite enough to draw him off the chaise longue, but at least the only tears he had cried this morning had been those of bitterness and not sorrow.

At last, when his muscles grew cramped from lolling, he forced himself to rise and summon his man. "I shall wear the pads today, Martin," he mumbled, not looking his valet in the eye. He knew that a gentleman of his beauty and wealth ought not to feel ashamed of anything—ought to move through the world with poise and speak with confidence. Yet it did shame him in some inexplicable way to make use of the pads.

Martin's expression gave nothing away as he helped Loftus into the tight undergarment with sewn in cotton pads that made his arse look fuller—and his waist smaller by comparison. But Loftus wondered whether the fellow was silently mocking him. He dressed for the afternoon in trousers of palest peach, a periwinkle waistcoat, and a dove grey coat that also had sewn-in pads in the shoulders. He put on a white hat with satin rosettes that matched the waistcoat, and left the house. He made his way to the Temple of the Muses. He intended to start reading more, so that he might have subjects of conversation at hand were he to find himself in a room with a true nonesuch like Soulden. The trouble was he did not really like reading and was not much good at it. The only book to truly hold his attention had been *The Maiden Diaries*. He had devoured volumes one through three, and was eagerly awaiting the next installment. It was hardly reading material befitting a gentleman, and yet the story had truly opened his eyes to the realities of...Well, he didn't know just how to put it. Only that two years ago, he had been unsure what was expected of a fellow on his wedding night. He had thought to ask his older brother, Geoffrey, but it seemed an awkward sort of conversation to initiate. And besides, Geoffrey had eyes only for women, and Loftus supposed it was a bit different with a woman than with another fellow. He had finally broached the subject—very delicately—with Geoffrey's friend Lady Olivia Wilton, as unconventional a woman as ever there was. She'd laughed until tears streamed down her face and then lent him her copies of *The Maiden Diaries,* promising they were more of an education than he'd ever receive at Oxford.

Now, thanks to the books, Loftus was slightly less confused about the act—although he suspected swiving generally did not require quite the number of garden tools, oblong vegetables, and observation by curious livestock that seemed usual for the rake Slyfeel. But the rather strange and perhaps somewhat embarrassing aspect of it all was the way in which the novel had awakened his fantasies. At first, he had been content to simply read some of the more shocking scenes over and over again. But soon he found himself making up further adventures for his favourite characters, arranging them in his mind the way some lads arranged toy soldiers for mock battle. Many a night he'd tossed and turned, spinning tales in his mind about Slyfeel and the stableboy Burnside, the bedcovers tented over a stand that wouldn't let him sleep until he took it in hand.

Even now he felt his breath quicken as he approached the Temple. He supposed, once he was inside, it would not hurt to check to see if a fourth volume had been published, in addition to purchasing a book on politics or art or some such. He wondered that no one stopped him to say hello. He had foolishly assumed that once he made his formal debut he would know everyone in the *ton* as if by magic, and would regularly be hailed and greeted on the street and invited on excursions and complimented on his wardrobe. But passersby generally kept their heads down, or spoke to their companions. He wondered anxiously if nobody wished to speak with him because they all knew of his humiliation the night before. If they looked at him and saw that stained, sopping frock coat.

He entered the Temple and fairly sighed with relief at being out of the street and away from that horrid crush of indifference. He forced himself to browse the endless shelves before selecting a book on the Greeks. That seemed respectable enough. The Greeks had been very important, after all, and any thought of the Greeks immediately brought on thoughts of Lord Soulden, which filled Loftus with a hazy warmth. Next, Loftus headed to the small alcove that housed books suited to very *specific* dispositions. It took him but a moment to locate *The Maiden Diaries,* and he was shocked and beyond delighted to discover there was indeed a fourth volume! How had he not heard the news sooner? He realised with an ugly sense of desolation that it was probably because he didn't have much in the way of friends. He was not sure he could count Olivia Wilton as more than an acquaintance, and he spent most of his time with his mother. If he was truly a diamond of the first water, why were peers not falling over themselves to spend time with him?

He must not let himself think that now. He must stride to the counter with confidence and purchase a book that could make him seem ungentlemanly. But he *was* a gentleman, and he had a right to do as gentlemen did—and that included reading scandalous literature. He squared his padded shoulders and started forward.

Then stopped.

There, browsing a shelf of books on the history of theatre, stood Lord Soulden. He was even more handsome than Loftus had remembered. He wore sober greys and blues, and yet was so radiant he might as well have been wearing colours as bold and vivid as a sunrise. Loftus doubted those broad shoulders were padded or—Loftus swallowed—that arse. As he watched, Soulden lifted a book from the shelf and perused it, frowning briefly when he found a scrap of paper someone had carelessly left inside it. He plucked the scrap from the pages and slipped it into his coat pocket, so smoothly the motion was nearly imperceptible, and Loftus had to wonder at his grace. Some gentlemen might have dropped the paper on the floor for the shopkeeper to clean up, but not Soulden.

The viscount studied the book a moment more, then put it back. Loftus must act quickly, must introduce himself. He took a step forward, then froze. What if Soulden had heard about the frock coat?

Poise. Confidence. He must introduce himself to Soulden as though there had never been an incident involving a frock coat. He must also hide the fourth volume of *The Maiden Diaries* underneath his arm.

"M-my lord." Good God. Was that his voice speaking? How dare it speak, when Loftus hadn't yet attained poise or confidence? "Lord Soulden?"

Soulden turned. There was a narrow wariness in his expression, but it vanished the moment the man's gaze fell on Loftus, replaced by a polite openness—the blank slate with which every gentleman approached an introduction. "Do I know you, sir?"

Loftus remembered to lift his chin, and also to turn his face infinitesimally to the left. His right side was his better side, and he wished Soulden to pay it the more attention. "I am Mr. Loftus Rivingdon, my lord."

He held out his hand, and Soulden took it. Neither of them was wearing gloves inside the shop, and Loftus's heart tumbled over an entire measure of beats at the touch of Soulden's skin against his own, and—his breath caught—the lingering brush of Soulden's fingertips against his palm as they disengaged. Was Soulden making an overture? Loftus was certain that he was.

"Ah, Rivingdon," Soulden said. There was nothing in his tone to suggest that the drag of his fingers against Loftus's hand had been intentional, but Soulden was a more worldly gentleman than Loftus, and bound to be more discreet. "Baron Rivingdon's youngest?"

"Yes," Loftus said dreamily.

"Then it must be your first Season, eh?"

"Yes." Loftus drowned for a moment in Soulden's eyes.

"How are you finding it?" Soulden asked him.

Loftus bloomed like a hothouse flower under the warmth of the man's gaze. "Oh, it has been most wonderful, my lord," he lied. Well, perhaps it was not a complete lie. In fact, perhaps it was not a lie at all, because standing here, with Lord Soulden's attention upon him was the most glorious thing that had ever happened to Loftus. Mr. Notley could tip an entire punch bowl over him right now, and Loftus didn't think he would even notice. "I have been most gratified to receive the friendship, and perhaps more, of several very eminent members of the *ton*."

Mother always said that the best way to gain and to keep a man's attention was to remind him that he wasn't the only fish on the hook. Of course, neither Loftus nor Lady Rivingdon knew much about fishing, but Loftus felt the analogy was sound.

"Ah, wonderful," Soulden said with a pleasant smile. His gaze fell on the book under Loftus's arm. "And what is it that you're buying today? Is that—*oh*."

"Certainly not," Loftus said hastily. "It is a collection of, ah, essays." He did not like the way that Soulden's mouth twitched. "Of *sermons*. A series of them, concerning the doctrine, principles and practise of faith."

"Ah," said Soulden, his eyes shining. "Yes, that is what I should hope a young, unmarried gentlemen like yourself should read. For his *edification*."

Loftus's cheeks burned. "Indeed."

Soulden smiled. "It's been a pleasure to meet you, Mr. Rivingdon. I do hope I shall see you again. Will you be attending the Kennilworth rout?"

Loftus dropped *The Maiden Diaries*. It opened, to his horror, on the title page, and Loftus bent down quickly to slam it shut. He rose again. Poise. Confidence. His slightly more beautiful right side. "Yes, Lord Soulden, I do hope so."

"Then I shall see you there," Soulden said. "Enjoy your...*sermons*."

And he winked, and swept out of the Temple.

~

*L*oftus arrived home in a state of jubilation. Why, he barely even registered that the footman handed him a note after taking his gloves and hat. Lord Soulden would be at the Kennilworth rout. He *hoped to see Loftus there.*

"Mother!" Loftus called as he barged through the inner hall, unfolding the note as he did. "I must tell you the most wonderful news." He glanced down at the paper, felt himself blanch, then stopped and read the note again. "Mother!" he fairly howled, his fine mood fast deserting him. "Billings! Billings, where is my mother?" The footman informed him she'd retired to her bedchamber after luncheon. Loftus pounded up the stairs. As he approached the bedchamber, he heard raised voices from within. His father was at home.

Loftus could not hear precisely what they were saying, but his heart began to race. He hated when his parents argued—though they'd been doing it since before he could remember; he ought to be used to it by now. He clutched the note in his hand so tightly that his sweat began to dampen the paper. Another few steps and he could make out what was being said.

His mother's voice was already as high as it could go before it reached that dog-whistle point. "If you cared for this family as you ought to, I wouldn't need to spend so much money making him shine."

"Shine?" his father shot back. "You could spend half a million pounds on coats and hats for him, and he'd still be a useless little sodomite who walks like he's got a stick up his arse."

Loftus stood very still. It was nothing he hadn't heard before. Nothing that still had the power to wound him. He ran his thumb along the edge of the note.

"Although really," his father continued, "if he had a stick up his arse, he'd probably bloody enjoy it."

"This isn't 1780, Robert! He's not your firstborn; what's it to you if he prefers men?"

"Let him fuck a carthorse for all I care, just as long as he stops mincing around like a girl, covered in *frippery*."

"Mind your language!" His mother's voice took on that impossibly shrill note.

"Oh, like you're some kind of saint?"

"He's beautiful. Nearly everyone says so—"

"Beautiful? I want a son who's *useful*."

"Useful like you? You've lost us damn near *everything*. Do you hear me? Everything!"

Loftus ducked his head, his stomach twisting in on itself. He closed his eyes and tried to draw a deep breath but could only get air in short, sharp bursts. He hurried to his room and shut the door. He lay on his great canopied bed, with its covers and drapes done in pale yellow and pink. His father's words had been cruel yet familiar, but his mother's... *"make him shine"*—those had cut deep. Didn't Loftus already shine? He'd thought she spent money on his wardrobe because she loved him and wanted his natural beauty shown to advantage. But what if it was really because he did not possess natural beauty in the first place?

Perhaps his parents' argument had come about over the bill from M. Verreau for the skirted frock coat. Loftus felt wretched with guilt. He ought not to have bought it, he supposed, but his mother *had* said they'd spare no expense for Loftus's first Season. He dug his nails into his palms—hard enough to hurt, but not hard enough to mar the skin. He realised the note still lay crumpled and soggy beside him on the bed. The ink was so fine, however, that it had barely bled at all. Loftus stared at it. Mr. Morgan Notley requested his presence at the Notley home in Curzon Street for tea and to discuss the replacement of Loftus's coat.

Loftus wished to seek his mother's advice—he hated Morgan

Notley, but he'd loved his frock coat, and certainly Mr. Notley should bear the expense of replacing it. But what if Notley's olive branch was a trap, as Loftus's had been? He sighed, his ribs pushing against his stays. Now that he knew the strain the coat had put on the family finances, he had no choice but to go to Notley and seek compensation.

The script on the note was flawless—elegant and curling. Had Notley written the words himself? He pictured Notley—that lithe little body, that pink bow of a mouth. Dark curls glossy as the satin of his ribbons. Large brown eyes whose innocence was a cruel deception indeed. He did not require his mother's advice. He would go to Curzon Street on his own, and he would be vigilant for any traps Morgan Notley might have laid.

He sat up, but found he couldn't move right away. Was his mother well? She often wept for hours after arguments with Loftus's father. Perhaps he should check on her? But what if they were not done fighting? Feeling much like the useless wretch his father thought him, he slipped out of the bedroom and hurried down the stairs, nearly bolting for the front door.

∼

Morgan was pleased that Rivingdon had accepted his invitation to tea. He was not pleased by the idea of seeing Rivingdon, but he was pleased with himself for coming up with the perfect solution regarding the ruined coat: He would offer Loftus Rivingdon one of his own coats from last year. He and Rivingdon were roughly the same size, though the other man was slightly taller. Morgan's clothes—even the items that were a year out of date—were, on the whole, nicer than Rivingdon's. Morgan would never be caught in anything he'd worn last year, and so he might as well give away one of the old coats.

At five minutes till the hour, Rivingdon was announced, and Morgan had one more go at practising the sort of easy smile that made it clear he did not care that Rivingdon had ruined his debut and purchased a skirted frock coat from that traitor Verreau and tried to break his foot. Then Loftus Rivingdon was in the Notleys' drawing room, looking pale and stiff as ever. What a blight his presence was on a room that to Morgan was pure comfort—done all in whites and soft pinks, as though one were sitting on a cloud at sunset. Deep green eyes caught Morgan's and regarded him warily for a moment before Rivingdon issued a greeting and a demure thanks for the invitation. Mama and Cecil were joining them for tea, both to protect Morgan's virtue and to distract him from fantasies of poisoning Rivingdon's tea. Morgan had asked Cook to make fairy cakes with frosting in rose and lavender for the occasion, and the tray of cakes was lovely indeed. Too lovely for the likes of Rivingdon.

Still, he greeted his guest graciously. His mother's greeting was colder, and Cecil's was more of a good-natured grunt than actual words. Then they all sat and commenced the most awkward tea Morgan had ever experienced. Rivingdon apparently had no conversation whatsoever, and so Morgan was forced to laugh with practised gaiety as he recounted the story of the skirted frock coat to his brother, who stared at him with a furrowed brow as though he couldn't imagine why Morgan thought he'd care. He had a fleck of pink frosting at the corner of his mouth. Morgan wanted to scream with frustration. The boor. Morgan turned away from him, only to have his gaze fall once more on Rivingdon. The fellow's expression, which Morgan had previously thought sour, was actually more sulky. An effect that worked well with his full lips and pale, sculpted brows. His nose was quite lovely too—small, with the slightest bump at its midpoint that lent it some character. His hair was so white-blond it looked ethereal. And those green eyes—Morgan might have killed for them.

What was he doing, thinking such things? He refocused on the story he was telling. "I cannot believe I was so terribly clumsy! And on the night of my debut! Why, if it hadn't been for Lord Balfour getting murdered in his own bedchamber, my clumsiness would probably be the talk of London right now."

Cecil's brow scrunched further. "Murdered?"

Rivingdon looked equally confused.

"Yes," Morgan said. "Lord Hartwell killed him to protect Warry's honour. I think it rather a grand romantic gesture. If someone threatened my honour I should like to be defended thusly."

Cecil burst into laughter so loud it gave Morgan an instant headache. "Hartwell didn't murder Lord Balfour, you idiot."

Mama tutted. "Cecil, language."

"Didn't he?" Morgan asked. "I mean, it *is* hard to imagine anyone threatening Warry's honour, but—"

"You *imbecile*," Cecil wheezed. "Balfour wasn't murdered. Lord Hartwell planted him a facer and now suddenly he's got plans to travel the continent. Which means he was probably about to ravish our Warry and got caught at it by someone who wanted to tup the little blighter even more."

"Cecil!" their mother exclaimed.

Cecil shrugged, reaching for more cake. "It's true, isn't it?"

"We have a guest!"

"Well, the thing is," Morgan went on, ignoring his brother's horridness. "Hartwell and Warry are now engaged. And if Hartwell is not to hang, I suppose all's well that ends well."

"Engaged?" Mama cried, and Morgan felt a rush of pleasure at having heard that bit of gossip before she had.

"Hang?" Cecil repeated.

"It is not official yet," Morgan said haughtily. "But I have it on good authority that Hartwell intends to ask Warry tomorrow." He glanced at Rivingdon to see if he looked impressed, or envious, or perhaps awed by Morgan's far-reaching knowledge of Society. But Rivingdon merely studied his plate, which irritated Morgan terribly.

"Anyway, can you ever forgive me, Rivingdon, old chap? For the business with your coat?"

"There is nothing to forgive," Rivingdon said with icy calm. "It was an accident."

But goodness, his eyes met Morgan's again, and something burned there that made Morgan rather uncomfortable. The next laugh he gave was a bit shaky. "Too kind of you. But of course I should like to make it up to you. I want there to be no ill will between us. I have a number of coats that I am certain are of comparable value to your frock coat. You may pick any one of them to take with you."

Rivingdon stopped chewing his fairy cake. Swallowed. "You are offering me one of your coats?"

"I know they are of a slightly different style to yours." He eyed Rivingdon's pale ensemble. "But the bolder colours I favour would not wash you out so much."

Rivingdon set aside his cake and did not speak for a long moment. Morgan was aware of his mother watching the exchange with hawklike sharpness and of Cecil blissfully stuffing his third fairy cake in his mouth. "You wish to offer me a used coat—a non-skirted, non-frock coat—in exchange for ruining my brand new, impeccably tailored, *skirted frock coat?*"

Morgan blinked at the flatness of the man's tone, but recovered his composure quickly. "My coats are very fine indeed."

"Yes," Mama said coolly to Rivingdon. "Whatever is wrong with Morgan's coats?"

The man stiffened visibly. "Nothing, my lady. I'm sure they are very fine, as Mr. Notley has said. It is only that my ruined coat was *very* expensive."

"Then you shall have *two* of mine," Morgan said. "You may sell them, if you like, and use the funds to purchase a new skirted frock coat from M. Verreau."

"It will not be available in time for the Kennilworth rout. And that is where I have promised to dance with Lord Soulden."

He said it deliberately, as though he were slowly pushing a blade into Morgan's breast. Morgan refused to flinch, but inside, a sudden faintness overtook him. Soulden would never have promised Rivingdon any such thing! Would he? "Well, then I am twice as sorry to have ruined the garment. It looked well on you, Mr. Rivingdon." There it was—the slightest spark of hope and uncertainty in Rivingdon's eyes. He was not so sure of himself as he pretended, not at all. Morgan could use this to his advantage. "I can only offer you my humblest apologies and two of my coats. Should you like to go upstairs and make your selections?"

"Morgan!" His mother's eyes widened. "One does not spontaneously invite guests to one's bedchamber to look at one's wardrobe."

"Cecil shall chaperone us, Mama."

Cecil looked up, mouth full of fairy cake. "By all means," he said, without swallowing. Ghastly manners. "Just what I need—a deeper knowledge of Morgan's wardrobe."

The three of them went upstairs. On the landing, Morgan took Cecil's shoulder and drew him several feet ahead of Loftus Rivingdon, hissing in his ear, "Do clear off, please, Cecil. I wish to speak to Mr. Rivingdon alone."

"Are you mad? Mama would have my hide."

"For God's sake, Cecil, I am not going to do anything untoward with Mr. Rivingdon. We do not even like each other. Just pretend as though you intend to sit at the door to the bedroom, and then go pick your teeth somewhere. We shall be done in a few moments."

"You little snake..." Cecil whispered, but Morgan had already turned to Rivingdon and gestured toward the door to his bedroom.

"Come, Mr. Rivingdon. My coats are all in here."

Morgan was a bit appalled at himself, for he really ought to be chaperoned. And yet...well, what was the harm? They were only going into Morgan's bedchamber for a moment, to pick out a coat or two. The rake Slyfeel would have most certainly seized this opportunity to deflower a virgin like Morgan, but Loftus Rivingdon was no Slyfeel. The very notion was laughable.

Morgan enjoyed watching Loftus—*Rivingdon*; when had he

started thinking of him as Loftus?—take in the grandeur of his bedroom. It had a high ceiling with whitewashed beams, pale green paper hangings, and tall, latticed windows that let in a flood of afternoon light. A carved table and matching draped sideboard were painted the same soft green as the paper hangings, and Morgan had not one but *two* massive gilt framed mirrors on adjacent walls. A fringed chaise longue sat along the far wall, a French-styled vanity beside it. The *pièce de résistance*, however, was Morgan's bed. It was large and feather-stuffed, with chintz hangings in a deeper green, accented with panels of rose that matched the rug. Morgan watched Rivingdon take it all in, and felt a thrill at the longing in the other man's eyes.

He made a point of indicating the oak wardrobe near the door, which was carved in a Turkish style. The round handles had been painted with flowers by an artist who had died shortly after, and whose death had considerably heightened demand for his work.

"That is where I keep this Season's clothing," Morgan announced airily, and then led Loftus to the armoire that housed last year's wardrobe and opened it. "Choose whichever two you like."

Loftus approached hesitantly. He inspected his hands—making sure they were clean enough to touch fine fabrics; Morgan recognized the gesture—then began perusing the coats. "These are beautiful." He was breathing shallowly, with envy or admiration, Morgan could not tell. Perhaps both.

"Yes, they've all served me well. Although some of them I never did find time to wear. This one would look good on you."

"I do not care for garnet."

"It is not garnet. It is much more of a currant."

Loftus continued to breathe rapidly. He took a step to the side and it seemed his knees nearly gave out. His envy clearly ran even deeper than Morgan had thought! Then he noticed the man had gone so pale as to erase even the tinge of yellow in his complexion. "Are you well?" Morgan asked.

"Forgive me. I am a bit short of breath."

"You wear stays, do you not?"

Loftus turned sharply to him and gave him that narrow-eyed look that Morgan was rapidly becoming familiar with and that now gave him a small tug in the pit of his stomach, for reasons he did not quite understand. "Of course I do. Any gentleman of fashion with the slightest concern for his figure would wear them."

Morgan chose to ignore what he supposed was a barb aimed at himself. "Perhaps they are too tight."

Loftus didn't answer. His sides moved in and out rather like a small animal, and Morgan had the sudden, unwelcome thought that the fellow's hair was probably as soft and silken as a small animal. It was too fine to be worn in the curls that were the current style, but the straight, shiny locks suited him.

"I can loosen them for you if you like," Morgan offered, and then clapped a hand to his mouth. How grossly improper! And yet he did not retract the offer. It seemed he could barely speak at all, in fact.

Loftus still made no reply. He closed his eyes briefly, placing a hand to his midsection. Morgan watched him, uncertain what to do.

Loftus spoke at last. "I don't like the stays. I thought I would. But they give me an odd shape, and I...perhaps they make me look even worse, in a way?"

"*Even* worse?"

Loftus shook his head.

"What do you mean, even worse?"

"I...I don't know." Loftus looked so distraught that it was difficult not to pity him.

"You need not wear them, if you don't like them."

Loftus's surprisingly broad shoulders squared. "My mother gave them to me, so clearly she felt they were needed."

"Your mother gave you stays?"

"She said I have a sweet tooth I indulge too often." Loftus was staring into the armoire, muttering almost too quietly for Morgan to hear. "And it is beginning to show."

"You are very slender," Morgan offered, trying to imagine Mama telling him he looked anything but perfect. It must be horrid to hear one's own mother declare that one was too thick about the waist.

"Not like you."

Morgan felt a burst of pride at the comment before unease overtook him. It was not a compliment offered with pleasure or admiration—or even raging jealousy. Loftus's tone was flat and hopeless. And Morgan truly did not know what to say.

At last, Loftus sighed. "I am fine. I was only dizzy for a moment." He touched the sleeve of a pale-yellow coat that would have looked all wrong on him. "I only wish I knew whether the stays are truly to the benefit of my figure."

"Remove your coat." Morgan's blood buzzed slightly at his own casual directive. Mama did not like to scold him, but oh, she would have had something to say about him asking his guest to disrobe in his bedchamber.

The suspicion in Loftus's gaze nearly made Morgan laugh before he reminded himself that they were mortal enemies, and he ought not to be feeling such sympathy for his rival.

"Go on."

"*Why?*"

"You can't trust me for much, but you can trust that I'll be honest with you about your stays."

"You must be mad."

"Some would say I am generous."

"Where is your brother?"

"Good heavens, I am not planning an assault on your virtue," Morgan snapped, smile vanishing. "This is fashion advice, no more." How dare Loftus even *suggest* Morgan desired anything improper from him!

"I have never sought your advice."

Morgan's lips twitched in spite of himself. "There is a first time for everything."

Somehow they had come to be standing quite close together. Morgan could just smell Loftus's cedarwood cologne over the scent of his own orange blossom toilet water. Cecil's unkind comment about the overturned fruit cart came back to him. Perhaps he should have applied slightly less.

"I cannot remove my coat without help," Loftus said tersely.

"Of course not." Morgan could not imagine undressing without assistance. "I shall help you, if you undo your buttons."

Loftus looked very much as though he suspected a trap, and yet his fingers moved slowly to his buttons. Once the coat was open, Morgan gripped its shoulders, discovering they were padded. He wondered if that had been Lady Rivingdon's idea as well. Loftus tensed beneath his hands, but Morgan merely eased the coat off his shoulders without comment, then helped tug the tight cuffs over his hands. His fingers brushed Loftus's knuckles, producing a curious sensation. Morgan swallowed and folded Loftus's coat, setting it upon his chaise longue. He turned back to see Loftus standing by the bed in his waistcoat and fine muslin shirt, his cravat pulled slightly askew by their joint effort to remove his coat. Morgan could scarcely breathe for a rather alarming moment.

"You may lift your shirt." Morgan's throat was dry, putting a catch in his voice that he hoped Loftus would not notice. "If you feel comfortable doing so."

Loftus breathed softly, and yet the sound seemed to echo in Morgan's large room. His hand moved at last to his waist, and then he hesitated. "Well, I suppose it's easier if I—" He hastily unbuttoned his waistcoat, shrugging out of it clumsily and then holding it balled in his hands.

"Here," Morgan said gently, hating to see such lovely fabric treated so.

He took the waistcoat and laid it with Loftus's coat. Loftus glanced at him, still wary. "Is this a trick?" he asked.

Morgan shook his head. Perhaps it ought to have been. But he knew what it was to need an honest opinion of the figure one cut. "I assure you, it is not a trick."

Loftus bit his lip, and Morgan felt an uncomfortable pull between his legs. Loftus's lips were—generously full, to put it mildly. It rather made one want to touch, which was, of course, absurdly inappropriate. He coughed.

Loftus at last lifted his shirt, very slowly, revealing stays of sage coloured satin that made a band around his narrow waist. Above was an expanse of pale skin that looked so soft, for moment Morgan could think of nothing but how it might feel to run his fingers over it.

They stood for a moment in breathless silence. Morgan knew he ought to say something, but he did not want to move. Did not want to do anything but look at Loftus Rivingdon.

"Do you think I'm very ugly?" It seemed Loftus hadn't meant to ask the question—and was deeply embarrassed that he had.

Tempting as it might have been to lie, to say yes and destroy all he could reach of Loftus's confidence, Morgan couldn't have made himself say it if he'd wanted to. "No," he whispered. "You are absolutely gorgeous."

They were perhaps the most honest words he'd ever spoken in his life.

For an instant, Loftus's eyes were wide and hopeful. And then a hardness returned to them, and their very colour seemed to darken. "You mock me."

"No." Morgan reached out involuntarily, and then realised he was not sure what he'd intended to do. It was only that he wanted desperately to touch the soft, pale skin above Loftus's stays. There was a red indent along the garment's upper edge where it had dug too hard into tender flesh. Morgan would have loved to trace it. To loosen the laces and feel Loftus sigh with relief, and then touch every single mark the dreadful thing had left.

He fairly shook himself, trying to reclaim as much of his composure as he could.

Loftus stared icily at Morgan's hand, suspended in the air between them. Embarrassed, Morgan let his arm drop to his side. Then he stuck his hand in his trousers pocket for good measure. "I was curious about the material," he murmured.

"It's satin over bone," Loftus said stiffly.

Morgan nodded. "I assumed."

Loftus went on, "I do not have much in the way of muscle definition. You no doubt noticed that my coat had padded shoulders. If you say anything to anyone—"

"Gorgeous," Morgan repeated.

"Stop." Loftus's tone was harsh, and he jerked his shirt back down over his stays. "Why do you insist on—? Well, but you must enjoy seeing that I am far from incomparable."

Morgan shook his head. "I should not consider you a rival if you were not formidable. I concede this point: you are beautiful."

He must be possessed. That was the only plausible explanation for the words he was speaking. Yet they were the truth.

"If it's a trick, will you just say so?" Loftus sounded pained. "I am not quite myself today, and I just—if you are doing this for revenge, you have already won. Not forever!" he added hastily. "I just…right now…I do not much like myself." He cut his gaze toward Morgan. "Do you ever feel that way? No, what a stupid question. Of course you don't."

"I do, sometimes. More than you think."

Loftus swallowed visibly and looked away.

"May I unlace your stays?" Morgan spoke very softly. "And we shall see how you look without them?"

"You are supposed to be giving me a coat." Loftus sounded uncertain again.

"I wish to help you."

"Won't your family wonder why we've been absent so long?"

"All the more reason to hurry."

Loftus sighed and slowly turned his back to Morgan. "Very well. Take care that your hands are not sweaty or greasy."

Morgan's temper flared. "I don't know what sort of barbarian you think me. And I have told you I do not sweat."

Loftus didn't answer as Morgan lifted his shirt and, trying not to draw too audible a breath, tugged the laces of the boned garment. Loftus was terribly slender, bending to the pressure of Morgan's tugs like a reed in the wind. Morgan could not imagine how his mother thought he required stays. It also occurred to Morgan that perhaps one not need be slender to be beautiful, and while that was not a thought he'd ever had before, it seemed a rather profound one.

He gripped the garment's edges, leaving his knuckles pressed for a moment against the warmth of Loftus's sides. Then he lifted the garment. The satin clung for a moment to Loftus's skin before coming away. The fellow's torso was covered with raw red lines, and it seemed to take him a moment to properly exhale. He kept his stomach sucked in, Morgan noticed, as though he could not even remember how to relax that part of himself.

"Does that feel better?" Morgan asked, reluctantly dropping the hem of the man's shirt. He set the stays on top of the growing pile of Loftus's clothes.

Loftus nodded, head bowed. He was still facing away from Morgan.

"Come, let us put your waistcoat back on and see how you look."

Loftus turned toward Morgan once more. His face, which Morgan had observed last week normally held just a hint of a yellow undertone, was flushed, and now Morgan found himself wanting to brush his fingertips over the splotches of pink on Loftus's cheeks. Oh, what a model of depravity he was turning out to be! He ought never have picked up *The Maiden Diaries*.

He also ought not to have thought about *The Maiden Diaries* just now, for in the most recent chapter he'd read, fingertips ran up and down all sorts of body parts, and he simply could *not* afford to recall those passages in detail. Not if he wanted to maintain the line of his pantaloons.

He quickly helped Loftus into the waistcoat. Stepped back as Loftus did up the buttons.

"There now!" Morgan eyed him critically. "Oh, you look well."

"I do not look bloated?"

"Not in the slightest. I don't think those stays were ever needed. Shall we put on your coat?" He held the discarded tailcoat out and assisted Loftus in the donning of it. "All right, take a few steps back now so I may see you properly. Loftus! You cut a stunning figure."

He realised he ought not to sound so enthusiastic. Indeed, dread was returning to the pit of his stomach. Suppose Lord Soulden really *did* come to favour Loftus over Morgan? It *could* conceivably happen, if Loftus wore the right colours.

Oh dear. What had he done?

Loftus gave the barest hint of a lopsided grin, which rendered him well and truly stunning, before he seemed to remember how much he loathed Morgan.

"It is said that your mother was quite fashionable, in her day. I suppose you take after her," Morgan offered.

"A week ago, you did not know who I was. Now you are versed in my mother's fashion history?" Loftus said bitterly.

Know thine enemy, Morgan thought. "I made enquiries."

"Well, then you may know that my father is a gambler." Any trace of a smile had disappeared from Loftus's face. "He has plunged the family far below our former standing. My mother has been most unhappy in her marriage. That is because she married for love instead of for practical reasons. And look how that turned out! I mean to rectify our family situation and marry a title. But if I disappoint her..."

Morgan didn't speak, just waited.

"Well, then, she will have nothing at all, will she? I am the only good thing she has in her life."

Morgan felt a stab of pity for the fellow that was quickly replaced by calculation. Loftus Rivingdon was deeply insecure. A nonpareil such as Soulden would be able to sense that insecurity with ease, and would find that trait most unappealing. He would inevitably discard Loftus, if he did not rebuff him straight out. And with Loftus out of the way, Morgan could make his move.

"Well then you must not fail her, Loftus," he said quietly, widening his eyes.

Loftus jerked as though he'd been slapped. "I know that! That's what I've just told you."

"Yes, but I'm not even sure you understand the full extent of it. My cousin Rebecca, she is forever telling me about the difficulties of a woman's position in society. Women have not the freedoms we do, you must remember that. For a woman to be trapped in a bad marriage, that is a dreadful fate."

Loftus's deep-set eyes took on that near pleading glint again. "I do know that. I want to help my mother."

"Of course you do! And in light of how much is at stake," Morgan said gently, carefully, "might it not be better to set your sights on someone a bit more…appropriate? Still a title, of course," he added hastily. "Still someone capable of restoring your family's good standing. But—I know you will think I say this because we are at odds with one another, but I do wish to help you here—somebody a bit more manageable. You are very beautiful, but Viscount Soulden is perfection itself. Even I am intimidated by the prospect of courting him. And you *are* only a baronet's son."

Loftus's eyes blazed, and Morgan realised he ought not to have included that last part. He was in the process of debating how to make an apology sound sincere when Loftus's expression softened, taking on that tinge of hopelessness again. "You might be right." Morgan disliked how defeated the man sounded. A rivalry was no fun unless both parties approached it with their wits sharpened. "Yet he is the perfect match for me."

"I know it seems so. Who could look upon him without wanting him? But there are many other eligible bachelors. I'm only thinking of how your mother might feel if you were to reach too high and then fall. Publicly."

He actually saw Loftus shiver.

"I will think on it," Loftus whispered. "I shall take that yellow coat there, and—and the currant."

Yellow is not your colour, Morgan wanted to say. But he held his tongue.

A quarter of an hour later, Loftus Rivingdon left Morgan's home in possession of two coats and with his stays tucked between the coats. He did not move as stiffly now that his waist was not bound so. Morgan had a sour taste in his mouth. He had one or two minor flaws, he knew. A touch of vanity, yes. A tendency to prattle. But for the first time in his life, he had the unshakable sense that he had done something truly terrible in exploiting Loftus's fears. Shame was nearly a foreign concept to Morgan, and yet he felt it now, imagining Loftus arriving home to a mother who criticised his figure, who put such pressure on him to succeed. Imagining that soft-looking skin marked red from the stays. He almost wished he could summon Loftus back by magic, retract what he'd said. Tell the fellow the truth: that if Lady Rivingdon was in any way disappointed in her son—physically speaking, of course; the fellow's character was still abominable—then she needed her head examined.

～

*L*oftus stared out his bedroom window for a while after returning to his home, a small smile curving his lips. What a little fool that Notley was. He could scarcely have believed things would go so well. All he'd had to do was widen his eyes a bit—a trick he'd learned from Notley—and murmur soft questions. *Am I truly beautiful? Do you really think I look well without my stays? Oh poor me, what if I should disappoint my mother?* Notley had swallowed it all. And he had done just as Loftus would have predicted. Tried to use Loftus's perceived insecurities to his advantage.

This was good. Let him think that Loftus was taking himself out of contention for Lord Soulden's hand. Let him think his path toward the viscount was clear. Loftus would make his move when he was ready, and it would be so very satisfying to see the look on Notley's face when Loftus commanded Soulden's attention at the Kennilworth rout in two days' time.

His smile slipped as he recalled with a sudden tug in his gut the feeling of Morgan's hands against his skin. The way Morgan had asked him, so softly, to lift his shirt. The next tug came somewhere lower than his gut as he thought of Morgan calling him beautiful.

His breath slid very slowly from his lungs. He did not care what impression his figure made on Morgan—Notley—no, Morgan; he ought to let himself think of his rival intimately, for a certain degree of intimacy would be required in order for Loftus to destroy the man. He did not care. He did not.

Yet he found himself reaching under the mattress for volume four of *The Maiden Diaries*. And thinking, every time Slyfeel ran his skilled hands over his latest conquest, of Morgan's gentle fingers drawing away his stays, brushing over his skin, seeming to hover as though Morgan would have liked to touch Loftus for hours on end.

CHAPTER 7

The Kennilworth Rout

Morgan fiddled with his ivory buttons all the way to the Kennilworth rout, jostled between his mother and Cecil in the carriage. Cecil was fidgety too—he was impatiently awaiting the birth of his first child, and Mrs. Notley had still literally failed to deliver. Morgan thought Cecil was taking a rather unseemly interest in matters. Last night he had even refused a second brandy with dinner, choosing instead to rush home and sit with his wife. He hadn't even thought that perhaps Morgan might like another invitation to Bucknall's! Really. It was lucky that Morgan was used to disappointment when it came to Cecil, or he might have been quite upset at his selfishness.

Morgan sighed as he thumbed a button. They were intricately carved and not at all garish—but Morgan thought that they were rather ruined for him now that he knew about elephants. Who would have guessed they did not drop their tusks like a stag shed its antlers? Morgan had never seen an elephant, but they looked quite wonderful in books, and it seemed a shame to have them reduced to buttons, even though buttons were one of life's true delights.

He sighed again as his thoughts drifted from ivory buttons to Loftus Rivingdon.

Two crises of conscience in one carriage ride; it was quite unprecedented. Poor Loftus felt so dreadful about his looks—understandably, because he was certainly not as beautiful as Morgan—and his mother seemed quite awful. And the matter of his father's gambling debts—terrible! Morgan tried not to think of Loftus with any pity but, as with the elephants, he couldn't escape that idea that by knowing, he was obligated to somehow act. Unfortunately, also as with the elephants, he had no idea what he was supposed to do. He certainly wasn't going to step out of the way so that Loftus had an unimpeded path to matrimonial bliss with Viscount Soulden, but perhaps there was another bachelor, only slightly less eligible, that Morgan could nudge Loftus towards.

And then, once they were both satisfactorily wed, Morgan would no longer have to worry that Loftus was sad, or feel guilty about having wielded Loftus's insecurities—however mildly—against him. He would no longer have to see those beautiful eyes shimmering with a film of tears, and think about how pale and soft and warm his skin was, and–

What?

Morgan jolted upright.

He was *not* thinking about Loftus's skin. Not now, and not last night when he'd fallen asleep after reading a new chapter of *The Maiden Diaries*. Somehow in his dreams it wasn't Lord Slyfeel whispering in his ear and making him shudder, but someone softer, prettier, with hair the colour of moonbeams.

"Cecil," he said meditatively, "what do you know of elephants?"

Cecil chewed his bottom lip. "The period of gestation for cows is almost two years."

"Elephants," Morgan said gently. "From Africa. With tusks and trunks."

Cecil gave him a strange look.

"We do not talk about gestation!" Mama exclaimed, and snapped him on the wrist with her fan. "Really, Morgan. What are you thinking?"

Morgan wasn't entirely sure himself, but he kept his mouth closed until they reached the Kennilworths' house.

And what a magnificent house it was! So much better than Lord Balfour's, and without the slightest taint of murder—real or rumoured—upon it. It was in Mayfair, because of course it was, and its rather austere facade turned out to hide a multitude of architectural treasures. The doors opened onto a glorious entry hall with parquet flooring. The chandeliers glittered, splashing the walls with shards of light. The footmen, all of them exactly the same height and weight and hair colour—what an eye for detail the Kennilworths had!—wore matching crimson uniforms. Their shoes were so highly polished that they too reflected the lights from the chandeliers. But Morgan was almost blind to the details because he saw, the moment he stepped inside flanked by Mama and Cecil, a man ascending the sweeping staircase in front of them.

Lord Soulden!

Morgan's breath caught in his throat. If only they had arrived a minute earlier, perhaps they might have crossed paths in the entry hall and walked up the stairs together! He consoled himself with the knowledge that he'd catch up with the viscount once they were inside the rout.

It was Morgan's first rout, and he hoped that his nerves did not show. While the ball had been his true debut, Morgan felt more comfortable dancing than conversing, and here at a rout there wasn't even any music so that he could pretend, if he needed a little more time to come up with something to say in reply to someone, that he hadn't heard them the first time. Routs were for sparkling conversation, and Morgan was afraid that he sparkled a little less when he was not in motion.

Still, he lifted his chin as he walked up the stairs with Mama and Cecil, because he was beautiful and indomitable. When he stepped into the large gallery overlooked by the portraits of what were presumably generations of Kennilworths, Morgan took a breath to steel himself, fixed a beguiling smile on his lips, and waited to be noticed.

And noticed he was, by both men and women who approached Mama and Cecil with polite overtures and sharp gazes, pulling Morgan into conversation the moment they were introduced. All of Morgan's nerves drained away, leaving him a little breathless with relief and delight. He was the centre of attention! A lady complimented him on the way he wore his hair. A gentleman asked him if he had seen Mr. Booth performing Richard III. Mama listened proudly while Morgan spoke to everyone who spoke to him. Cecil ate a small cake and kept checking his pocket watch.

At length, Morgan was able to slip away from his small crowd of admirers, and Mama and Cecil, on the pretext of fetching a drink. He had glimpsed Soulden on the other side of the gallery, and had noticed Loftus Rivingdon weaving stealthily towards him. Morgan's flare of jealousy warred with a stab of pity: Loftus was wearing the yellow coat, not the currant. Was he *blind*? Yellow did his glorious complexion no favours at all. It made him look waxy and ill. He ought to have worn the currant.

Morgan caught up with Loftus. "Good evening."

Loftus's mouth wavered as though he was not certain if he ought to smile or not, and his gaze darted to Lord Soulden and back. "Good evening."

They both stared at Soulden. He was a little further down the room, standing in profile and looking as perfectly handsome as always. He had the sort of face that was made for portraiture. He stood with one hand tucked into his coat, and he was speaking in a low voice to an uninteresting looking man who was round of figure and somewhere in his middle years. Whatever Soulden was saying must have been compelling, because the round little man nodded intently every few moments.

"We cannot just approach him," Morgan fretted.

Loftus said, "Well, *I* can. I have already been introduced."

Morgan gasped.

Loftus raised his eyebrows. "I introduced myself, actually."

Morgan wished he hadn't wasted a gasp on Loftus's initial statement, because he felt it rather took away the impact of his second, more important gasp. "You did not!"

"I did," Loftus said proudly.

"That is scandalous!" Morgan hissed.

"Oh, please." Loftus brushed a hand down the front of his coat. "You speak to *me* of scandal? Even if the Season were a hundred years long, I doubt I could commit any scandal remotely as shocking as your cousin's."

"Yes," Morgan said, wondering if he meant Warry, or Becca, or both of them for different reasons. Probably Warry. "Well, Warry and Hartwell are marrying this Sunday, and it turns out that Hartwell didn't murder Balfour after all, so that is no longer a scandal. It is in fact rather a triumph."

Loftus gave him a dubious look.

"Well," Morgan said, "if you have already been introduced to Lord Soulden, you can introduce *me*."

He strode towards Soulden, leaving Loftus hurrying to catch up.

The little round man saw them approaching and said something in an undertone to Soulden before moving away. Soulden turned, an eyebrow raised as he watched Morgan and Loftus bear down on him.

"Ah," Soulden said. "Mr. Rivingdon. How nice to see you again."

Morgan halted, and jabbed Loftus in the ribs. "Introduce me," he hissed under his breath.

Loftus cleared his throat. "My lord," he said, "please allow me to introduce my..."

"Friend," Morgan whispered sharply.

"My *friend*," Loftus said between clenched teeth. "Mr. Morgan Notley."

Soulden bowed. "A pleasure, Mr. Notley."

Morgan managed to squeak a reply even though he suddenly

had no air in his lungs at all. He and Loftus stared at Soulden. Soulden stared back at them, a faint line appearing between his brows.

"Um," said Loftus.

Morgan continued to stare.

"Oh, I see," Soulden said after a moment. His cheek twitched. "Allow me to be bold, gentlemen. You are both quite lovely, but I am afraid I am not in the market for a husband. While I am sure you are both"—his gaze flicked between them—"*delightful*, I would advise you to set your sights elsewhere, for I fear I shall only disappoint you."

"You could *never* disappoint me, sir," Loftus said, breathy and pink-faced.

Morgan nodded, wide-eyed.

Soulden glanced around and then leaned in close. "Boys," he said, his voice low and rough, "find a couple of milksops to set your caps at. I'm not the gentle ride you're looking for, trust me."

And then he bowed and walked away, leaving both Morgan and Loftus with their jaws on the floor.

~

Morgan drank a glass of punch quickly, and then fanned his face with his hand. Loftus, lurking suspiciously nearby but possibly too afraid to approach him after their last encounter over punch, looked just as breathless as Morgan felt.

Morgan set his glass down and stepped away. He caught Loftus by the end of his sleeve and tugged him behind a column. They were still in sight of the people in the gallery if they chose to look, but the cool marble offered at least an illusion of privacy.

"What did he mean?" Morgan asked, fanning his face again. It did nothing for the heat that had settled there. "He is not a *gentle* ride?"

Loftus glanced around before whispering, "Do you think he is a Slyfeel?"

"I have no idea to what you are referring," Morgan said primly.

Loftus rolled his eyes.

"Fine," Morgan huffed. "Yes, I think he is a rake just like Slyfeel! And perhaps that is not where the resemblance ends!"

Loftus gasped, which was really more Morgan's thing, though he did not comment on it.

"I think," Morgan said, "that Viscount Soulden is as rough as a stallion!"

"And as big?"

Morgan tore his gaze away from Loftus's damp bottom lip and tried to pretend he had an air of worldly knowledge. "Oh, certainly."

"And does he imagine that we are too willowy and frail to handle such dimensions?"

Morgan gasped, and did it rather better than Loftus. "I do not think I could handle a *stallion!*"

For a moment Loftus looked uncertain. "Slyfeel's paramours seem to manage with a great degree of enthusiasm and good spirits."

Morgan considered that. "Yes, that is certainly true."

He was uncomfortably aware of the paucity of his knowledge of such matters. While Mama was forthcoming with him about the ways in which to navigate both Society and a marriage, she had rather glossed over the details of how to navigate the acts one was expected to perform in the marriage bed. Morgan had never suspected that his innocence might be off-putting to a man as experienced as Soulden, but now he saw his own uncertainty reflected in Loftus's eyes.

"I do not wish to marry a milksop." A scowl creased Loftus's perfect brow. "I wish to marry Lord Soulden."

Morgan wondered why it was a rush of solidarity he felt, not a spike of hot jealousy. "As do I."

Loftus looked at him cautiously, and something passed between them that Morgan thought was a little more than understanding, and perhaps something approaching camaraderie. Was it the first faint stirrings of friendship? Morgan had never had friends before, so he could not be sure. But it was strange that he no longer hated Loftus with a fierce, fiery rage. Instead of being rivals, Morgan thought that they were almost brothers in arms. Of course he still wanted to be the one who wed Soulden, but he no longer wished to strangle Loftus in a ditch in order to have that happen. It was quite perplexing.

Morgan cast his gaze around the gallery. "Do you suppose there are people here who are accustomed to"—he lowered his voice—*"rough rides?"*

Loftus curled his mouth into a disdainful smile. "I'm sure there are the sons and daughters of factory owners and shipyard owners and cotton mill owners who have no breeding at all, and who know exactly how to take a stallion!"

Morgan gasped at his vulgarity, delighted and appalled in equal measure. "I *know*! It is appalling that almost anyone can make their debut these days. Whatever next? Will the denizens of the Isle of Dogs soon be lined up to meet Prinny?"

Loftus's eyes brightened and he threw back his head and laughed. Morgan's gaze caught on his slender throat, which gleamed under the lights of the chandeliers, and on his Adam's apple, which gave an intriguing angle to the line of his throat. Morgan's hand twitched, and for a moment he fought the reckless urge to reach out and touch Loftus's beautiful neck.

Loftus's laughter faded, and his expression grew pinched once more. "How rough do you suppose he means?"

"I don't know." Morgan shivered, but the sensation wasn't entirely unpleasant. "Oh, do you think this is why Slyfeel always has a riding crop at hand?"

Very soon they were comparing chapter notes in an attempt to discern what was credible about *The Maiden Diaries*, and what was entirely fantastical. Morgan was bothered by not knowing the difference, and he suspected Loftus was as well.

"In your *mouth?*" Loftus squeaked at one point, slapping his hands over his lips as his tone caught the attention of a pair of ladies passing. "But wouldn't it taste funny?"

"I don't know," Morgan said. He wrinkled his nose. "It doesn't sound very nice, does it?"

"You truly think that aspect of the story is credible?"

"Well it happens quite a lot, especially in volume two. Would the author really have used such descriptions over and over if the very idea were utter nonsense?"

Loftus swallowed visibly. "I did wonder…" He took a breath. "Do you remember the *particular* scene in volume two, chapter three, where Slyfeel and Lord Stanhope are on the knoll…"

"Yes! Oh it is deli—I mean, frightful. The way Slyfeel—well, he does…in Stanhope's mouth—" Morgan lowered his voice so that Loftus would have to lean in to hear, and his heart thumped as he caught Loftus's scent—that lovely, light note of cedarwood—"and then they—well, I don't need to remind you what Stanhope does. And then they *kiss*."

"Yes, precisely." Loftus nodded with vigour. "Frightful."

Morgan cleared his throat. His heart was now going rather fast, and his drawers suddenly felt uncomfortably tight as he recalled the description of Slyfeel grabbing Lord Stanhope's hair, and Stanhope yielding helplessly to Slyfeel's insistent tongue, his mouth still bitter with the taste of his debaucher's seed. "Would *you* ever…?" Oh, what was the matter with him? Yet he was desperate to know the answer. "But of course, this is hardly a subject of conversation for gentlemen."

"Oh, hardly."

A long silence.

"But *would* you?" Morgan's voice was barely audible.

Loftus looked at the wall, the floor—anywhere but Morgan. "Would *you?*" he asked finally.

That was not fair. Not fair at all. Morgan had asked first. And yet, maybe if he answered, Loftus would answer too…

He had just lifted his chin to perform a slight nod that he might be able to pass off as something else should Loftus recoil in horror, when Mama bustled over to fetch him. "Morgan! What are you doing lurking back here? You are here to be *seen*, my darling." Her gaze found Loftus and narrowed. "Mr. *Rivingdon*."

She said his name as though it were a curse. Morgan really must find out the cause of the animosity between his mother and Loftus's. He searched frantically for something to say that would convince Mama to leave them to their conversation, but all he could think of was whether or not Loftus would ever…in his *mouth*.

Loftus bowed. "Lady Notley."

Mama took Morgan by the elbow and began to steer him away.

"Oh!" Morgan exclaimed, disappointed. He and Loftus had only just got to the juiciest parts of *The Maiden Diaries*. "You must come to tea, Mr. Rivingdon! Do say you will!"

Loftus looked surprised, and then a cautious smile spread across his features. "I would like that, Mr. Notley. Thank you."

Mama made an impatient clicking sound with her tongue, and pulled Morgan back into the rout.

CHAPTER 8

The morning after the Kennilworth rout, Loftus slept late. He woke when Martin brought him tea and opened the curtains to allow the watery sunlight to wash into his room, but when Loftus enquired, Martin said that his father was still taking his breakfast in the dining room. Loftus fell back against his pillows unhappily and pulled his blankets over his head. No, he would wait until his father had left the house before he ventured forth from his bed, even though the day outside looked lovely and he wished for nothing more than to take a walk. The house was on Bruton Street, at the end closest to Berkeley Square, but Loftus disdained the trees and hedges of the square, preferring to set out the other way down the street—to Bond Street. There, his desires and delights were always met, because the tailors of Bond Street were the greatest in the world.

Loftus hunkered under his blankets and thought of his father's anger at the amount he spent on clothes. They were not fripperies though—they were necessities! Not that Loftus would have had the courage to burst in on his parents' argument to defend himself thusly. His father would eat his words when Loftus married Lord Soulden—Loftus would gladly be the one to shove them down his throat until he choked—but, until then, Loftus would have to bite his tongue.

No, Loftus did not think he would enjoy Bond Street today. Not if he would only hear his father's ugly disdain in his ears the entire time he was there. He stared at the patterns of light on his ceiling and wondered what he might do instead.

His thoughts drifted to Morgan, and he pulled them back again. Morgan—no, *Notley* was not his friend, whatever fellow feeling they had shared last night, and however much of *The Maiden Diaries* he had also read. Notley was his rival, and Loftus was lulling him into a false sense of security. He was the swaying viper to Notley's gormless bunny, and he would strike when Notley least expected it. Only one of them could win Soulden's hand—as well as all the other parts of him, however stallion-like they were—and Loftus was determined it would be him. He would invite Notley to the wedding, of course, and Notley would cry. It would be delightful. And then Loftus and Soulden would laugh about it afterwards.

Notley had invited him to tea. Should he go? He had no wish to sit in the company of Lady Notley or Cecil again. Though it could be enjoyable to talk with Notley of *The Maiden Diaries* once more. Morgan's question still set his face burning when he recalled it. *"But would you?"* What precisely had he even meant? *Would you put a prick in your mouth? Would you let—that happen while the prick was in your mouth? Would you kiss the fellow afterward?*

He huddled into himself. Would Viscount Soulden *expect* that? Loftus was not sure at all he would like the taste. But if he was to marry Soulden, then he must learn to like a rough ride. Or at least tolerate one.

He sat up suddenly, struck by an idea. He would call on Notley today, and he would bring volume four of *The Maiden Diaries* to lend him, as Notley said he had not read it yet. He would carry it in discreetly, of course, and try to get the fellow alone for a moment to make the offer. Then perhaps he could lean close to Morgan's—

Notley's—ear and whisper, *I would*. And let the man guess what, precisely, he meant.

Oh, that would be jolly fun.

Cheered, he rose from his bed. Perhaps by the time Martin dressed him, his father would be gone. He considered the items in his wardrobe. Spotted the stays, which had fallen to the floor. He had not worn them since that day with Notley. Not even to the Kennilworth rout. And truly, he did not miss them.

~

Morgan was painting in his sitting room when Sedgewick knocked at the door. "Mr. Rivingdon is here to see you, sir."

Morgan tried to ignore the way his heart skipped. Loftus? He frowned at the large canvas before him, on which he had rendered an excellent likeness of Soulden. He had been so busy over the years cultivating fine manners and breathtaking beauty that he had sorely neglected the arts. But his muse had come to him today, and he was rather enjoying a peaceful afternoon at the easel, an old damask robe that he no longer had use for wrapped around him to protect his clothes. Should he allow Rivingdon to see him like this? He was not even wearing a neckcloth.

He *did* want Loftus to see his painting and envy his skill.

"Send him up, please." he said without looking away from his masterpiece. "Is that Mama at the piano downstairs?"

"Yes, sir."

That was good. When Mama lost herself in her piano-playing, she had no concern for what Morgan got up to.

"Shall I send Grady to chaperone, Sir?"

"No, Sedgwick. Mama has determined that Loftus and I do not require a chaperone due to our mutual loathing."

"Very good, sir." Sedgwick did not sound convinced.

Morgan ignored the man and dabbed a spot of paint on his

canvas. Then he took a step back and tilted his head, unsure if the placement of the dab pleased him or not. He used to have a much better eye for painting, he was certain. He had been much praised for his painting by his childhood tutors, but Mama felt that once such praise had been attained there was no further need for Morgan to spend time on painting—as though one attained proficiency and then moved on to the next goal. In Morgan's case, the next goal had been singing, but he could not sing half as well as he could paint and, he thought a little despondently, he did not *like* singing. But singing, Mama thought, was a better skill for an incomparable to practise. One did not entertain guests by painting for them. A song was an ephemeral delight. A painting persisted even after a golden afternoon had faded and skirted, Morgan thought, perhaps perilously close to being considered the tangible result of *labour*.

Last year Morgan had visited the Dulwich Picture Gallery with Cecil and Mrs. Notley—although she had still been Miss Harriet Linley back then, and Morgan's presence had been for the sake of propriety. He and one of Harriet's cousins had trailed around the gallery while Cecil had grunted like a warthog at Harriet and Harriet had, rather astonishingly, been quite charmed by him. Morgan had found himself drawn particularly to the work of the Flemish and Dutch masters at the southern end of the gallery. He had stood in front of paintings and felt, for the first time in his life, invisible. It had not been frightening. It had been, strangely, freeing. Morgan hadn't imagined himself as one of the figures preserved for eternity within a gilt frame; he'd imagined himself the invisible hand applying the brush strokes that made it possible. Not his face on a painting, but his signature.

But Mama said he had to practise his singing.

"Mr. Rivingdon, sir," Sedgwick said, and Morgan jolted and turned.

Loftus looked divine. He wore pantaloons of red—Morgan had never seen him in pantaloons before; they suited him—with braiding on the fall, a dark blue coat, and a grey cravat. His waistcoat was mossy green. How splendid that he had worn no yellow!

"Good morning," Morgan said.

"Good morning." A pinch of colour stained Loftus's pale cheeks. "I have brought you a book that you may borrow."

"How kind. Sedgwick, please send up tea and cakes."

Sedgewick bowed and slipped away.

Loftus set his book down on a chair, and came to stand beside Morgan. He raised his brows as he studied the canvas. "What are you painting?"

"What—" Morgan huffed out a breath.

"Is it supposed to be Lord Wellington?"

"No!" Morgan glared at him. "It is Lord Soulden, obviously!"

Loftus looked abashed. "Oh."

Morgan pressed his mouth into a thin line. "Well, he clearly doesn't care about buttons, and neither does he care for our looks, so I thought I would impress him with my artistic ability, but it seems that in your opinion I have none!"

"I didn't say that," Loftus said. He gave Morgan a wary look. "I mean, you paint much better than I can, but..."

"But?"

Loftus wrinkled his nose. "But much worse than Sir Thomas Lawrence."

Morgan huffed again. He had decided this morning to try huffing in lieu of gasping. He rather thought it suited him. "Well, of course I am much worse than Sir Thomas Lawrence! He is a master!" His anger deflated. "And Mama thinks painting is a waste of my time. She thinks that it is acceptable for the future spouse of a lord to draw little scenes in a diary or in letters for the amusement of their friends, but one must be careful not to appear to be more than an amateur, do you understand? Whether that is in art, or science, or letters, or anything at all."

Loftus nodded, and then his gaze slid back to the painting. "Do you... do you think you ought to have started smaller? Perhaps with a miniature?"

Morgan sighed. Loftus was right. He had been foolish to attempt a canvas as large as this one when he had hardly picked a brush up in the last few years. "Perhaps, yes."

"Also, if one has to squint," Loftus said, "it might present your work in a more, ah, favourable aspect."

Some of the rage that had caught Morgan at Lord Balfour's ball seized him again—before he could even stop himself he had jabbed Loftus in the temple with his paintbrush, and smeared a line of cobalt blue paint through his beautiful white-blond hair.

Loftus sputtered, his jaw dropping. "Why—" And then, to Morgan's surprise, Loftus began to laugh. "I wasn't even trying to be cutting, I swear!"

"I'm sorry!" Morgan exclaimed. He made to set his paintbrush down, but Loftus leaned forward and snatched it from him. Morgan darted out of the way, so Loftus shrugged and grinned and painted a blue stripe down Lord Soulden's face.

"There! I have made it better!" he announced.

Morgan blinked at the painting. He could not agree at all that Loftus had made it better but, if he was being honest, he had to admit that he hadn't made it any worse, which also stung. He took another brush from the cup on the table and swirled it in the green paint on his palette. He approached the canvas. He hadn't been able to get the shade of Soulden's hair right at all. A thrill filled him as he swiped his brush against the canvas, the green paint mixing with the brown already there and creating a shade not unlike Loftus's mossy waistcoat.

"It suits him!" Loftus's eyes shone, seemingly brighter thanks to the blue streak in his hair.

Morgan laughed, oddly weightless, and gave Soulden another green lock of hair. He and Loftus worked silently together, slowly turning Morgan's unflattering portrait of Viscount Soulden into a patchwork of muddy colours, like the dappled surface of a leaf-clogged pond. It was dreadful, but Morgan couldn't stop smiling.

"Perhaps I will paint miniatures," he said, idly dabbing some paint on the tip of Soulden's nose. "Loftus, did you know that they *kill* elephants to make ivory?"

Loftus blinked at him. "Was I not supposed to know?"

"No," Morgan said. "It seems everyone knew but me. Does that not seem wasteful to you? Elephants are so large, and while I cannot think of what purpose they serve, it seems rather needless to kill them just for the sake of their ivory. Surely they have more use than that. Why, is there not some way to capture the elephants and saw their tusks off? Would they regrow, do you think?"

"I do not know." Loftus's brow creased. "I have never thought on it."

Morgan sighed and thumbed the ivory buttons of his coat, leaving a green smear on one. A week ago he would have shrieked in despair at his own recklessness, but he could no longer love his buttons as he once had. "I think that I shall stop wearing ivory buttons."

"No *ivory*? But, Morgan, what else compares?"

Morgan. Loftus had called him Morgan.

"Pearl," Morgan said decisively. "Brass can be very pretty. Embroidered buttons are lovely, and, why, my father has an old coat that was once quite the height of fashion, and the buttons are decoupage!"

"Nobody has worn decoupage buttons since before Mr. Brummel made fashion fashionable, and you know it!"

"And look at what happened to him."

"He may be living in poverty and disgrace," Loftus said, "and in *France*, but that doesn't mean he wasn't right about buttons! And Bath coating and buckskins! One can be perfect without being garish!"

Morgan looked him up and down. "Says the man wearing red pantaloons."

Loftus made a sound of mock outrage and jabbed Morgan in the cheek with his paintbrush.

Morgan smirked. "Anyway, there is no reason that decoupage buttons could not become fashionable again. Or—or *painted* buttons! I'm sure it would get Viscount Soulden's attention if I wore buttons with his miniature on them."

"How large would the buttons be?" Loftus asked dubiously.

"La! Button-sized, of course."

Loftus's eyes widened. "He would have to get very close to you to see his own likeness on them, in that case."

Morgan bit his lip. "Yes, he would, wouldn't he?"

Loftus looked both scandalised and delighted. "Oh!"

Now that they had covered Viscount Soulden's portrait in dabs of colour that rendered it entirely incomprehensible, Morgan set his brush down. Loftus did the same. For a moment they both studied the messy canvas.

"It is not *terrible*," Loftus said.

"It *is* terrible," Morgan decided, "but it was also a lark."

Loftus smiled at him. "Yes, it was a lark."

Sometime in the midst of their painting, Sedgwick had left tea and cakes. He had set the tray on the small table just inside the room and left it there. Morgan went and poured a cup for Loftus, and one for himself. Then he noticed the book Loftus had brought with him.

"Oh, what book is it that you are allowing me to borrow?" he asked.

"It is, ah..."

Morgan studied Loftus's pink face, and then picked the book up. He flipped the cover open to the title page. "Oh! It is volume four of *The Maiden Diaries*!" His throat felt dry, and he sipped some tea to soothe it. He set the book down again.

When Loftus spoke, it was from directly behind him. His breath was hot against Morgan's ear. "Do you remember what we spoke of last night?"

Morgan swallowed. "We spoke of many things."

"You asked me a question." Loftus's breath tickled Morgan's hair and made the strands dance against his earlobe. "And I have an answer for you. *I would.*"

Morgan's insides turned to embers and then crumbled into hot ashes, all in the space of a single breath. His head spun. What did Loftus mean? He would *what*? He would take a man's prick in his mouth, just as Slyfeel had done to so many gentlemen, and had them do to him in return? He would keep it there even when it—

Morgan shuddered.

He would *kiss* the man afterwards?

All of it, perhaps.

"I would too," he rasped, and Loftus's sharp intake of breath was his only answer. Morgan turned, only to find Loftus had danced out of his reach. He was back at the painting, dabbing dots of blue across where Viscount Soulden's face had once been. "Loftus."

Loftus did not look at him. The back of his neck was bright pink.

Morgan picked up *The Maiden Diaries* and carried it with him over to the easel. "I have not read this volume yet, but—oh! I am terrified to say it!"

Loftus turned his head to stare at him with wide eyes. "Tell me. Please."

Morgan lifted his chin. "But I think I would probably do any of the things inside its pages!"

Loftus dropped the paintbrush. "You cannot mean that!"

"Why not?" Morgan demanded, suddenly angry. "Why shouldn't I? You are the one who brought this here. You are the one who—who answered you would! Why should I not say that I would too?"

Loftus gave him a wild look. "Because if one of us says yes, the other one needs to say no, Morgan! Or—or just think where it might end!"

"Then *you* say no," Morgan said.

"I..." Loftus's throat bobbed when he swallowed. "I don't want to."

Morgan drew in a shaky breath. "Loftus, don't you want to tell Soulden you can handle a rough ride? Don't you want to know what your husband will expect of you? I have talked to Mama, and she says that everything I need to know is in the Scriptures, but it's not, because I've checked! I think *this* book"—he held up *The Maiden Diaries*—"is a better bible for our purposes, don't you?"

"I don't even know what you're saying anymore!" Loftus hissed.

"I am saying," Morgan said, leaning in so close he could smell Loftus's cedarwood toilet water, "don't you want to *practise*?"

CHAPTER 9

Near the toe of his boot lay the paintbrush Loftus had dropped, splatters of blue paint on the floorboards. He could only stare at it, thinking, *Oh, but that will be a devil to clean up.* At some point, he must acknowledge Morgan's question—must answer it. But for now, it was probably best to just stare at the paintbrush.

Was Morgan serious? *Practise?* He had only meant to tease Morgan, not to incite him! Surely he had only meant to tease?

"Practise what, exactly?" he asked faintly.

"Well, just… One of us will marry Soulden—almost certainly me, but presumably you will also marry *someone*—but neither of us knows how to—surely you take my meaning, Loftus!"

Loftus shook his head slowly. Days ago they had been ready to kill each other, and just moments ago they had been laughing as though they were friends, their arms tangled, paint on Morgan's robe, in Loftus's hair, the canvas ruined. And now…all Loftus could think about was Morgan's closeness. And that question, dreadful and thrilling: *Don't you want to practise?*

"But *how* would we practise that?" A thousand fantasies

converged on his mind all at once, all of them a danger to both the line of his pantaloons and his immortal soul.

"Well." Morgan stepped away from the easel, and Loftus was absurdly devastated to lose his proximity. The other man shrugged off his paint-stained robe. Beneath, he wore a shirt of fine muslin, the top two buttons open, exposing the delicate line of his collarbone. No neckcloth. A simple, dove grey waistcoat that reminded Loftus of the one Soulden had been wearing that day in M. Verreau's shop. And pale-yellow satin pantaloons.

Loftus became aware Morgan was watching him. The fellow shifted so that he was holding the robe in front of him, as though suddenly shy. Then he tossed the garment aside and gazed at Loftus. "It would just be a game, you see. We could—we could pretend that—for instance—you are Viscount Soulden. And I am myself."

"But what would we do?"

Morgan laughed lightly, but it sounded forced. They were still close enough that Loftus could see the pulse jerking in Morgan's neck. "Well, you would speak to me as though you are Soulden. And you would—tell me what your intentions are. And then we would…um…"

"Intentions?"

"Well, yes. That you intend to kiss me—and not gently either— and that I must comply. And then I could say something like, 'My Lord, if I had known what you brought me here for, I should never have come.' And you could say, 'Oh, you would have come. You've been craving this since the day we met.' And I could start to walk away, but you could take my arm."

"This sounds exactly like the scene on the knoll in *The Maiden Diaries*," Loftus could not help but point out.

"Oh, does it?" Morgan said with badly-feigned surprise. "Why Loftus, you're right, that's jolly! We could use that scene as a script, of sorts."

Loftus could not make order of all the sensations within him.

His heart still raced. The skin on the back of his neck prickled. His stomach seemed tied in knots, yet the feeling was not altogether unpleasant. "But that is the scene where…"

In his mouth!

"Ah yes." Morgan gave a jerky nod—perhaps the first inelegant movement Loftus had ever seen from him. "Well, we don't have to go that far, certainly. But there is much that leads up to that. Talking, and…kissing…and such."

"You want to practise kissing?" Loftus's voice seemed to echo in the room.

"Well, we do not have experience! And Soulden is the sort who would probably ravage our mouths, much like Slyfeel. And he would be disappointed if we did not even know how to kiss in return."

Loftus's breathing was impossibly loud and humiliatingly unsteady. Though he knew he ought to bolt from the room, from the house, from this devil of a man who plagued his thoughts and made him feel such—inappropriate things…he instead said, "You're right."

"It would just be a game," Morgan repeated.

Just a game. And then Loftus would not feel like quite such a novice when it came time to lie with Soulden on their wedding night. Really, it was such a good plan, he was surprised he had not thought of it himself. And yet he could not move from his spot on the floorboards. Indeed was not sure he would ever be able to move again. Because he could not stop looking at that V formed by Morgan's open shirt, and the smooth skin framed by white fabric. That absolutely divine hollow where his collarbones met. What sound might Morgan make if Loftus pressed his lips to that spot? Traced the shadow of the bone with his fingers until he slipped the muslin off one shoulder, just as the rake Slyfeel might do, and kissed newly bared skin?

"Yes," Loftus whispered. "All right."

"You must be forceful," Morgan informed him. "Lord Soulden

would be every bit as confident in his mastery of seduction as Slyfeel."

"Why must I be Soulden? I do not know how to—"

"Well, we can take turns," Morgan said impatiently. "But you must be Soulden first."

"What should I do to start?"

Morgan huffed. "I have given you your lines!"

"But your line is first."

"Oh. Well, all right." Morgan's fingers flexed at his sides. "If I had known what you brought me up here for, *Lord Soulden*. I should not have come."

Loftus's throat was nearly too dry for speech. "But you have craved this from the first day we met."

"You must sound forceful! You sound like a nervous schoolboy reciting his letters."

"But you have craved this from the first day we met," Loftus said more loudly.

Morgan heaved a sigh. "Rivingdon, you are hopeless. Imagine that you mean to seduce me, but I am resistant. I *want* to comply with your every touch and demand, but I am naive and frightened, and you must teach me not to be."

Loftus nearly fainted. "I—all right."

"I shall walk away right now. Unless you stop me." Morgan started for the door. "*Unless you stop me!*" he called back.

Without thinking, Loftus reached out and caught his arm.

"You brute!" Morgan cried, pulling against Loftus's grip. "Unhand me!"

Loftus let go, bewildered. Morgan looked furious.

"Do not unhand me! My God, man."

"But you *said*—"

"Pull me to you and kiss me until I am rendered quite senseless! Please," he added.

Loftus's blood surged. He was tired of endless humiliations suffered at the hands of this horrid, demanding fellow who always thought he knew best. Who thought Loftus ought to play the part of Soulden because Morgan was the one who was sure to marry the viscount. Who feigned manners, but was hardly any model of decorum. He could not let this wretch best him. He could not!

"I shall try again." Morgan spun on his heel. But before he could step forward, Loftus grabbed him and pulled him around. Morgan's head snapped back, and then tipped forward, and Loftus felt heat rush to his groin.

"You little minx." He stared into Morgan's wide eyes. "Where do you think you're going?"

The black expanded in the centres of Morgan's eyes, and the man's mouth fell open. "I—let me go."

"Not a chance." Loftus spoke calmly, gripping tighter. "Look at you. Why, you've never had a rough ride in your life, have you?"

"N-no?" Morgan's voice trembled as he tried to yank his arm free. "And I shouldn't like one!"

Loftus tugged him a little closer. Morgan gasped. "How would you know, if you've never had one?"

"I am a gentleman," Morgan whispered.

Loftus laughed—genuinely laughed—at the ridiculousness of the claim. Morgan was no gentleman. But he was beautiful, and there was something about him that made Loftus want to...touch him. Touch him until the staged reactions fell away, and Morgan responded honestly, helplessly, to Loftus's hands and lips. He wanted that with a fierce pang that felt almost like sorrow. But his blood was still hot, and Morgan's pulse still beat visibly beneath the pale skin of his neck, driving Loftus wild, and he continued. "A gentleman, are you? I hardly think so." He leaned forward and whispered into Morgan's ear, "I should like to make you forget all your nice manners. Make you *demand* to feel me inside you like the impetuous little brat you are."

"*Rivingdon!*"

The genuine horror in the cry jerked Loftus out of the scene. He drew back. "What? I was being Soulden!"

Morgan's lips worked around a stuttering exhale. "That was very—"

They stared at each other, both breathing hard, and Loftus had the horrible sense he'd gone too far. Yet he could not stop picturing Morgan stamping his foot, demanding Loftus give him a rough ride, and then Loftus doing so, driving the sense of entitlement right out of Morgan Notley and reducing him to incoherent begging. Oh no. No, he was taking this much too far, and perhaps Morgan could see his thoughts and would mock him for—

Morgan stepped forward and kissed him. His mouth was sweet and warm and surprisingly gentle. Loftus leaned back, startled, and then tilted his head and kissed Morgan in return, cautiously at first and then harder as desire surged again between his legs. Morgan raised his arm, still trapped in Loftus's grip, as though in surrender, and Loftus squeezed his wrist then eased his grasp, rubbing his thumb along Morgan's wrist bone and relishing the soft sound Morgan made against his lips. He had never kissed anyone before, had thought it might be repugnant—wet and messy, with hands running everywhere and spoiling his clothes and hair. But this was wonderful. Every soft movement of Morgan's mouth made Loftus want to answer by pulling Morgan against him, using his tongue to tease Morgan's lips apart. He released Morgan's wrist, and Morgan clasped Loftus's hands in his, holding them between their chests. Loftus's body seemed to throw sparks like a fire log.

"We cannot," Morgan murmured, then kissed him again and again. "Oh, we cannot." But apparently they could, because they were.

Loftus stopped for a moment to catch his breath. He was dizzy. Not the horrible, sick dizziness of when he wore his stays too tight and for too long, but a light, bubbly sensation that nearly made him laugh. His stand strained against his pantaloons, and he had to close his eyes against a vivid fantasy of Morgan reaching between his legs to cup and stroke, rubbing harder and harder until…

Oh. Oh no.

He rested his forehead briefly against Morgan's, squeezing the other man's hands and running his thumbs along Morgan's knuckles. "We cannot," Loftus agreed. And then brushed Morgan's lower lip with his own before sliding his tongue into Morgan's mouth. Morgan gasped. The fellow gasped all the time; it ought to have been annoying, but right now it made Loftus smile. Morgan released Loftus's hands and brought one of his own up to cup the back of Loftus's head. His other clutched Loftus's elbow as though he feared Loftus might try to escape. The next time Loftus's tongue entered Morgan's mouth, Morgan sucked on the tip of it, and Loftus's knees nearly buckled. He put both arms around Morgan's slight waist and pulled their bodies together, kissing him painfully hard until they both required air.

"Loftus," Morgan whispered, and Loftus was so glad to be rid of *Rivingdon*, to hear his name whispered so desperately by that small, perfect mouth.

Loftus stroked the back of Morgan's muslin shirt, feeling the shift of muscle beneath the fabric. "Yes?"

"Are you still—are you still Lord Soulden?"

No, Loftus wanted to say. *I am me, and you are you, and we are doing this.* But he made himself nod.

"May I tell you something then, my...my lord?"

"Yes," Loftus whispered, kissing him again, for he could not seem to help himself.

"Hmmhhhh," Morgan breathed, tipping his head back, forcing Loftus's lips to meet the softness of his neck. Loftus attacked his new target eagerly, pressing his hips forward so that they met Morgan's, drawing from Morgan the best gasp yet. Loftus too inhaled sharply at the feel of Morgan's stand against his through their layers of fabric, and could not help rubbing his own stand against Morgan's for just an instant before pulling back. He made himself slow his kisses, for the hitching of Morgan's breath was so delectable Loftus wanted to savour every small sound of surprise and need. Morgan said, "I—am—" each word was a breath; Loftus had to strain to hear. "I am very badly behaved." Small shocks coursed through Loftus's groin at that, and he stifled a moan against Morgan's skin, which caused Morgan's chest to swell against his own. "And I need you to—to—to—"

"To teach you your place?" Loftus ventured.

Morgan whimpered once more, nearly wrenching Loftus's shoulder from its socket. "Yes, my lord."

A shiver went down Loftus's back, and he felt, for a moment, as though he might well be Lord Soulden, or the rake Slyfeel—strong and sure of himself, prepared to give Morgan the rough ride he needed.

He locked his teeth in the delicate skin at the side of Morgan's neck. Morgan yelped, and Loftus let go, raising his head. Morgan stumbled back a few steps, swiping the air in front of Loftus like a cat with claws extended. "You fool! That is too high on my neck! It will show over my cravat."

"There is barely a mark!"

They faced one another again, their panting horribly loud in the high-ceilinged room. Morgan reached up slowly to touch the spot on his neck. Ran the pad of his finger over the redness of it. "Slyfeel does not *bite* Stanhope."

"Not in this scene. But in chapter—"

"—Seven," Morgan finished, chest still heaving.

Loftus made no reply for a moment. "And anyway, I thought I was Soulden, not Slyfeel."

"You are. We are simply using *The Maiden Diaries* as a guide."

Loftus put a hand to his hot forehead, smoothing back his hair. "Be thankful I did not bite much harder. For you very much deserve it."

Morgan moaned almost inaudibly, and swayed as though he wanted to come forward—either to attack Loftus or fall helplessly into his arms.

"We could finish the scene," Morgan whispered at last. He gazed at Loftus, uncertainty, hope, and a truly breathtaking hunger in his eyes.

"You mean…" Loftus couldn't believe what Morgan was suggesting.

Morgan laughed, but the sound was not light as he'd clearly intended—it was desperate and shaky. "It is only practise, Loftus. Correct?"

Loftus closed his parted lips. Swallowed again, and nodded. "Correct."

And then Morgan sank very slowly to his knees.

Loftus simply stared. Morgan Notley on his knees. Those lovely pale-yellow pantaloons touching the floorboards, dangerously close to the streaks of paint. His small, gloveless hands on his thighs. His dark eyes somehow even larger than usual, looking up at Loftus with an unmistakable plea in them. He lowered his gaze, and his long lashes touched the ever-so-slight bluish circles under his eyes—the only imperfection Loftus could have found on the man. Had he not slept last night because he had lain awake, as Loftus had, thinking of their conversation at the Kennilworth rout?

Loftus stepped forward as if in a trance, the front of his trousers level with Morgan's face. He stopped before he got too close, afraid Morgan would be repulsed by the clear evidence of his stand. But Morgan's tongue flicked out and wet his lips. "Right then," he said, clearly trying to sound brusque and failing as his voice cracked. He reached for Loftus's buttons.

Loftus almost stopped him. Almost asked if he was sure, almost said this was a terrible idea. But he forced himself to take a breath. All they were doing was practising. It was the act of having a fellow spend inside you that ruined one; other forms of pollution you could ask forgiveness for. Or so that was what Geoffrey had said when he'd told Loftus of a young lady he'd got overly familiar with while at Eton. At the time, Loftus had covered his ears, not wanting to hear any details. Now he wished he had any reference besides

The Maiden Diaries for how he might please Morgan. Or rather, how he might one day please Soulden.

His heart stormed against his ribs as Morgan's fingers worked his buttons. He had to cant his hips backward to keep from spending on the spot, and the glare Morgan flicked up at him suggested he knew that. Morgan finished undoing his trousers, then parted the split of his drawers. Loftus's stand sprang out, and he felt himself flush violently. He was not sure what size a man ought to be. He was larger than Greek statues, at least, but that was not much of an accomplishment. He was no stallion, that was certain. Was Morgan disappointed?

Morgan did not look it. He gazed at Loftus for a long moment, appearing—Loftus almost would have said longing. Then he repeated, "Right then," and leaned forward. Stopped. "I'm not sure how to do it," he said fretfully.

Loftus blinked down at the dark head. "Um. Well." In truth, he was not sure what Morgan was supposed to do, exactly. He just knew he was painfully desperate for the man to do *something*.

"Lord Soulden would know precisely how he wants his pleasure!" Morgan snapped. "Tell me what to do!"

"Take me in your mouth," Loftus said immediately, surprised his voice did not shake.

"What if the whole thing doesn't fit?"

"You could start with a bit of it."

Morgan mumbled something Loftus didn't catch.

"What's that?" Loftus asked breathlessly.

Morgan kept his head bowed. His shoulders twitched. "They often choke on Slyfeel's—his—length. In *The Maiden Diaries*. I do not want to choke."

"You don't have to do this," Loftus whispered. "If you don't want to."

"No!" Morgan looked up at him, his face bright red, his eyes blazing. "I *do* want to." He licked his lips again, and Loftus suddenly couldn't breathe. Morgan's perfect lips parted, and he whispered, "Teach me. Teach me how to take a stallion."

Loftus reached out and placed a hand on Morgan's glossy hair. Morgan's breath shuddered through him. He bowed his head again. Loftus stroked his fingers through the thick waves, and Morgan's shoulders hunched briefly before he drew another breath. Loftus stroked his nape. The skin there was, if possible, even softer than Morgan's hair. Morgan sighed and bowed lower, exposing more of his neck to Loftus's fingers.

Loftus didn't rush him, but when Morgan lifted his chin and leaned forward, Loftus increased the pressure ever so slightly on Morgan's head. It felt more like he was steadying Morgan than guiding him. Steadying himself, perhaps.

Morgan's lips closed delicately on the head of Loftus's prick. Loftus inhaled sharply, fingers tensing in Morgan's hair, nails digging into the other man's scalp. Morgan slid his lips down tentatively. Pulled back before he was halfway down Loftus's length. He moaned softly, and Loftus had to work to keep his hips still as the vibration sent pleasure shooting through him.

"Ohhh," Loftus exhaled. This was better than anything he could have imagined. Certainly better than his hand. Morgan looked so *beautiful* with his mouth around Loftus's prick, dark hair shifting with each movement, becoming slightly disarrayed as Loftus's fingers threaded more deeply into it. "Morgan," he whispered. And in response, he got a soft sigh that rushed warm air along his shaft, made him squeeze his eyes shut for a long moment.

He could never have imagined feeling any sort of reverence for Morgan Notley, but there was no other word for this tightness in his chest, the swell of tenderness in his throat. Morgan was trembling slightly, but whether from need or nerves, Loftus didn't know. He did not want Morgan to be nervous. He wanted Morgan to experience all the pleasure he himself was experiencing as pressure built in his balls and heat coiled in his gut. His harsh breathing came in counterpoint to

Morgan's moans and the slick noises of his mouth. Morgan grew bolder, sliding farther down Loftus's prick until he was nearly to the root. He whimpered as he attempted that last fraction of an inch to take Loftus fully, and the sound did Loftus in. His stand pulsed, and he tried to push Morgan back, but Morgan clapped a hand to his thigh and pulled determinedly on Loftus's prick, his cheeks hollowing. Loftus spent hard, clutching a handful of Morgan's hair to stay upright, and that seemed to startle Morgan. The other man jerked back, his lips not quite closed, placing the back of his hand to his now-full mouth.

"It's in my mouth!" he said, the words garbled.

"I tried to warn you!" Loftus panted.

"What do I *do* with it?" Some of Loftus's seed dribbled from his lips.

Loftus tried to think, but his brain seemed to have taken a rather sudden hiatus. "Spit it out!"

"*Spit* it?" It came out *"Thpih-eh?"* "I am a *gentleman!*"

This was hardly the time to point out that Morgan looked far from gentlemanly on his knees with his mouth full of Loftus's spend. "Well, I don't know what else you should do!"

Unless he did what Lord Stanhope had done on the knoll. Which was…frightful.

Morgan was flushed again. He clenched his eyes shut, and Loftus felt a stab of empathy. He reached out automatically to stroke his hair again. "It's all right. You could spit into the cup that holds your brushes. Then we can wash the cup."

But as Loftus watched in shock, Morgan screwed up his face and swallowed hard. After a moment, he opened his eyes, keeping the back of his hand pressed to his mouth. He looked up at Loftus, misery and—amusement—warring in his eyes? "I can't believe I did that," he said softly. Then snorted a laugh. "I never thought I would."

"Did it taste funny?"

"Yes!"

"Very bad?"

"No…but it was strange."

Loftus was quite embarrassed. He knew any fellow's spend probably tasted strange, but he did not like to think that his had been unpleasant for Morgan. Even though he knew he should be wishing Morgan Notley every unpleasantness in the world. He still couldn't believe Morgan had let him do that—*in his mouth*!

Loftus ventured, "At least it did not seem like so much as Lord Stanhope had to swallow. It sounded as though Stanhope was about to drown!"

They both burst into laughter, Morgan steadying himself with a hand on Loftus's leg as he shook with amusement. At last he looked up again, knuckles pressed once more to his mouth. "Was it—was it good?"

Loftus huffed out mingled amusement and disbelief. "It was incredible."

"Really?" There was no mistaking the hope in Morgan's expression.

Loftus nodded. "Yes. Really. You were very good at that."

Morgan smiled and dropped his gaze. "I—must admit I rather enjoyed myself."

Loftus drew a few more breaths. "I suppose I should—" He awkwardly tucked his damp prick back in his drawers. Fumbled with his trouser buttons. Then he looked at Morgan's bent head and felt an overwhelming urge to touch him again.

He almost didn't. They were only supposed to be having a ridiculous bit of fun after all. Practising for their futures. But there was still a welling in his chest that he couldn't explain, a strange sort of longing, even though he had just got everything he ought to have wanted.

He placed his hand on the dark hair once more. The tips of his fingers seemed to buzz. He stroked as gently as he could, sliding his thumb down onto the smooth skin of Morgan's nape. He half expected Morgan to demand to know what he was doing. Instead Morgan pressed his head against Loftus's thigh, rather like a cat.

"Do you think I would please Viscount Soulden?" Morgan whispered.

Loftus's mood soured at once.

Of course. Morgan wanted Soulden, not Loftus. That was why they were here. *Loftus* wanted Soulden too. Didn't he?

Loftus made a sound that was no answer at all. Morgan looked up. "You don't think I would?"

"Since when have you cared for my opinion on anything?" Loftus enquired brusquely.

Morgan glanced sideways, toward his easel and the horrifying attempt at portraiture. "That is true. You offered your opinion on my painting and then you ruined it." He snorted quietly, his gaze on the canvas they'd ruined together. "The truth is…I am a little afraid to marry. I will do it, obviously. I intend to have many prospects and to choose Soulden over all of them. I think I am quite suited to being a husband. To ornamenting a handsome man's home. I just… my looks and my manners are so overwhelmingly impressive, I am only now realising I have cultivated few practical skills. And while I think I shall age quite beautifully, like my mama, what if—what if when I am older, I am—less appealing, and…" His voice had grown tight.

Loftus's hand stilled in his hair. "Get up."

Morgan started, turning his face back up to Loftus again. Those eyes. Loftus had never seen anything like them. Gorgeous, dark, and determined. They were begging, but for *what* exactly?

Loftus truly was not sure his already trembling legs could withstand another wide-eyed gaze from Morgan on his knees. He took Morgan's arm and helped him to his feet. They stood face to face, Morgan's brow delicately wrinkled. Loftus leaned forward, and then they were kissing again, Morgan's tongue deep in Loftus's mouth, a slightly bitter taste to it. He realised with mingled shame and pleasure what that must be. He ran his hand down Morgan's body, cupping the strained front of his pantaloons. Pulled back from Morgan's mouth for a moment as he undid the buttons,

Morgan whimpering desperately, trying to help, their fingers tangling together.

At last, Loftus got Morgan out, using the dampness at the head of Morgan's prick to ease the slide of his palm along the shaft. The feel of it in his hand was a new sort of bliss—rigid flesh, soft, damp skin that Loftus found he could draw back from the head just a little to make Morgan gasp into his mouth, make the man's hips buck. Morgan's kisses faltered as Loftus increased his pace, for Morgan was gasping too hard and too frequently to keep his lips on Loftus's. Loftus steadied him with his other hand between his shoulders, their foreheads pressed together, both of them breathing hard.

"Loftus!" Morgan whispered in a rush. His hips shifted back, then forward again. Loftus kept his fist curled loosely, letting Morgan drive into it until his hand was wet and sticky and Morgan's knees had half buckled. "Oh God." Morgan's voice was hushed. "Oh God."

Loftus nodded breathlessly, his forehead, damp with sweat, rubbing against Morgan's. Morgan's hand was tight on his shoulder, as though he were struggling to stay upright.

"It was so good. Loftus, it felt so good."

They didn't say anything else for a while. Loftus's sticky hand curled reflexively. He was unsure how to clean it.

Their breathing gradually slowed and quieted. They lifted their heads. Morgan straightened his knees.

And quite suddenly, Loftus panicked.

What had they done?

Good Lord, what had they done?

He had come here to lend Morgan a *book*; he was supposed to be engaged to Lord Soulden already, and instead—*instead*— "Oh God."

"What? What is it?" Morgan sounded alarmed.

"I—" Loftus could make no answer.

"Loftus, *what*?"

"We have…"

Morgan's eyes widened. "Loftus…"

"We should not have done this."

"It's all right. It's all right. It was a game."

"Yes." Loftus nodded a little too vigorously. "A game."

"We were merely practising taking—"

"—taking a stallion, yes."

"We cannot afford to jeopardise our futures because we do not know how to pleasure a husband."

"I know." Loftus was still nodding, soiled hand flexing convulsively. "That is the only reason we did this."

"The only reason," Morgan agreed firmly. But he was gripping Loftus's shoulder too hard, and shaking. "Oh God. Oh God. You're right. We have…Oh no."

"No, we just said it is all right."

"I know, but—"

"Morgan—"

"Loftus, what have we done? What will Mama say?" Morgan's voice was rising.

Loftus's brow furrowed with mingled confusion and horror. "She must never know."

"I tell Mama everything!"

"Well you cannot tell her *this*!"

"*Loftus we are ruined!*"

"No." Loftus's voice was weak.

"Yes!"

"You were the one with my prick in your mouth; this whole thing was *your* idea—"

"No! Loftus—*Rivingdon*, you swine, it wasn't like that! We *both* wanted to." Morgan was as white as the sitting room's lace curtains.

Loftus attempted to get hold of himself. "Yes, I'm sorry. I am sorry, that was horrid of me. We did this together." Just…it *had* been Morgan's idea. So if scandal should plague anyone for eternity, it should be Morgan.

"It doesn't count unless one party spends inside the other. That's what Cecil says."

Loftus sighed with relief. "That's what my brother Geoffrey says too."

"So we're fine." Morgan gasped. "But—but does my mouth count?"

"I—I don't know. I don't think so. I think that was Geoffrey's point. That he had, um—done—as we did—with a young lady. And it was not sinful. Because—"

"Right." Morgan was nodding as vigorously as Loftus had.

"So it's all right," Loftus said, wanting Morgan to stop nodding quite so frantically.

"Yes." Morgan glanced down. "Loftus!" he shrieked.

Loftus jumped. "For Christ's sake *what?*"

"Look there!" Morgan motioned to his pantaloons. There was a wet stain on the lovely fabric.

"Oh."

"Oh? Is that all you have to say?"

"Calm down, man!"

"I cannot calm down, it is on my pantaloons. The very evidence of my shame *is upon my pantaloons!*"

"I shall clean it off."

"Hurry then!"

Loftus glanced around, then grabbed a clean paint rag and strode to the basin of water. He dunked the rag, wiping his own hand as he hurried back to Morgan. He began to dab at the stain, trying to ignore the fact that Morgan's prick was still out, dangling soft and spent in its dark curls.

"Do not rub so *hard!*" Morgan yanked the rag from him.

"There, it is clean now."

"The mark is still there!"

"It simply needs to dry."

Morgan looked at him, and that combination of misery and

reluctant amusement was back in his gaze "Do you think Lord Soulden knows how to clean spend off his pantaloons?"

"Of course he does. He probably does it with some frequency."

Morgan gave him a wavering smile. Then he unexpectedly reached out and brushed Loftus's hair behind his ear. "Loftus?" His voice was hushed. "What if I am not sorry at all?"

Loftus was quite sure that if he did nothing but stare into those deceptively innocent eyes for the rest of his life, he would die satisfied. "I...am not sorry either."

Morgan touched the satin of his pantaloons. "It is *crisp*."

"It will come out in the wash."

"What will the servants say?"

Loftus sighed. "Truly, have you never—accidentally, of course—polluted your bed sheets in the night?"

"No! I told you, I do not sweat, and I certainly do not...emit. And even if I did, Loftus Rivingdon, it is quite a different matter to have this substance on your bedclothes than to have it on your pantaloons!"

Loftus supposed that was true. "I should leave. Perhaps your mama is still at her piano, and we shall pretend I left long ago."

"Yes. Yes, that is a good idea. Let us go. I will show you to our side door so you will not have to go past the music room." Morgan tucked himself back into his pantaloons and worked the buttons. "Come, quickly."

They hurried from Morgan's sitting room and into the hall. They each looked both ways, then headed for the stairs.

"Oi!"

Loftus jumped. Morgan yelped. They clutched each other, fingers grabbing wrists as Cecil appeared at the end of the hall.

"Cecil, what are you doing here?" Morgan fairly screamed.

"I am part of the family, and I do visit occasionally, you know. Why are you two—?" Cecil froze, staring hard at Morgan. "Oh no. No. No, Morgan, tell me you haven't—"

"We didn't do anything!" Morgan insisted, far too loudly to be at all convincing. "So do not tell Mama!"

Cecil folded his arms. "If you didn't do anything, then what am I supposed to not tell her?"

"Don't tell her that we didn't do anything!" Morgan's voice was shrill and borderline hysterical. "Or, I mean, don't tell her anything, because we didn't *do* anything!"

"Morgan. You little *sod*."

Loftus's heart pounded as he watched the exchange.

"You said it didn't count unless—"

"Christ, Morgan, stop talking! If I don't know the details, I can pretend this conversation never happened." Cecil let his arms drop and heaved a sigh. Glanced at Loftus. "Why is his hair blue?" Loftus had nearly forgotten about the paint. "Never mind, I don't want to know. Get Mr. Rivingdon out of here. Then go find a mirror, do something about *your* hair because I couldn't give two fucks about bloody *style* and even I know a man's hair ought not to look like that, and practise an expression that does not make you look guilty as an egg-sucking dog!"

Loftus jolted at the word "sucking," which caused Cecil to roll his eyes again. "Oh, Christ."

"Stop *swearing*, Cecil!" Morgan snapped savagely. "You know I hate when you swear."

"Oh, that's rich. Ever the little gentleman, eh?"

"Stop it! I *am* a gentleman."

Cecil laughed, his tongue between his teeth. "Right then. Go on. If God smites you right here, you little liar, I don't want to be in range."

Loftus could feel Morgan shaking with rage, and realised they were still holding onto each other's wrists. Morgan released Loftus and started for the stairs. Loftus followed quickly. He glimpsed Morgan's face. The fellow looked near tears, which made Loftus feel quite small and terrible.

Morgan led him past a little yellow drawing room and to a door near the stairs to the servants' quarters. "Here." He yanked the door open, letting in cool spring air. Birds chirped, and the sound of a rattling cart reminded Loftus that the world had gone on while he and Morgan made the biggest mistake of their lives. He didn't move. Morgan shifted and ran a hand through his hair as though recalling what Cecil had said regarding its state of disarray.

"My hat," Loftus said at once, recalling that his own hair had blue paint in it.

"I shall see it returned to you. Please go."

"But—"

"I suppose it is best that we do not see each other anymore except where it can't be helped. I must focus on courting Lord Soulden."

"Morgan—" Loftus began.

"No." Morgan shook his head, blinking rapidly. "No. Good day, Mr. Rivingdon." When Loftus didn't move at once, he snapped, "*Leave*," and put a hand on Loftus's back in what seemed a mockery of all they had done before and fairly shoved him out the door.

CHAPTER 10

The Harringdon Ball

At the Harringdon ball, Lord Christmas Gale, who was known by everyone, danced with Mr. Benjamin Chant, who was not. This was much remarked upon, as nobody could remember the last time Lord Christmas Gale had danced with anyone, let alone someone who was practically a no-one. Loftus was pleased to note that this was not the only thing remarked upon: Lady Overfall remarked upon the lustrous nature of his complexion, Lord Fortescue remarked upon how well he danced the quadrille, and Prinny himself—*yes, Prinny himself!*—remarked that Loftus appeared as a rose amongst the thorns. Loftus glowed with the Prince Regent's praise, and felt as light as a feather as he danced the night away with a series of attentive partners. He could not even feel the ache in his feet.

He caught glimpses of Morgan throughout the night, although he could not summon the courage to approach him. After what they had done—God! Loftus could hardly think on it, except at the same time he could think of nothing else! Every time he closed his eyes, whether to sleep or even just to blink, he saw Morgan on his knees before him, his dark eyes staring up at him and his mouth stretched wide around Loftus's prick. Loftus could not believe they had done such a reckless, wicked thing—but the fluttering in his stomach that attended him whenever he thought of it was not all guilt. He wanted to do it again. In Loftus's fantasies, he did for Morgan what Morgan had done for him.

Loftus, finally taking a break from dancing to catch his breath and have a drink of punch, glanced around the crowded ballroom. He saw Mother standing with a group of her friends. Father was here too, but probably already ensconced in a darkened room playing cards, so Loftus did not expect to see him tonight. He caught Mother's eye, and she smiled at him proudly and raised her glass of punch in his direction. He puffed his chest out and straightened his neckcloth. Yes, despite his rather inglorious start to the Season, at last he was, as he had always intended to be, a diamond of the first water.

He sipped his punch slowly, his gaze travelling over the crowd. Everyone looked quite glorious, but none of them, he noted with satisfaction, looked as glorious as he did. He was a little breathless with that knowledge, but mostly breathless because he had been dancing and because he had worn his stays again. He had thought about not wearing them, but his mother would have known just by glancing at him, and Loftus did not want to argue with her whether he looked too plump. Not when her opinion would not be swayed. Why, if she could draw up more than a pinch of flesh on his stomach between her thumb and her finger, she would have him eating nothing but bread and water for the rest of the Season.

His gaze fell on Morgan, who was in conversation with his cousin, Lady Rebecca. If there was anyone here tonight who could match Loftus for his beauty it was, of course, only Morgan. Usually Loftus would have seethed with bitterness at having to acknowledge such a thing, but his feelings for Morgan had softened, and grown a thousand times more complicated—since they had—

Heat climbed in his face and he took another sip of punch.

Since they had *practised*.

"Loftus."

Loftus tensed at the sound of his father's voice, and turned. "Father?"

Baron Rivingdon glowered at him. Glowering seemed to be his favourite expression when it came to his youngest son. Charles and Geoffrey, Loftus's older brothers, were permitted to bask in their father's pride, but Loftus had never shared in that. He had been, since the moment he was born, his *mother's* son. If it wasn't for the fact that he looked so much like his father, Loftus might have formed some wicked suspicions about his mother's conduct, but no, there was no denying his paternity, much though the baron might have wished to. When Loftus had been younger he had hoped that his father might one day like him, and perhaps even buy him a commission with the Royal Dragoons—Loftus was an excellent rider, even on old Hercules—but his father had laughed at the very thought of paying for a cornetcy for Loftus, and said something about throwing good money after bad. No, it was, as his mother had always said, up to Loftus to marry well. His future was in matrimony, not in the red coat, gold braiding, and dashing Waterloo helmet of a dragoon.

Baron Rivingdon raised an eyebrow. "How the hell much did tonight's finery cost me?"

Loftus blanched at his father's language. "It—it is an investment that will be recouped once I have made a match that—"

His father sneered. "You sound just like your mother. Pair of bloody witless fools."

"Please do not make a scene," Loftus said in an undertone. His night had been such a success, he could not bear it if his father ruined it for him.

His father snorted.

Loftus drew a breath and held it, smiling and bowing at a woman who smiled at him. And then he caught a glimpse of a familiar figure half hidden behind the feathers in the woman's elaborate hairstyle, and as the woman moved past him his heart beat faster as he saw that the figure was Lord Soulden. He was wearing a deep blue coat and white pantaloons. He looked, as always, perfectly turned out. His dark curls shone in the light cast by the chandeliers, and his full mouth was turned up at the corners in a handsome, expectant smile, as though he was just waiting for the evening to gift him some delight.

Now. It had to be now. His night had been so splendid thus far, surely good fortune would follow him this last brief distance.

"Excuse me," Loftus murmured to his father, and approached Soulden.

He was aware of movement approaching from the corner of his eye, and walked faster. He reached Soulden before Morgan did.

"My lord," he said, and bowed.

Soulden returned the bow. His gaze settled first on Loftus, then flicked over his shoulder to where Loftus imagined Morgan was lingering hopefully, and then back to Soulden again. "Mr. Rivingdon. How nice to see you again."

"The pleasure is all mine, sir." Loftus lifted his chin. "If I may be so bold—"

"I do not dance," Soulden said, cutting him off rudely. His eyes, Loftus imagined, were at least kinder than his manners. "If I have not made myself abundantly clear, to both you *and* Mr. Notley, I am not interested."

Loftus panicked that his father was watching them; he could not let his father see Soulden snub him thus. "If you are not interested, my lord, then perhaps it is because you do not *know* me. In which case the fault is yours, surely, for I have only endeavoured to become known to you."

Soulden's eyes narrowed for a moment. "*Known*, Mr. Rivingdon? In which sense of the word?"

Loftus somehow managed not to blush. "Only in the most proper sense of the word, I assure you, my lord."

Which wasn't at all true. If Soulden were to express any desire to know Loftus in the biblical sense, Loftus was certain he would cave faster than any one of Slyfeel's conquests, who at least put up a moment's token resistance.

An expression that Loftus couldn't read flitted over Soulden's handsome face. When he spoke again, he sounded almost weary. "Mr. Rivingdon, I have plenty of friends. I am simply *replete* with friends and have no need for more. And as for anything other than a friend, I believe I have already discussed with you, and also with Mr. Notley, how you are neither, delightful as I am sure others find you, to my taste."

"Impossible," Loftus said, keeping his head high even as his heart beat faster and his stomach lurched at his own audacity. "I am to everyone's taste, my lord."

"Good God." Soulden drew a hand over his face briefly. He exhaled heavily, and narrowed his eyes at Loftus. "Plainly it is. For God's sake, man, leave me the devil alone, won't you? You and your little friend."

He struck Loftus's shoulder with his own as he pushed past him.

Loftus spun on his heel to watch him go, the weight of his failure, yet again, a dark, heavy mass on his chest. It left him barely enough room to breathe.

Morgan sidled up to him, his eyes ridiculously and unnecessarily large. "I—my brother is a member at Bucknall's. He could get you in too, if—if perhaps Lord Soulden is rather a bear at balls. He seemed happier at the club."

Loftus nodded woodenly. He could hardly hear Morgan over the buzzing sound in his head. And over the horror of realising that he had been rebuffed, yet again, except this time it wasn't only Morgan who had noticed. It was much worse than that.

Baron Rivingdon stood watching his defeat, his lip curled in derision.

∼

Morgan sat in the Green Room at Bucknall's three nights after the Harringdon Ball, as miserable as he'd ever been. He had been invited by Warry, who, rather than appearing guilty and melancholy as would befit a fellow so recently at the centre of a scandal, held his head high as they entered and broke into a broad smile when they discovered Hartwell seated in the Green Room, a newssheet and a half eaten pie on the table before him.

"Were you reading the news?" Warry sounded surprised. He took a seat beside Hartwell, and Morgan sat to his cousin's other side.

Hartwell hastily pulled the sheet away. "Yes, and it's ghastly. Not fit for your eyes. Ah, hello Mr. Notley."

Morgan mumbled a greeting. Warry attempted to snag the newssheet, but Hartwell pulled it away again.

"It really is ghastly, darling."

"Mm. Thank you for protecting my virtue." Warry signaled for a drink.

Morgan's brows lifted. What an utterly tasteless comment, given recent circumstances! Yet Hartwell only laughed—albeit a little uncertainly. Morgan was not in the mood for any of it. The looks they cast each other. The way they fell immediately into banter that was neither clever nor interesting to anyone but themselves. One would think they had been married decades rather than days. One would think they'd married because they actually cared for each other, and not merely to avoid a scandal. How ludicrous.

"You've just missed Gale," Hartwell told Warry. "Or rather, I don't know if you've missed him. He left the room, but he may be coming back. It's strange; sometimes I could swear I am in mid-conversation with him and then suddenly he is gone."

Warry said, "He doesn't like me anyway."

"He asked where you were."

"To ensure he would not have to speak to me, no doubt. Oh, hello Gale," Warry said, as Lord Christmas appeared at their table.

"Warry," Lord Christmas said stiffly. He had an unbecoming lankiness to his frame and a sour disposition, and Morgan wished he would not join them. But he sat on Hartwell's other side, one of his long legs jiggling under the table. A crumpled paper stuck out from the inside pocket of his unfashionable coat, and it rattled with the movement of his leg, making such an irritating sound that Morgan could scarce keep from snapping at him. Then he saw that the fellow had *mud* on his buckskins—buckskins! Mud! How was it this man was adored by all of London?—and he realised what a mistake it had been to come here tonight.

Warry enquired after Mr. Chant, which caused Lord Christmas to shoot a dark look at Hartwell, which caused Hartwell to insist he had not told Warry anything, which prompted Warry to wonder aloud what there was to tell. When neither Lord Christmas nor Hartwell would answer, Warry apologised and said he had merely asked because they'd left Lord Christmas in Chant's company last night. This made Lord Christmas's leg jiggle all the faster, and he stated rather sharply that Chant was well. Which he then amended to, "How should I know how Chant is?" Then port arrived at the table, which seemed a great relief to everyone. Lord Christmas drained most of his in one swallow.

"Ah, Stratford's here," Hartwell remarked, watching a dark-haired man cross the Green Room into the Blue.

"Poor fellow," said Warry.

"Why do you say that?"

"He hates to be in London. He comes once in a while because his business is horses—very fine horses, I might add—but he despises the city."

"He is such a quiet man." Hartwell appeared to consider the door Stratford had walked through. "Is it not difficult to be so quiet?"

"For you," Warry replied, "certainly. For Stratford, I think quite the opposite. I recently overheard him discussing a sale with a gentleman here, though. He is quite commanding in matters of business."

"Why, I have tried on occasion to make conversation, and each time he is like a mouse peering up at a hungry cat, and then I feel horrid about myself."

"Perhaps you should leave him be," Warry suggested.

Hartwell looked as though that had never occurred to him. "But you've spoken to him?"

"Briefly. He is wonderful to talk horses with."

"Yes, I imagine he knows more about their tracheas than I."

"It was their oesophagi I tried to discuss with you, and yes, I imagine he does."

Hartwell clapped Warry's shoulder gently and rubbed. "I loved what you told me about horse throats, darling. Never think I didn't."

Warry rolled his eyes and picked up the remainder of Hartwell's pie, then began to eat it slowly and, Morgan thought, a bit oddly—opening his mouth wide and running his tongue along the crust. Hartwell watched him, seemingly transfixed. Lord Christmas's brow furrowed.

Morgan tried to shut them out. It was as though no one at this table cared at all that he was downtrodden. That he witnessed such a horrid scene at the Harringdon ball three nights prior. He still shuddered to think of how Loftus's father had looked at his son. How Soulden had shoved Loftus with his shoulder—hardly the behaviour of a gentleman! How he had said *and your little friend*, making it clear that he did not want Morgan either, which seemed impossible. But Hartwell and Warry ensured that he could get not a moment's peace in which to feel sorry for himself. Also, the port was making his head a bit fuzzy.

"If you'll excuse me." Warry stood, patting Hartwell's knee as he did. "Talking of horses reminds me that there is a book I wish to look at while I am here. I shan't be long." He stood and moved toward the Blue Room and its carved bookshelves.

Hartwell said, "I shall find him two hours from now, sitting by the fire, having read the whole damn thing." He stared after Warry with a longing in his eyes that made Morgan want to hurl his glass against the wall. Morgan nearly stood and excused himself as well so that he could storm home and fling himself upon his bed and pull all the covers around him and *not* think about what he had overheard between Loftus and Baron Rivingdon when he had been hovering—admittedly—near Loftus at the Harringdons'. Baron Rivingdon calling Loftus and Loftus's mother a pair of bloody witless fools.

Lord Christmas eyed Hartwell. "Have some self-respect, man. You are practically salivating."

"I cannot help it." Hartwell sounded wistful. "He is perfection."

"Mere weeks ago, you had determined that he was an obnoxious whelp who made poor choices that irritated you to no end."

"The poor choices were mine," Hartwell said quite seriously. "You know that as well as I. I was a terrible fool, and it is a wonder that he has forgiven me, let alone agreed to be my husband."

"I'll drink to that." Lord Christmas lifted his glass and drained it. "And once you've put up the money for the horse he longs to buy off Lord Stratford, I'm sure he'll consider you even."

Hartwell looked startled. "What?"

Lord Christmas stretched his long legs to the side of the table and yawned. "He is not going to look at a book. He is going to ask Lord Stratford about his horses, as he is one of the few people Lord Stratford does not mind talking to. And later, I imagine, once he has selected the perfect specimen from among Stratford's stock, he will rehearse all the reasons this purchase is a splendid idea and lay them out before you. Your household will soon have a new family member. I'll bet he's already picked out a name."

Hartwell's lips parted, but he did not speak at once. "Did he tell you this?"

Lord Christmas sighed. "Hartwell, I am quite literally famous for my deductive reasoning. Have you not read the *Gazette?*"

"It's just that Warry and I have made so many purchases recently, what with the wedding and the merging of our lives, and of course I have recently lost a title..."

Lord Christmas cocked a brow. "But he *is* perfection."

"Of course he is," Hartwell said quickly.

"And you *do* love him."

"More than any man has ever loved anyone in all the history of time."

"And you *were* horrid to him."

"Yes, but I have apologised. On my knees. In every sense."

Lord Christmas made a face. He stood and clapped Hartwell on the back. "I'd say you owe him a horse." He tucked the folded paper deeper into his pocket. "I'm off. Mr. Notley." He nodded to Morgan.

Morgan could barely make himself nod in reply.

Lord Christmas left.

Hartwell tipped his empty glass forward and stared into it. "Lord Stratford's horses sound very expensive," he remarked quietly, as though to himself.

Morgan could think of nothing to say, which was rare. Perhaps not so rare these days. Loftus Rivingdon's existence had reduced him from a beautiful social butterfly with delicate, colourful wings, to some horrible crawling worm. Or a caterpillar. Whatever the opposite of a butterfly was. Why, he could barely recall his triumphs of that night, so occupied was his mind with Soulden's harsh rejection of Loftus.

Hartwell turned to him. "Are you enjoying the Season thus far, Notley? I have been so focused on my own, ah—challenges, I have scarcely paid attention to what's gone on around me."

"I am enjoying it fine," Morgan said shortly.

Hartwell tilted his head. "That sounds as though it is not the truth."

Morgan glanced at his own glass. When had he finished the

port? His head buzzed and his chest felt very warm. "I had heard that you murdered Lord Balfour to preserve Warry's honour. I thought that a rather romantic gesture, but I am told you did not actually murder anyone. I also thought ivory buttons very becoming, but I have since been told that elephants must die to make them. So I wonder if goodness exists anywhere on this earth, or whether everything is simply terrible all the time, and if there is a point to life at all."

Hartwell nodded as if he were quite familiar with the sentiment. "I did sometimes feel that way, before I married Warry. And I will probably feel that way again once he buys a very expensive horse. But things are much better now. I rather think the sense that everything is terrible is one that comes and goes."

"Well, Lord Soulden treated my friend—I mean my rival—Mr. Rivingdon very badly at the Harringdon ball. I hated to see it. I mean, I loved to see it. For he is my rival. But—no, actually, I did not love to see it. People should treat each other better than they do. But I myself have treated people very badly. Including Mr. Rivingdon. I don't know what to think anymore."

"Mr. Rivingdon is your rival?"

"Well, yes. I suppose. Even so, he did not deserve what I did to him. And when I tried to—to be a bit kinder at the ball, he fled."

"Ah." Hartwell nodded, yet seemed somewhat confused.

"I do not want him to flee from me! I want him to feel he can confide in me."

"But he is your rival."

"Yes, I know. If he confides in me, then I may use what he says against him, and—" Morgan stopped, shaking his head suddenly as though in blinding pain. "No. No, that is not right." He took a breath and tried again. Why did nothing make sense? "I wish I had not treated him badly in the first place. That is what I wish."

"Oh, I quite sympathise," Hartwell assured him. "Gale is right. I behaved terribly toward Warry recently. And when we were younger as well. Nobody but Becca ever asked me to think of anyone but myself, and so I lived for many years in a world where I was the centre. I know that is not an excuse, but…when I think now about how very self-obsessed I was all my life, I feel considerable shame. And I do wish I'd murdered Lord Balfour—you're right, that would have been a wonderfully romantic gesture. I did kick him in the face, but that is not the same as murder."

Morgan nodded in agreement.

"Anyway, I find myself wanting to apologise a great deal for the past. And one of the people I most enjoy talking to about, well, anything, is Warry. But as he was often the victim of my boorishness, it feels unfair to ask him to reassure me each time this guilt comes upon me."

"So what do you do?"

Hartwell seemed to ponder this. "I don't know. I don't really do much of anything, now that I think of it. I try to behave better, I suppose."

"My uncle Francis says a man might give another a fine walking stick made of olive wood when he wishes to make amends."

"A walking stick, now that is a lovely idea. I would certainly feel more charitably toward a fellow who had given me such a gift. I don't know about Warry, though." Hartwell stroked his chin. "I suppose he would prefer a horse."

Morgan sighed and slumped. It was the first time he had ever slumped in his life, and it was oddly satisfying.

"Why don't you try giving a walking stick to this Rivingdon fellow, if you feel badly about your actions?"

"Perhaps," Morgan said doubtfully. "But I don't think he wishes to have anything to do with me anymore." The back of his neck heated as he imagined what Hartwell would say if he knew about how Loftus and Morgan had *practised*. For days now, he had thought of nothing but the feeling of Loftus's stand in his mouth. The way Loftus had stroked his hair. The slightly bitter taste of his seed. He had stolen a cucumber from the kitchens last night and tried putting it in his mouth and stroking his own hair, but it had not been the same. At all. And then this afternoon Mama had berated the kitchen staff for being unable to provide the cucumber sandwiches she'd requested for tea.

Hartwell mused. "I suppose you could give him the walking stick regardless. And whether he forgives you or scorns you, he will still have the stick. And then it would be a selfless act, you see. For you are giving the gift without the expectation that you will benefit from having given it."

Morgan bit his lip—rather harder than usual. Hard enough, perhaps, to leave a mark. "What you said about never being expected to think of anyone but yourself..." He trailed off. "I think that is what I was taught as well. I have always thought of myself and myself only. But if I had known, for instance, that elephants died to make buttons, I should not have wanted to wear ivory buttons."

Hartwell's brow knitted. "Are the buttons somehow related to Rivingdon? I apologise. I am often several steps behind in a conversation, as Warry is fond of pointing out."

"I think they are," Morgan said. "Though I am not certain precisely how."

Hartwell was silent for a moment. "I am not sure I know the youngest Rivingdon. His brothers, yes."

"Well, he is quite horrid." Morgan paused again. "No. He is not. His mama and his father are, though. Don't repeat that," he added hastily. "I don't mean it as gossip. But I think he feels a great deal of pressure to succeed on the marriage mart."

"And Soulden treated him badly, you say? That's not like Soulden. Well, it is rather like Soulden. But Soulden usually behaves badly in jest."

"This was not a jest. He pushed Rivingdon with his shoulder. It was dreadful."

"I shall have a word with him, if you like."

"Is Soulden a..." Morgan leaned closer to Hartwell, and his head swum for a moment. "A Slyfeel?"

Hartwell drew back. "Mr. Notley! Are you not a bit young for—well, no I suppose you are only a year younger than Warry. Still, you do not strike me as the sort to… Ah, it is never the ones I suspect."

"I have read all the way through volume three," Morgan confessed with a small moan. "I feel I am coming undone all on my own lately, with no help from a rake like Soulden. I mean Slyfeel. I mean…" Morgan trailed off and let himself slump once more. It felt wondrous. He ought to have slumped his whole life, for all the good remaining upright had done. "You have read it?" It was quite a forward question, but much like slumping, asking it felt very freeing.

Hartwell's eyes darted about the room. He shifted with a small inhale, hesitated, then spoke, his voice low. "Well, yes. More as an experiment than anything. But I'll confess I did become quite captivated."

"Is the information in it very useful, do you think? Soulden said he is not a gentle ride, and I—"

"*Soulden* said—Well, I suppose he would." Hartwell cracked out a laugh. "Oh, Pip." He frowned. "Is the information *useful*? Mr. Notley, this is hardly a conversation for—"

"How is it that I am a gentleman and yet I know nothing?" Morgan asked loudly.

Hartwell cleared his throat. "It is not my usual habit to encourage such pollution of the mind, but the series is informative."

Morgan looked at him wearily. "It is not pure fantasy, do you think?"

"Some of it is—I hope. I was troubled for days by the shallot scene. But the story also illustrates—well, not just what one might insert where, but the importance of saying lovely things while inserting. Slyfeel is rather fond of Spanish coin, I think. He is someone who would say what needs to be said to get a lady into his bed. Or a gentleman, or a stablehand, or an actress, or that rather old fellow who liked it surprisingly rough in Volume Three; do you remember him? I was worried for his poor heart, the way Slyfeel was riding him, but Warry assured me this is the sort of story where everything turns out well for everybody. The only novel I had read previously was *Frankenstein*. Very different. Anyway, where was I? Ah. Yes. But it is not all Spanish coin, what Slyfeel says. Sometimes he and his paramours speak so deeply from the heart that I am quite moved by it. And then I find if I say what I am honestly thinking when I am with Warry in that sense, it makes the experience even more…It makes me feel even closer to him. Sometimes he says I should not talk so much and get on with the business at hand, as it were. But if he had any idea how many times throughout the day I wish to tell him that he is just splendid but hold my tongue so that he may concentrate on his book or his cake or the sheets that list sheepdog pups for sale, he would be impressed that I manage to keep my feelings to just a few short speeches in the bedroom."

"That sounds very…nice," Morgan said honestly, not entirely able to recall how they'd got on this subject. "I should like someone to say beautiful things to me. I should like to be married. I should like for Soulden to have been kinder to my friend. I mean, rival."

"Pip is Pip," Hartwell said. "I should not take it too hard."

Morgan wished to rest his forehead on the table and groan, for taking it too hard from Soulden was precisely what he had wanted for so long, and now it would never happen.

Instead, he thought for a moment. "I suppose he and I—Rivingdon that is—have been badgering Lord Soulden somewhat lately." He frowned. "Perhaps I should give Soulden an olive walking stick as well."

"Oh, Soulden likes sticks of all kinds." Hartwell guffawed. "You can tell him I said that. Oh my, yes, he'll get a good laugh out of that."

Warry entered the room again, and Hartwell straightened. "Oh, here he comes. Do you think he's bought a horse? He would at least tell me first, I should hope. Joseph Warrington the younger?" he called out.

Warry approached the table. "Lord William Hartwell, former heir to Ancaster. What is it?"

"You don't have a book."

"Yes, I only needed to check something in it." He took his seat. "Did I miss saying goodbye to Gale?"

Hartwell gazed at him for a long moment, then leaned back. "You did. But of course he doesn't like you anyway."

Warry coloured up. "Do you think he heard me?"

"Oh yes. Ears like a bat, that one. Or some such. Do bats have ears? Ears like a *horse*, perhaps." He put a bit of emphasis on 'horse,' and then watched Warry carefully. Warry didn't react that Morgan could see.

"What was all that when I mentioned Chant?"

"Nothing. They are investigating a murder together and I think Gale is becoming rather fond of him. But he is Gale, so naturally he's making a complete hash of it. The Chant part, I mean."

"I see. You didn't order more port, did you?"

"No. Your cousin and I were only talking. Did you see Lord Stratford in there?"

"I said hello to him, yes. Why?"

"No reason. I just wondered if you'd seen him." Hartwell shot Morgan a plaintive glance. Then smiled pleasantly at both of them. "Shall we play cards?"

Morgan shook his head. "No, I...I think I ought to go." He rose. He knew somebody who deserved to hear beautiful things said about himself. Somebody he ought not have treated badly. Somebody he should like to apologise to on his knees, in every sense. But he needed time to think. Right now, he needed to be—not the fellow in the portrait, but the fellow holding the brush. To look outside himself so that he might truly, *truly* see someone else.

He only hoped Loftus had not shut him out for good.

CHAPTER 11

A series of grey, gloomy days followed the Harringdon ball, and Loftus couldn't help but think the weather was apt. The drizzle that settled over the city didn't stop Lady Rivingdon from attending a myriad of teas and luncheons, and taking Loftus with her. Loftus performed beautifully—even Mother said so—sipping tea and politely declining cakes, and yet he found himself dissatisfied. After all, it was not his mother's friends he wished to impress—he was not sure who he wanted to impress anymore. He could not think of Lord Soulden without shame and bitterness. And he could not look at any other peer with the same adulation he'd felt for Soulden.

He thought of Morgan more than he should have. And, just to confound matters, he didn't *always* think of Morgan on his knees. He thought of Morgan's awkward kindness at the Harringdon ball. He thought of the way the light shone in his large, dark eyes. And he thought of Morgan's painting, and wondered if he'd begun work on his button miniatures yet. He would have liked to visit him and enquire, but Mother seemed relentless in her pursuit of cucumber sandwiches and small seed cakes, and she expected Loftus to remain at her side.

Why, he'd even secured an invitation to Bucknall's one afternoon through a Lord Crauford, who had admired the embroidery on his lapels and listened to him spout off a few facts about the Greeks he was not entirely sure he'd got right. He'd seen Soulden at the club and had been so overcome with humiliation and desire that Crauford had tried awkwardly to fan him with his handkerchief. But Soulden had hurried on to a different room, and Loftus hadn't pursued.

Loftus awoke on a Wednesday morning to discover the day had dawned brightly, the clouds having vanished overnight. His small delight at discovering the change in weather didn't last any longer than it took for him to dress and go downstairs—he could hear his parents arguing over the breakfast table from the hall. He passed one of the maids on his way to the dining room. She caught his eye and gave a guilty start, her face reddening.

Of course the argument was about him, and of course the servants had heard every word.

Loftus suddenly had no appetite at all, so instead he hovered just outside the doorway to the dining room and listened.

"—made quite a stir!" Mother said shrilly.

"But he hasn't got a suitor," Father said. His voice was calmer, more even, but Loftus heard each word clearly, and every one of them was wrapped in a tone of low delight, as though his father wasn't just recounting his failures, he was reveling in them. "It's been weeks, and I've not had a single enquiry."

"Loftus is beautiful, and—"

"And empty headed!" The baron raised his voice. "Just like his mama!"

"He has conversed several times already with Lord Soulden."

His father's laugh made Loftus's stomach clench. "Oh, yes, I saw that. Soulden cut him the other night. You're as deluded as that little wretch you call a son if you think Soulden a prospect! Marry him? Soulden couldn't even bear to speak with him!"

The maid was back, although Loftus could barely see her through the sudden tears in his eyes.

"Oh, *sir*," the maid whispered, and she sounded so full of pity for him that Loftus wanted to fling his arms around her and wail like a bereft child.

He shook his head instead, and flapped his hand at her to leave. It was only when she was gone that he allowed his lower lip to wobble, and he tugged a handkerchief out from the inside pocket of his coat to hold in readiness in case any of his hot tears spilled over.

He heard the scrape of a chair, and moments later his father strode out of the dining room. "Loftus, with me."

Heel, Loftus.

But Loftus obeyed. He heard the rustle of skirts as he fell into step behind his father, and cast a look over his shoulder at his mother. She was watching them from the doorway, her fist pressed to her mouth as though to prevent a cry escaping.

Loftus barely had time to take his hat from the footman as he followed his father out of the house.

The carriage was already waiting, and Loftus climbed in after his father. He stared out the window as they pulled away. His father did not speak to him, and Loftus did not even attempt to begin a conversation. He couldn't even hazard a guess at where they were going until they had arrived: the Auction Mart Coffee Room in Throgmorton Street.

He followed his father up the steps and into the coffee room. The glass domes in the ceiling let the sunlight in. Men sat in booths along either side of the wall, reading news sheets and discussing business. It did not seem busy to Loftus's eye, but perhaps there were no auctions scheduled until later.

Baron Rivingdon scanned the room for a moment, his hat in the crook of his elbow, and his customary scowl on his face. Then his mouth turned up. "Ah!"

He headed for a booth about halfway down the length of the room, and Loftus followed him.

"Wilberforce!" he exclaimed.

The gentleman in the booth stood. "My lord."

The man was in his middle years, Loftus guessed, with grey curls piled on the top of his head like dollops of curds. He had a thin face and a beaky nose, and lines at the side of his mouth that were deep and shadowed. He turned his gaze on Loftus. His eyes were the same drab brown as a sparrow. He was not an ugly man, just unremarkable.

"My son," Baron Rivingdon said, jerking his head at Loftus. "This is Captain Wilberforce."

"Sir," Loftus said, and shook the man's hand.

"A pleasure to meet you, young Loftus."

Loftus tried not to bristle. He was not a *child*. At least he hoped that was what the captain's familiarity intended to convey, because the captain might have been a gentleman, but Loftus was the son of a baron. He had an *Honourable* in front of his name. He was to marry a *peer*. The captain ought to have addressed him as Mr. Rivingdon, not Loftus. But along with the annoyance he had at the captain's dreadful manners, Loftus slowly became aware of unease settling over him. How did the man know his given name, and why did he speak it in such a familiar way?

"Sit, sit," Baron Rivingdon said, and slid onto the bench on one side of the booth.

Loftus sat beside him. Better the devil he knew. He balanced his hand on his knee, rubbing the ribbon of the band anxiously, aware that Captain Wilberforce was staring quite openly at him.

A man came to take their order. Loftus asked for just a coffee, hoping the bitterness of it would settle his stomach. His father ordered soup and bread, as did Captain Wilberforce. Loftus sat and listened while his father and the captain settled into talk of things that flew above his head—finances, and stock prices, and lots to be auctioned here today. Loftus suspected that half the conversation flew over his father's head too. God knew Baron Rivgindon's grasp on money began and ended where he lost it over cards. But Loftus forced a pleasant half smile on his face, careful not to let his feelings show.

"I shall stay for a few more weeks," Captain Wilberforce said in answer to something the baron asked him, "then I am travelling to Spain."

That caught Loftus's attention. "Do you not attend Town for the whole Season, sir?"

The captain's dour facade broke with what seemed like a genuine smile. "Good Lord, no! I have business to attend to."

"Business in Spain?" Loftus asked curiously.

"Sheep," Captain Wilberforce said, as though that explained everything. "Merinos. Fine animals. I'm looking for those bred from the same ancestors that were sent to the Cape Colony, d'you see?"

Loftus did not see.

"Very high clean yield," Wilberforce said, nodding his head. The lines around his mouth deepened. "Extraordinarily good fleece. Do you know anything at all about sheep?"

"No," Loftus said. "I fear I do not, sir."

"Well, you could learn, I expect," Wilberforce said, eyeing him speculatively.

"Learn?" Loftus echoed faintly. "Why would I learn about sheep, sir?"

His father laughed, and dug his bread into his soup. "Well, you would have to, wouldn't you, if you were to marry Wilberforce? He's got thousands of the things!"

He felt as though he had been thrust under tepid water, and was viewing this conversation through the swirling lens of the surface of a pond. Everything felt distant and muted, and the loudest sound in the world was the thump of his pulse in his skull. He thought of Morgan's painting, of how it had looked like leaf-dappled water by the time he and Morgan had finished with it. He wanted to cling to the memory of that moment—what a lark it had been!—except there was a burning pressure in his chest, and he was desperate to breathe. He was afraid that when he opened his mouth to draw air into his lungs he would discover that he was drowning.

He caught Wilberforce's gaze, afraid of what he would see in those eyes—and even more afraid of what his own might reveal. Not just shock, but fear. He did not want to marry Wilberforce. He did not want to marry this man who was a stranger to him. He wanted to marry—for a moment his brain froze like a clockwork toy with the mechanics gummed up, before it jerked into motion again and spat out the correct name—*Soulden*. Yes, he wanted to marry Soulden, so he could not imagine why he was thinking of Morgan, his fingers stained with paint and his mouth pulled into a smile.

"You've no other interest in you," Baron Rivingdon said sourly, "so you needn't look so put out."

Loftus caught a glimpse of pity in Wilberforce's gaze, and he felt suddenly much younger than his years. He felt like a small frightened child, and he did not like to feel that way.

"We'll post the banns as soon as possible," Baron Rivingdon said. "Get the whole thing done in a month, eh?"

Wilberforce cleared his throat. "That would be agreeable."

Loftus's hands shook. He wanted desperately to be angry with his father, but he could feel nothing but disbelief at the callous way his father had done this—surprised him with this meeting without even a hint of what it was about. And he hated that he didn't believe it, because when in Loftus's entire eighteen years of life had his father ever shown him any consideration at all? This should not have come as a shock. Loftus should have known his father would delight in the cruelty of it, just to lord it over Mother that he'd taken all her hopes and dreams—and her *son*—and sold them off to a—to a *sheep farmer*?

He became aware that the captain was speaking to him, and he struggled to listen.

"I beg your pardon, sir," he said, "but did you say you live in *Wales*?"

Oh, how awful. How unspeakably awful! Loftus couldn't think of anything worse. He would surely be miserable so far from home.

Baron Rivingdon laughed suddenly.

Wilberforce's gaze darted to the baron, and then back to Loftus. "No," he said, his tone uncertain as though he wasn't sure what part he was playing in the unfolding drama of Loftus's life, but feared he might be the villain. "I...I said I live in New South Wales."

~

"Mama?" Morgan called out, entering the inner hall. Mama paused in the donning of her gloves. She was clearly ready to go out; on the small carved table by the window sat her reticule, Little Lord Byron already resting comfortably inside it, his small furry face tilting to study Morgan. "Yes, darling?"

"I apologise. I didn't realise you were leaving." He hesitated, suddenly awkward. The hand in which he held the small gift for his mother clenched at his side.

She smiled. "I am on my way to Lady Follett's for tea and whist. She claims to have the story on this great mystery Lord Christmas Gale has just solved."

Morgan sighed, rolling his eyes. Lord Christmas was rumoured to have days ago solved a rather harrowing mystery, the details of which eluded society, but which may have involved, in any combination, a missing tiara, a pack of vicious dogs, several cannibal pirates, an escaped circus monkey, and some poisoned crumpets. Morgan thought the whole escapade sounded unnecessarily extravagant and attention-seeking. Especially since now, instead of whispering about how Morgan had been seen two days hence riding in Hyde Park with the Marquess of Huntly, all anyone seemed to whisper about was how Mr. Benjamin Chant had solved the case along with Lord Christmas. They said it as though 'solved the case' were a euphemism—and perhaps it was. How grotesque. Lord

Christmas and Mr. Chant were not wed! Were there no rules in society anymore?

He thought guiltily of his practise session with Loftus, and clenched his fist tighter. "I...I wished to give you a gift."

"A gift?" Mama's face lit up quite genuinely, and Morgan found himself smiling in response.

"Yes. It isn't much. But I have been working on these this past week, and..." He brought his hand up and uncurled his fingers, revealing three buttons in his palm. They were enamel set in metal, each painted with a flower—one a rose, one a daffodil, and one a hyacinth. It had taken him a while to learn to paint on such a small surface, but he was proud of the progress he'd made.

"Oh, Morgan!" His mother inhaled, reaching out to take the buttons. "How lovely. Wherever did you purchase them?"

Morgan drew back his hand, sliding it into his pocket. "I made them."

Her eyes came up to meet his, a half smile freezing on her face. "You what?"

"Well, not the buttons themselves. But I painted them." He smiled tentatively.

She studied the buttons in her gloved palm, her own smile fading. "Darling, whatever possessed you?"

"My muse," he said honestly.

"I must admit, I'm concerned."

Morgan's heart beat faster. "Why, Mama?"

"It is one thing to paint an occasional canvas. Indeed, it is a pastime that might enhance one's reputation and improve one's circulation. But these paintings are very small, Morgan." She lifted one button and examined it. "Painting a surface this small might strain your eyes, or cause your fingers to cramp."

"But it did not, Mama. I felt quite well after painting them."

"But over *time*, my dear... Oh, to think how you must have had to squint!"

Morgan felt his chest and neck prickling with chagrin. "I did not squint. I was careful."

She sighed, fingers closing over the buttons in her palm. "My sweetheart. I know you meant well. It is fine to have a hobby. But sometimes there is a fine line between hobby and *labour*."

Morgan shuddered instinctively at the word. "It felt...enjoyable, Mama."

Mama walked to the table and set the buttons down next to her reticule, cooing to Little Byron before turning back to Morgan. "Perhaps I ought to take you with me to tea. Perhaps I ought to have been taking you out more all along. Then you would not feel the need to fill your hours with stressful work. Lady Rivingdon's son has been doing so well this last week—much to, I think, everybody's surprise."

"I rode with the Marquess of Huntly," Morgan reminded her, a familiar cold dread mixing with the heat of his temper.

"Yes, I know. But I think it worth pointing out that perhaps Loftus Rivingdon is shining so brightly because he has made himself seen about town while you are in here painting very tiny..." She glanced down at the buttons. "Clowns?"

"Flowers," Morgan said, his throat tight.

"Of course." She smiled.

"It was Rivingdon who suggested I paint miniatures."

His mother's face shifted at once from false brightness to genuine anger. Her jaw stiffened, and her eyes narrowed. "Did he really?"

Morgan nodded numbly.

"Well, doesn't it all make sense, then? He was trying to sabotage you, sweet."

"I don't think he was," Morgan said before he could stop himself.

"Oh." She made a little sound in her throat and put her gloved fingers to the hollow of her collarbone. "You are so sweet-natured, of course it would not occur to you that people can be deceptive.

But I know the family, love. That boy is as devious, as conniving, as wretched as his mother." Her cheeks had grown red, and she looked like a stranger—her neck corded and her face suddenly contorted with remembered rage.

Morgan nearly took a step back. "Mama...won't you tell me what happened between you and Lady Rivingdon all those years ago? I have wanted to ask so many times, but I have been afraid of..."

Afraid of this stranger, he realised suddenly. These past few weeks, he'd looked forward to getting this delicious tale out of her, imagining that it would give him a jolt of vicarious delight to hear how his mother had battled and bested Loftus Rivingdon's. Yet something had stopped him from asking. The knowledge that Mama carried in her an anger and resentment so powerful it might distort her very appearance, make her someone other than the lovely and kindhearted woman Morgan adored. But he did need to know, for his own sake. Because he could no longer pretend he despised Loftus Rivingdon, and that thought was terrifying. Let Mama give him a reason to hate Loftus again. Let her banish his foolish fantasies of Loftus in his bed, Loftus on his knees, Loftus wearing Morgan's currant-coloured coat.

"Of bringing back bad memories," he finished softly.

"My sweet." She reached out and stroked his cheek. "I think you're right: It is time you knew everything. The whole sordid story." She passed her thumb over his cheekbone, and he closed his eyes briefly. "But I must warn you, it is ugly. And I shall not sugarcoat any of it."

He nodded as she drew her hand away. "I am ready, Mama."

"Come. Let us sit in the parlour."

"What about your tea?"

She shook her head. "It is very important that you know this. I need you to understand why you must never paint miniatures at Loftus Rivingdon's urging again." She took his elbow and guided him gently into the parlour. His heart was pounding once more as she walked him to a chaise longue upholstered in light green and gold stripes. Many times when he was a boy, he had practised fainting onto it, imagining the day when he might be able to faint before a gentleman as handsome as Soulden, and have the gentleman come to his rescue. His mother had watched, interspersing her praise with constructive critique: *"Do not allow your arm to dangle like a dead hare on a hook. Bend the elbow and place your hand near your head, as though you are in becoming repose."*

What fond memories he had of this chaise longue. Would he ever be able to love it the same way again, once his mother told him what wickedness lurked in Loftus Rivingdon's soul, planted there by his horrible mother? He did not want to think badly of Loftus, not anymore. And yet he must know the whole truth.

They sat, and she took his bare hands in her gloved ones. "My sweet. I wish I could keep the truth of the world's horrors from you but a little while longer."

"It is all right, Mama. I am a man now."

She took a breath. "I know. And yet you are still my beautiful, innocent boy."

His stomach clenched as he recalled Loftus's prick in his mouth. Also the cucumber.

"You must remember that even in a world of decent people, there walk among us some beasts who wear human disguise."

He nodded, brow wrinkling. "Yes. Of course."

"It was a chilly April evening in '96. The night of Lady Allen's ball. An unseasonable breeze blew through the trees. I had on my new rose-coloured satin coat over a stunning round gown—the very height of fashion it was. And my hair—oh, Morgan, you've never seen such curls! All natural, too. I did not augment with false hair as many did. As Lady Rivingdon—or Miss Jarvis, as she was then—did."

Morgan could picture it: His beautiful mother, dressed to perfection for an evening out. He smiled fondly.

"I had arranged to seek the company of several other young

ladies at the ball so that we might gossip. Once I arrived, I found the group: Lady Helen Rowley, Miss Storey, Miss Caney…and Miss Jarvis. I had never felt entirely comfortable in Miss Jarvis's company. But I was just out that Season and did not know her well. I thought I had only to get to know her better, and she would accept me." She shook her head, staring off at the far wall. "What a fool I was."

Cold fear gripped Morgan. What had Lady Rivingdon—nèe Miss Jarvis—done to Mama? Had she hurt her physically? Humiliated her? Spilled punch on that stunning round gown? He was fairly shaking with suspense.

"The Allen home was large, with many hallways and a rather disorienting number of portraits. When Miss Jarvis took my elbow and said, conspiratorially, that we ought to go get punch, a strange sensation came over me. I did not trust her, as I've said. And suddenly we were crossing the ballroom together, and in every direction I saw a hallway, or a portrait. I believe even then I had a sense I was being led to my doom. But there at the refreshment table stood Miss Storey —such a pleasant young woman she was, always so jolly."

Oh, the sense of foreboding was nearly too much for Morgan!

"Miss Storey told a joke. I cannot recall what it was, something about Mr. Hayward's teeth resembling a donkey's—I suppose you had to be there—anyway, I threw back my head and laughed merrily. And that was when it happened."

Morgan stared at her, wide-eyed. "What happened, Mama?" he breathed.

"Miss Jarvis looked at me. And right there, in front of Miss Storey and several others, she said, "My, your laugh is a bit shrill, isn't it?"

Morgan watched his mother's jaw quiver, his heart going out to her. This next part must be too difficult for her to speak aloud. Except several minutes went by, and Mama neither burst into sobs nor continued her story. Perhaps she was too traumatised to even recall where she was. That had happened to Morgan once when a button had popped off his waistcoat at age twelve, in the middle of a tea with Mama and some of her friends.

"Mama, it is all right," he whispered. "If you cannot tell the rest of the story, it is understandable."

Her gaze met his and narrowed. "The *rest* of the story?" she repeated.

"Why, yes. Whatever Miss Jarvis did to make you hate her so for the next twenty-odd years."

"My dear," she said coldly. "That *is* the story."

"Oh." Morgan paused, stunned. "It is?"

"Perhaps you didn't understand me, Morgan. She said my *laugh* was *shrill*."

"Right, right. That was very rude of her. It's just…"

Mama was glowering at him, and Morgan gulped. He realised suddenly that there was a time, not two weeks ago, when he would have heard this story and been outraged on Mama's behalf. He would have demanded to know if she'd tried suing Miss Jarvis for libel! And yet, after seeing how Loftus's parents treated him—to see what it truly meant for someone you loved and trusted to cut you— Lady Rivingdon's long ago comment did not seem so terribly wicked. He rather thought it worse that she'd told her son he needed to wear stays to hide imagined flaws in his figure.

"I just mean—" he said. "Well yes, that was horrible indeed. No wonder you despise her." But he couldn't make himself mean the words.

Mama studied him suspiciously. "And you must think, Morgan —think how high-pitched her voice is. Then imagine her having the *nerve* to call my laugh shrill!"

"It is too terrible, Mama. I am sorry you had to endure such treatment."

"I have not laughed in twenty-two years without thinking of her comment." His mother was staring into the distance again.

"I do not think your laugh shrill," he assured her. "It is beautiful. Like bells."

Her face softened, and she looked at him again. "Thank you, my dear. I am sorry to tell you such an awful tale. But you see now why I cannot allow you to go on straining your eyes making your charming little clown buttons when *that woman's* son is out there with perfectly functional eyes, capturing the attention of the *ton*."

"They're flowers," Morgan whispered, too softly for her to hear. More loudly, he said, "Yes, Mama. I understand."

"And you understand too that, as much as I admire your generosity in inviting him for tea the other day after that dreadful accident with his coat, I cannot ever again tolerate his presence in my home?"

Morgan gasped. Then put a hand to his mouth, hoping she had not heard the gasp. "I…" He tried to get hold of himself. It was not as though Mama had forbid him to see Loftus ever again. They would still see each other at soirees and routs and balls and teas. But unless Morgan could manage an invitation to Rivingdon House, and unless Loftus had a private room where they might be together unchaperoned, they would never again…

Not that they would anyway, Morgan reminded himself, trying not to feel Loftus's full lips against his, that insistent tongue sliding into his mouth. Trying not to smell cedarwood or see a streak of blue paint in silver-blond hair.

"Of course, Mama. I only had him over to apologise for my clumsiness."

"And that was the right thing to do." She stroked his cheek again, then glanced around, straightening her spine. "I must get to my tea." She rose. "Have a splendid afternoon, darling. A promenade in the park would not go amiss!" She walked to the door, and he heard her crooning once more to Little Byron as she gathered her reticule. After a few more moments, he heard the front door open and then close.

He let out a breath, leaning back on the chaise, hands folded on his lap. What to make of Mama's story? To think that she had, in some way, let so small an incident dictate the course of her life. It seemed rather...pitiable.

For the first time in memory, Morgan wondered if his mother was happy.

Could she be, if she were holding onto long ago slights? If she wished for Morgan to be as angry as she was at other people's foibles, real or perceived?

Did it matter that he and Loftus both loved Soulden? Or rather, did it matter as much as Morgan's desire not to hurt Loftus more than he had already been hurt? This was the connection with the buttons, Morgan finally understood. Did the beauty of ivory buttons matter as much as the fact that elephants had to die to make them? Of course not. And in this scenario, Morgan and Loftus both loving Soulden equaled the beauty of ivory buttons. And Morgan's desire not to harm Loftus was an elephant's death. Oh, it was all so very symbolic and deep and true!

He rose slowly and walked back into the hall. On the table beneath the window, the reticule was gone. But sitting there were the three flower buttons Morgan had attempted to give Mama. He picked them up, a tightness in his throat. Did *he* matter as much to Mama as a long ago slight? Did his feelings matter as much as her desire to see him win the Season? Had he ever mattered to her as her son? Or was he simply another little dog in a reticule. An accessory. A conversation piece. Something very small and amusing in its smallness. Now his entire body felt tight. He picked up the buttons and curled his fingers around them, then slipped them into his coat pocket. As he did, there was a knock at the front door.

He peered through the inner hall into the front hall, hoping for a glimpse of the visitor as the footman opened the door. He strained to see—oh, perhaps Mama was right about his eyes—and made out a slender silhouette against the bright afternoon light coming through the door. He heard low voices, and his ability to breathe returned, albeit shallowly. Could it be?

Morgan was entering the front hall before he could think about it. The footman announced his guest, but the announcement was unnecessary. Morgan stopped just a couple of feet from Loftus Rivingdon, and found himself fighting a smile.

Then he saw Loftus's face. That smooth, ever-so-slightly yellow complexion was red and blotchy. His eyes looked swollen. And his teeth were chattering despite it being a rather lovely spring day. He stared at Morgan, and for a long moment, neither said anything. Then Loftus said, "I'm so sorry. I...I know I shouldn't... I didn't know where else to go."

And Morgan, not caring if the footman saw, not caring if word got back to Mama, stepped forward and hugged him.

CHAPTER 12

◈

Morgan's hand was tight around Loftus's as he drew him from the front hall into the parlour. Loftus, shaking and unanchored, felt that it might have been the only thing still holding him to the earth. If Morgan let go, something terrible was sure to happen. Loftus didn't know what, but he was certain it would shatter him into a hundred pieces. He was no longer crying; he had shed all his tears on his way here, and now he felt empty and flimsy, like a water bladder with every last drop squeezed out.

Morgan's too-large eyes were pools of sympathy. "Do you want to borrow my fainting couch?" he asked, and gestured towards the furniture in question.

A choked-off sob rose from Loftus's sore throat. Morgan was being so kind to him! They had started the Season as sworn enemies and now Morgan was offering him the use of his fainting couch. Such a selfless gesture on top of a day that had provided nothing but cruelties was almost enough to break him. He managed a watery smile, and sat on the edge with Morgan beside him. He did not have the strength to fling himself backwards and sigh; for perhaps the first time in his life, Loftus was too wrung out for dramatics. He just wanted to sit here quietly, with Morgan holding his hand, until his shock had receded enough that he was himself again.

"Tea," Morgan said to one of the servants. "With plenty of sugar." He squeezed Loftus's hand. "Mama says sugar is excellent for restoring oneself when one has had an upsetting moment."

Loftus did not think his mother would like him to have too much sugar, but right then he found it difficult to care what she wanted at all. His whole life he had strived to be the best for his mother, and where had it got him? It had made him an enemy of his father, and his father was even more vindictive than Loftus could have guessed before today. Loftus was nothing but a pawn in a decades-long cruel game between his parents, and if his mother had finally lost, well, Loftus had lost even more. He was being banished to the other side of the globe, just because his father did not like the way his mother spoiled him. He wanted to protest that it wasn't fair, but it seemed deeper than mere unfairness. It seemed much colder too.

"Tell me, Loftus, please," Morgan said, "what has happened?"

The story spilled out of him in short, wavering bursts of words, and his eyes stung as he watched Morgan's expression shift between pity, and outrage and—at the very end—horror.

"New South Wales!" he exclaimed.

Loftus nodded, pulling his gaze away from Morgan's and looking down at where their hands were clasped.

A maid brought tea, but neither of them unclasped their hands to take their cups.

"I suppose," Morgan ventured tentatively after a moment, "that at least you will see elephants."

Loftus hesitated. "Oh, I think that there are not any elephants in New South Wales, Morgan."

Morgan's lovely brow creased. "What am I thinking of, then?"

"Sheep?" Loftus asked.

"I am sure it must be elephants," Morgan said primly. "I do not see how one could confuse them with sheep, after all."

Neither did Loftus, but here they were. His mouth twitched in the first smile, faint and weak though it was, that he'd been able to summon since his awful meeting with Captain Wilberforce at the Auction Mart Coffee Room.

"But this is all too terrible!" Morgan exclaimed. He unpeeled his fingers from Loftus's at last, and picked up the tongs from the tray the maid had left them. He began to transfer lumps of sugar from the silver bowl into a cup of tea. "Too terrible."

Loftus missed the clasp of his hand.

Morgan passed him the tea. "We must do something!" He chewed on his bottom lip for a moment. "Oh, I told Warry I would join him this afternoon for a walk. If he cannot be kneeling in the muck with some farm animal, he has to make do with the ducks in the park. But I shall cancel, of course!" He rang a small silver bell, summoning one of the footmen.

Loftus found his thoughts wandering while Morgan instructed the footman to send a message to Hartwell House. Of course it would be Hartwell House, because Warry was married to Hartwell now. Not a scandal after all, but a triumph. That hardly seemed fair. Loftus had done everything right while Warry had done everything wrong, and yet Warry was the one currently married to a peer.

"Now," Morgan said when the footman had left, "what can we do to get you engaged to someone better before your father posts the banns for your wedding to this captain fellow?"

Loftus almost laughed in despair. "Morgan, we have both tried for *weeks* to become engaged! Do you really think we can find me a new fiancé in a matter of days?"

Morgan's gaze was intent. "Yes! Because it will not be Soulden —no, do not look at me like that, please. This is not about my becoming engaged to him now that you, in your desperation, must look elsewhere. Loftus, we both set our caps at Soulden, and in doing so we made ourselves unavailable to anyone else! But it is Lady Grosvenor's garden party tomorrow evening—she has a maze, you know?—and you must come, and so must I, and we shall find you a match who does not live on the other side of the globe!"

Morgan sounded so sure of himself that Loftus wanted to believe it. Unfortunately, he found himself bereft of hope, and the places that it had leaked out of were filled now with trickling doubt instead, slimy and unpleasant. Because Loftus wanted to trust that Morgan would not take this opportunity to dart in and steal Soulden away now that Loftus's hands were tied, but how could he? Had their positions been reversed, Loftus was sure he would have at least considered it. It was Soulden he wanted, even though it was Morgan he'd fled to today, and Morgan who was making him drink tea—it *was* Soulden he wanted, wasn't it? Loftus straightened up. Yes, it must be. It was the only thing that made sense.

He set his cup back on the saucer on the table, the porcelain rattling. "I did not mean to make you miss your walk with your cousin."

Morgan flapped his hand. "It is nothing. Warry cares nothing for things of import, and he gets so very pinched around the mouth if I try to tell him how to improve his wardrobe. Not that he needs to now, of course, because he is married to a *marquess*! He could have been ruined, you know? And Hartwell could have been hanged for murder!"

"But nobody was murdered, surely."

"No," Morgan agreed. "But that is how I first heard the story, and it is much more thrilling that way."

Loftus nodded, thinking of plain, dull Joseph Warrington, and how he had trapped Hartwell into marriage by being caught undone with him. What a risk! But then Hartwell was a marquess, and would be a duke one day if his father ever stopped rumbling about disinheriting him, so the risk had more than paid off for Warry. Loftus could never imagine–

Or could he?

His heart beat a little faster.

A day ago, perhaps, he could never have imagined doing something so reckless, but a day ago he hadn't been threatened with New South Wales and a sheep farmer. A day ago he hadn't been afraid of leaving England and never setting foot on her shores again. Loftus didn't know much about New South Wales—though apparently he knew more than Morgan, given the fellow's elephant comment—but he knew one thing for certain: there was no Bond Street in Sydney Town. And nobody, not even his father, could deprive Loftus of his beautiful clothes and exquisite hats. At least, not without a fight.

Loftus had nothing left to lose.

"Loftus?" Morgan looked at him worriedly, and Loftus wondered how much of his reckless plan was showing on his face.

"I am fine," he said. He forced a smile.

"I was just saying that I had rather a good talk with Hartwell the other day. And I—well, I wish you to know that I—"

"Yes, I'm certain we can find me a better suitor at Lady Grosvenor's garden party tomorrow." Loftus interrupted, unable to concentrate on what Morgan was saying.

Morgan studied him, looking a bit taken aback. "Oh. Well, yes. I...Loftus, you seem very distracted."

"I am just thinking of what we might accomplish together." Loftus hoped he did not sound too wooden. Oh, what a terrible risk he would take tomorrow! He must hope he was better at gambling than his father.

Morgan's face lit up. "Oh, of course! You really are so very beautiful, Loftus, although you oughtn't to wear as much yellow as you do."

Loftus pressed his mouth into a line. "There is nothing wrong with yellow!"

"Not in theory, no, but you are a little sallow, and–"

"Sallow! I am not sallow! What an awful thing to say..." His lip wobbled. "And I have had a dreadful day, Morgan!"

"I am sorry. I truly don't mean to make you feel worse." Morgan took his hand again, and Loftus could not tell whether the heat that flashed through him was pleasurable or frightening. "But this is important. The only way to get you out of this horrible scheme of your father's is if you make a better match—one he cannot argue with. And to do that, you're going to have to wear bold, deep colours. Why, your hair! Nobody else in all of London has hair like yours. Imagine yourself in a hedgerow green coat. Or perhaps the currant one I gave you."

Loftus nodded blankly.

"Are you paying attention? I do not wish to lose you to despair. We will make this right."

"What if we can't?" Loftus voiced the question before he recalled that he alone would decide his fate tomorrow. He indulged in a brief fantasy in which he and Morgan attended Lady Grosvenor's garden party together. They would compare notes on the cakes and sandwiches served and whisper to each other about the volume of *The Maiden Diaries* Loftus had lent Morgan. Loftus would pass several hours quite happily in Morgan's company. No anger. No scheming. Just the pleasure of one another's company. He felt a stab of guilt at the idea of leading Morgan on, letting him believe that they would work together tomorrow night. But he pushed the pain of it aside.

"We *will*," Morgan insisted. "You are a catch by any standard. I will not let you go and live among the sheep."

A sudden ache in Loftus's chest. "Why do you care?" he asked softly. "I should think you would want me as far away as possible."

Morgan cleared his throat. "New South Wales is a fate I would not wish on my worst enemy." His lips curved in another small smile.

Loftus nodded. He felt surprisingly calm now. "I suppose I should go. I have much to think about and plan for tomorrow night." He realised his hand was still in Morgan's. Morgan appeared to notice as well, but instead of letting go, he tugged Loftus into another embrace. Loftus felt weak enough to need the fainting couch for its designed purpose: warmth and uncertainty, desperation, and tenderness flooded through him. He breathed in, his face buried first in Morgan's shoulder, then seconds later in Morgan's dark curls. The man smelled of orange blossoms. Loftus could have stayed there for a very long time.

Alas, the door opened, and a voice said, "Jesus Christ!"

They both straightened so fast they knocked heads, yet one of Morgan's arms remained around Loftus as they faced Cecil.

"*Cecil!*" Morgan screamed. "Get out of here! Why aren't you at home with Harriet?"

Cecil had angled his head and shoulders toward the door, as though trying to avoid the sight of Morgan and Loftus entangled. Yet he couldn't seem to avert his eyes. "I just came for a visit! Harriet says my constant presence distresses her, as I ask too many questions about her wellbeing. What is *wrong* with you? Do you want to ruin our family?"

"We were simply embracing! Loftus has just had terrible news. Are you trying to make him feel worse?"

"Good Lord, stop *shouting*!"

Morgan took a deep breath. "I'm sorry. That was unbecoming of a gentleman." He said, far more calmly and quietly, "I would like you to leave, Cecil. Now."

"You don't have to tell me twice," Cecil mumbled, stepping toward the door. "But Morgan, I swear, if I see something like this one more time, I am telling Mama."

"You do that," Morgan said evenly, his chin tilted up. "You do that, and you just see what happens, Cecil."

Loftus wondered if he ought to say something to try to smooth things over, but all he could concentrate on was the warm, gentle weight of Morgan's arm around his shoulders. Cecil left, and Morgan turned back to Loftus, heaving a dramatic sigh of relief. "He is so vexing! And I do not know why he is always *here* of late." Morgan glanced down at his arm as if noticing for the first time where it was, and then slowly withdrew it from Loftus's shoulders. "Well then," he said quietly. "Let me know what time tomorrow."

Loftus didn't answer, just stared into Morgan's absurdly wide eyes. He could not have put a name to what he was feeling. So instead he said, "Morgan? If I do have to marry Captain Wilberforce—"

"Do not say such things! You won't."

"But if I do!" Loftus was desperate to make Morgan understand. "If I do, I'm afraid I shall not even have to worry about pleasing him in the bedroom, for he seems too old for such acts."

Morgan gave a nervous laugh. "Perhaps he is. Oh Loftus, how terrible. Although, which is more terrible? Having nobody to commit such acts with, or having to commit such acts with Captain Wilberforce?"

Loftus shook his head, for he could not say. Certainly, once, he had longed to be an ornament. To exist for a spouse's pleasure—so long as that spouse's pleasure was to shower him with attention and gifts. But what if Wilberforce *was* still able to perform his conjugal duties? Would Loftus be expected to…to serve him? And if he was not able, would Loftus truly never know a lover's touch again? Panic forced his next words out. "Well, might we…practise? Just one more time? In case I do not ever get a chance to experience such things as have recently roused my curiosity?"

"Oh Loftus." Morgan's voice was barely above a whisper. "We are playing a dangerous game."

"I suppose." All he wanted was to feel something besides dread. Dread over what his father intended for him, and dread for what he knew he must do tomorrow night. If he could just have one good thing to carry with him through all of it, then whatever happened in the future, he would always have memory to cling to. His hands in Morgan's hair. Morgan's soft lips around his prick. The awe he had felt for Morgan, watching him go to his knees. At the very least, Loftus needed to kiss Morgan one more time. "Please?" He said it so softly that the word could plausibly have been just a breath.

"You shall be the very ruin of me," Morgan whispered, but he was leaning forward. Loftus shifted the rest of the way and met him, their lips touching gently at first. Loftus tilted his head, savoring the press of Morgan's mouth against his, shivering when Morgan yielded, parting his lips, kissing Loftus more deeply. Their arms were suddenly around each other, Loftus forcing Morgan back against the fainting couch, unable to get close enough to him.

Then something quite splendid happened, which was that Loftus found himself lying with his full weight on Morgan, his hardening prick trapped in his trousers and rubbing against Morgan's similarly constrained stand. He moved his hips slowly, sliding his tongue deep into Morgan's mouth as he did, then withdrawing to kiss him feather-light. Morgan whimpered. Loftus rocked his hips a little faster, and Morgan began moving his too, panting hard, digging his fingers into Loftus's shoulders. Afraid Cecil might hear them, Loftus closed his mouth firmly over Morgan's, swallowing the man's soft but increasingly desperate cries. And then came a great wave of pleasure that had Loftus lifting his head—gripping the fainting couch with one hand, holding tight to Morgan with his other arm. His hips bucked erratically, and Morgan grabbed him and pulled him back down, rubbing first against Loftus's softening stand and then against Loftus's thigh, his breath catching. The sensation of Morgan trying so frantically to use Loftus's body to claim his pleasure sent a new wave of heat through Loftus, and he spent in his drawers with shuddering force. He leaned down to kiss the hollow of Morgan's collarbone, the way he'd wanted to for so long. Morgan's back bowed and his chin tilted up so that Loftus had no hope of swallowing the sound of Morgan crying his name. He still tried—albeit too late—pressing his lips to Morgan's and muffling Morgan's repeated gasps.

They lay together, Loftus on top of Morgan, both of them breathing roughly.

"You'll remember this?" Morgan whispered at last. "No matter who you marry?"

Loftus propped up on his fisted hands, one on either side of

Morgan's shoulders. He gazed down at him. "I will." He hesitated, momentarily lost in what he saw in Morgan's eyes: a dazed sort of contentment, an innocence Loftus had once thought deceptive. Now it seemed so genuine—that combination of sweetness and uncertainty. Perhaps Morgan was just as confused by his feelings as Loftus was. "Will you?"

Morgan nodded, swallowing on a harsh breath. "Yes."

On an impulse, Loftus leaned down and kissed his forehead, which was warm and smooth. Morgan made a small sound and closed his eyes. Loftus found himself wondering what it would be like to kiss Morgan's eyelids and feel the flutter of those long lashes against his skin.

They rose slowly together. Morgan reached into his coat pocket and took something out. "Let me see your hand."

Loftus obliged, and Morgan placed three buttons in his palm.

"Something else to remember me by. It shall be your wedding gift. When you marry somebody far superior to Wilberforce, naturally."

The buttons were enamel with very small painted flowers on them. The daffodil on one of them was a bit lopsided, but they were lovely. Loftus swallowed. "They're beautiful." *Like you.* His gaze met Morgan's.

"You told me I ought to paint in miniature. And you were right. I have far more skill with buttons than I do with canvas."

"You don't want to keep them?"

"I shall make many more in the future. No matter what Mama says about me straining my eyes with labour."

"She does not like you making them?"

"I'm starting to wonder if she even likes *me*."

Loftus closed his fingers over the buttons. "I think that too sometimes, about my mother. My father despises me, I know that. But I always thought my mother treasured me. That if I just followed her advice, I would make her happy."

"I seemed to make Mama happy. Until recently. I cannot tell if I quite misunderstood the situation all along, or if she did think highly of me at some point."

"Your mama ought to love you," Loftus said sincerely. *For you are a treasure.*

"Yours too."

They exchanged the slightest of smiles. Loftus's throat was too tight to say more.

He left the Notley's beautiful town home and stepped out into what had become a rather grey and dismal afternoon. He felt as though he had left the sun itself sitting there in that lovely little parlour. And he should have liked more than anything to go back and bask in it just a little while longer.

CHAPTER 13

Morgan and Cecil arrived at the Rivingdons' house in Bruton Street the next evening. They had two hours to dress Loftus for Lady Grosvenor's garden party, which Morgan fretted was not enough time, and Cecil said was poppycock. Cecil was attended by a number of rotating footmen; whenever his location changed he dispatched one home immediately to inform Harriet, and to see if there was any news. Harriet had looked a little flushed over breakfast, apparently, and Cecil seemed to think the baby's delivery into the world was imminent, and for some reason he didn't want to miss it.

Despite all Cecil's silliness, Morgan was almost glad to have him with him. His presence gave the entire endeavour an air of propriety, which Morgan felt he and Loftus could sorely use, and despite his clear unwillingness to be there, Cecil was as good as his word and hadn't yet spilled the beans to Mama about his suspicions that Morgan and Loftus had behaved improperly together.

Loftus also had a watchdog—a sharp-eyed servant who glared at Morgan and Cecil as Morgan picked through Loftus's wardrobe, and Cecil stared out the window at his small army of footmen waiting on the street below.

Loftus seemed distant today, and Morgan ached at losing the closeness they had shared yesterday, though at the same time he blushed to think on it. He had called it a game, this thing between them, but he had wanted it with a clarity and an urgency that was too, too real. He hadn't cared yesterday that Cecil had been lurking in the house, that a servant might have walked in, or that he'd made a mess of his lovely trousers—he had been blind and deaf to anything other than Loftus, and how much he had needed him in that moment, and how he had wanted to be needed in return.

Yet today, Loftus would hardly meet his gaze.

Morgan bustled about with coats and waistcoats and shirts, pretending that he did not ache. "Yes," he said decisively, "you must wear the currant coat. And the grey waistcoat, I think, which will bring out that hint of blue in your eyes. You have such lovely eyes."

That won him a glance, wide and hopeful, and a faint blush on Loftus's cheeks.

At last he had Loftus dressed perfectly. The currant coat looked wonderful on him, and made his hair look even more striking, as Morgan had known it would. The colour suited Morgan with his darker autumnal tones, but it made Loftus look just glorious in the way it contrasted with his pale complexion and his white-blond hair. Morgan gazed at him, awestruck, and only half as envious as he could have felt, because he had grown as a person now and felt complicated things about ivory and elephants and Loftus Rivingdon.

"There," he said, letting the word out on a breath. "You look simply divine, Loftus. Cecil, what do you think?"

Cecil tore his gaze away from the window. "I like the red."

"It's *currant*." Morgan flapped a hand at him. "Just ignore him, Loftus. He is a terrible beast."

Cecil grunted, which Morgan felt only proved his point.

"Please fetch my walking stick, Martin," Loftus said, and the servant nodded and hurried from the room.

"Will your mama see us off?" Morgan asked, looping his arm through Loftus's.

Loftus set his jaw. "No, I do not think so. I have told her that Mr. Notley will be chaperoning me, and that is where her interest began and ended. She has rather cast me off like, well..." He gestured at all the discarded coats on the end of his bed, and shrugged. "What is the phrase that one uses when playing cards? She has thrown in her hand."

"Oh, Loftus," Morgan said, his heart clenching, and even Cecil's thick jaw dropped.

Loftus tried to look unaffected, but Morgan wasn't fooled by his blank expression for a moment.

"Come," he said, "we shall go to Lady Grosvenor's garden party, and you shall dazzle everyone there, and by the end of the evening we shall have you engaged to a peer!"

Loftus nodded, and caught Morgan's hand and squeezed it.

"Wait," Cecil said as he followed them out of Loftus's bedroom. "We're doing *what*?"

~

To call Lady Grosvenor's event a garden party was, Loftus felt, rather unfair to mere gardens. Grosvenor House, in Chiswick, was set in twenty hectares of grounds, most of which put Hyde Park to shame. The garden party was in what Lady Grosvenor called the pleasaunce: a section of the gardens near the lake and the maze, where one could stroll down corridors of marble columns and see delicately carved nymphs and satyrs peeking out of the greenery. On dusk it was beautiful indeed. Tiny lanterns glowed and twinkled. Musicians played from a hidden place behind screens decorated with Arcadian scenes, and handsome young men and women had been paid to dress as shepherds and shepherdesses, complete with lambs. It was utterly extravagant and delightful, but Loftus could barely enjoy it even for a moment.

"Oh, but this is magical!" Morgan exclaimed as a lamb skittered across the path in front of them.

Magical was hardly the word Loftus would use. Any other time, perhaps. But tonight, his heart pounded hard enough that the force of it made him ill. His very insides felt clammy, and his head seemed hollowed out. What if he had not the strength to do what needed to be done?

Cecil grunted. "Where are the drinks?" He peered through the drifts of finely dressed ladies and gentlemen trailing across the lawns like peacocks. "Is that Crauford? Lord, it is. I suppose the whole useless lot from Bucknall's is here. Oh, yes, I think that's Hartwell, isn't it?"

"Hartwell is married to our cousin," Morgan said. "You ought not to call him useless. Also, he's a marquess."

Cecil rolled his eyes. "Look at them comparing neckcloths, the flock of idiotic popinjays!" And then his sour expression softened as he looked at Morgan and Loftus. "I mean no offence."

Morgan blinked. "Why would I be offended, Cecil?"

Cecil mumbled something and cleared his throat. "Oh, and of course Soulden is here too."

Loftus's breath caught in his throat. *Soulden.* There was a time that name had conjured such sweet thoughts. Of a future as Soulden's husband, the object of all of his affection, the envy of the *ton*. Tonight, it made his head pound in time with his heart, until he felt sure he would faint with the ache of it. What if his plan did not work?

Oh, but it must.

Soulden was the prize of the Season now that Warry had snatched Hartwell up—and wasn't the *ton* still talking about *that* in hushed whispers? Let them whisper about Loftus Rivingdon now. He stared across the lawn at Soulden, and felt a slow burn of anger rise up in his stomach. He thought of his mother standing there— just standing there, saying nothing, doing nothing, as his father led him away. He let the pain of that moment ignite his determination.

Morgan wanted to find him a peer, but not just any peer would do. Loftus would have the best. Loftus could still ensnare the catch of the Season, and prove both his parents wrong in one fell swoop.

He smoothed his fingers down his currant coat.

He would forgive Mother one day, perhaps, if she was suitably chastened, but his father? No. Baron Rivingdon would never be welcome in the stately home that Loftus would share with Lord Soulden.

And speaking of the viscount, he was approaching with a man Loftus did not know, but who was far too plain to be his paramour. Loftus swallowed hard. Wasn't he? It was a testament to how nervous Loftus was that he scarcely even noticed what Soulden was wearing. He heard Soulden's companion say in a dull, dry voice that he had heard there was quite an impressive sculpture of Leda transforming into the swan somewhere in the maze's eastern quadrant. Soulden remarked that he had heard the same, and as he was not much in the mood to dance tonight, he would go and see if he could find the sculpture. His companion said he required refreshment but would perhaps meet Soulden there shortly.

Loftus fought another wave of nausea. This was his chance then. Perhaps his only chance.

"Loftus?" Morgan's voice was soft and tugged at something in Loftus's chest.

He closed his eyes briefly. "Yes?"

"You have not been yourself all evening. Are you well?" Morgan said it too low for Cecil to hear, and Loftus was struck by the genuine concern in Morgan's voice.

Loftus hoped his own voice would not shake as his legs did when he answered. "I am well."

Morgan gave him a long look up and down that alarmed him even as it warmed something in him. Morgan did not believe him. Morgan knew Loftus well enough to know when he was not himself. He had taken Loftus into his arms yesterday when Loftus had been near to drowning in despair, and he had declared that together they would find a way out of Loftus's predicament. He was, Loftus realised, perhaps the only true friend he'd ever had.

And right now, Loftus had to find a way to be rid of him.

"Is there food?" Cecil asked.

Morgan cast Loftus a despairing glance, and Loftus attempted to return it. Cecil was so crass. It was astonishing that he and Morgan were related at all, and yet Loftus felt a faint twinge of envy. Cecil was an awful brute, but he was here with Morgan, which was more than Loftus could say for his own brothers.

"Let us walk this way," Morgan said brightly. He steered both Loftus and Cecil away from Soulden and the other gentlemen from the Bucknall Club. But Loftus kept an eye on Soulden as best he could, tracking his whereabouts.

Presently, they found themselves within sight of one of the entrances to the maze. The maze was indeed spectacular, although Loftus thought it seemed a little ominous in the gathering darkness. As he watched, a woman darted out of it, laughing. One of the shepherdesses. A shepherd, looking a little rumpled and sated, strolled out a moment later. He caught Loftus's gaze, and winked.

Loftus gasped. The audacity! And yet it thrilled him too, because the shepherd, though undoubtedly lowborn, was almost as handsome as Soulden.

A servant hurried through the crowd, heading for them. Loftus thought he recognised the fellow.

"Sir!" the servant said to Cecil. "Mr. Notley, sir, you must come home at once!"

Cecil's rather red complexion went as ghostly white as the emerging moon. "Morgan," he said, gripping his brother by the shoulder, "we must go. Harriet–"

"No," Morgan said, jutting out his bottom lip. "*You* must go, but Loftus and I must stay here."

No. No, Loftus must find a way to convince Morgan to go with his brother. "Morgan, perhaps—"

"I wish to stay," Morgan declared.

Loftus could see the agony of indecision writ large across Cecil's face.

"Go," Morgan urged him. "Cecil, we shall be fine!"

Cecil held up a trembling index finger. "Do not make me regret this more than I already do, for the love of all that is holy!"

Morgan huffed.

"I am *trusting* you," Cecil said.

"Yes, yes." Morgan waved. "Off you go, dear brother. Hurry along! Mr. Rivingdon and I will keep one another company."

Cecil groaned. "Morgan..."

"Go!" Morgan shooed him like a horsefly.

Cecil gave him a baleful glare, and then spared one for Loftus too. Then, grunting like a bull, he spun on his heel and hurried away.

"He really has such dreadful manners," Morgan said, an eyebrow raised at his brother's retreating back. "Now, shall we do a round and review our options? I thought I saw Lord Fotherington before, and while he isn't exactly an oil painting–"

"One of yours, perhaps," Loftus suggested, the tease coming naturally in spite of the terror now roiling within him.

"Oh! You wound me!" Morgan exclaimed, but he laughed, and the laugh caught Loftus in his very core. "Anyway, while he isn't terribly handsome, he *is* terribly rich, and I think he will be an earl when his father drops off the perch, so he is certainly worth consideration. And he has never been more than fifty miles from Westminster, which counts very much in his favour."

"Yes," Loftus said softly. He cast another glance over his shoulder and saw Soulden approaching the entrance to the maze, alone. He ought to have fled Morgan's side while Morgan's attention was on Cecil, and yet he hadn't been able to make himself leave the warmth, the steadiness of the man beside him. Perhaps he could simply tell Morgan what he had planned? Perhaps Morgan would approve? Assist him, even?

But no. Morgan may have understood that Loftus was not

himself, but he did not truly understand Loftus's situation. This next part must be undertaken by Loftus alone.

They walked for a moment and stopped again beside the statue of a nymph who was in danger of losing her impractical drapery. It appeared to be solely held up by her nipples. How strange that statues such at this were admired, and yet if Loftus were to even unpin his neckcloth it would be as scandalous as if he were entirely naked. His hand began to shake at the thought. Just how large a scandal would he create tonight?

"Or Lady Grosvenor herself," Morgan said, raising his eyebrows. "She is a widow, and quite the merry sort. I am sure she would lavish her spouse with gifts. Also, she is rumoured to have an army of lovers, so I wouldn't expect you would be required too often to perform those duties."

"Yes," Loftus said again. Let Morgan compile his list, for all the good that it would do.

Loftus caught a glimpse of movement from beside the maze entrance, and looked over to see Soulden check his watch in the lamplight and then slip it back into his pocket. And then, his expression hidden in the darkness, he vanished into the maze.

Loftus, not even caring that Morgan was halfway through extolling the depressing virtues of yet another marriageable peer of the realm, hastened after him.

CHAPTER 14

"Loftus!"

Morgan dashed into the maze after Loftus. He thought he had only been one or two steps behind him when he'd started running, but by his third turn in the gloomy maze—there were lanterns at each corner, but their light did little to soften the darkness—he realised he had lost him. Tears blurred his vision as he stumbled through the corridors of yews, passing hidden nooks where statues stood, or benches waited for the tired or the amorous, or fountains bubbled. A lamb careered past him and then turned back and joined him, bleating pitifully. Morgan wiped his tears away and scooped the little animal up. It wasn't its fault that it smelled bad, after all and, in a shocking turn of events, for once Morgan didn't care if he got his beautiful clothes dirty.

He blinked to try to clear his vision.

He wasn't crying because he didn't know what was happening —he was crying because he *did*. He'd seen Loftus notice Soulden slip into the maze. He'd seen the moment of desperate calculation flash through Loftus's eyes, and realised why Loftus had been so strange since yesterday. Why he'd hardly seemed interested in Morgan's plan to find him a match. He already had a plan of his own. But it wouldn't work! Soulden had rejected them both soundly, repeatedly, and if Loftus was undone by him, what would happen if afterward Soulden rejected him *again*? Morgan's heart broke to think about it. Even his sheep farmer wouldn't want him then! The whole of Society would shun him. It would be a fate worse than death and, yes, even a fate worse than New South Wales!

He rounded another corner, the lamb under his arm wriggling unhappily, and caught a glimpse of movement: a flash of a currant-coloured coat gleaming in lamplight before it was swallowed up again in the darkness.

"Loftus!" he cried. "Loftus, wait!"

The lamb bleated in agreement.

Morgan reached a crossroads in the maze and hesitated, unsure which turn to take. He hurried left, moving even deeper into the twisting paths of yews. "Loftus!"

And then, there he was, silver-haired in the darkness, framed by an arch of leaves, turning back to look at Morgan. Behind him was a statue of a woman who was half swan. His skin was not at all sallow in the faint glow of the rising moon that mixed with lantern light. It was pale and perfect and flawless. He looked like a fairytale prince.

Except...he had untied his neckcloth.

Oh no. Oh dear. This was very bad indeed.

"Loftus," he said weakly, reaching out a hand toward him but stumbling as the movement shifted the lamb's weight.

Loftus narrowed his eyes. "Why do you have a sheep?"

"I am learning humility and grace," Morgan said. "It started with elephants, and now I find I am the very image of Francis of Assisi. I should like to paint this lamb, I think, and perhaps one or two of the swarthy shepherd boys running about the place. It would make a lovely nativity scene, don't you think?"

If only he could distract Loftus for such time as it took to get close to him. Close enough to knot his cravat for him once more.

Loftus stared at him hollow-eyed. "You would not paint me as a shepherd boy?"

"Oh no." Morgan exhaled shakily. "No, Loftus, you would be the *angel*."

Loftus's bottom lip trembled. "Go." He spoke the word softly, but then his expression and his voice grew harsh. "Go! You must not be here."

Morgan set the lamb down. "Loftus, I cannot let you do this! Whatever you are planning, it will not work out as you hope!"

"Why not?" Loftus asked, taking a step back as Morgan closed the distance between them. "Why shouldn't I have what I want?"

"Because he will not marry you!" Morgan exclaimed. "He is a rake, and a cad, and he does not want you!" He caught Loftus's hands. "He does not want to marry either of us. And he's a fool. He is a blind fool, because you are lovely, and far, far better than he deserves!"

"I am the third son of a baron." Loftus's mouth thinned, and he yanked his hands free of Morgan's. "Which is not much, but it is still *something*. I was supposed to be an incomparable! A diamond of the first water! And what am I?" He shook his head, his expression twisting into something so ugly that Morgan couldn't bear it. "What *am* I?"

"You..." Morgan swallowed around the lump in his throat. "You are an angel, and I won't let him ruin you, Loftus. I won't."

"He does not have to ruin me. Society need only think that he has." His fingers went to the buttons of his coat, and Morgan gasped.

"What sort of marriage would that be, even *if* you could get him to agree to it? He would despise you for entrapping him."

"Then let him despise me. Just so long as he is my husband." Loftus undid a button. "Will you be my witness, Morgan? Say that you have seen us together, here, myself in a state of dishabille?"

Morgan stared, horrified. "No! *Think*, Loftus! How can you even be certain he will—"

"It's quite perfect, really. Soulden moments ago told his companion that he would seek out this sculpture. The companion said he would join him shortly. If you will not be witness to my ruin, then surely when his companion comes through—"

"This is *madness!*" Morgan hissed. But even as he said it, he heard footsteps. The lamb bleated. The golden glow of the nearby lantern caught dark hair as Lord Soulden came into view.

Loftus stepped back from Morgan. "It is too late to stop me." He started to turn in Soulden's direction.

"No!" Morgan reached out and grabbed Loftus's neckcloth. He tugged it free with one hand, while his other one tore at the buttons on the currant coat he loved so much.

"What are you doing?" Loftus exclaimed, attempting to fend him off but then going strangely still and staring into Morgan's eyes. "Are you *mad?*"

Morgan thought that yes, he was completely and utterly mad.

He was holding Loftus by the wrist, buttons on the ground between them, when Soulden's voice boomed, "What on earth?"

And without thinking, Morgan pulled Loftus in and kissed him.

~

Loftus's first thought was to pull back from Morgan's kiss. But his body would not obey. Morgan's hands were on either side of his face, his lips pressed bruisingly hard to Loftus's, and instead of pulling away, Loftus leaned closer. Somewhere in the horrid mess of his brain he registered that this kiss was probably the last good thing that would ever happen to him, and so he might as well enjoy it. His arm hovered at Morgan's waist, not quite embracing the other man, but longing to. And with that longing came a rush of heat unlike Loftus had ever experienced before, even when he and Morgan were practising. He had quite simply never wanted anything more in his life than to have Morgan pressed against him like this, forever.

Which was ridiculous, for the thing he ought to want more than anything else in the world was to be married to a peer who was not a sheep farmer. Why, Morgan smelt a bit like a stable—Loftus presumed from holding the lamb—and Loftus simply could not go the rest of his years smelling like that. Yet he would not have cared in that moment if Morgan had rolled in sheeps' dung before kissing him, just so long as they were kissing.

Soulden's voice came again, "You two! What is going on here?"

Loftus reluctantly pulled away from Morgan, panting, one palm resting on Morgan's chest. His own eyes were half shut as he stared first at Morgan's lips, the moonlight shining on the dampness of their kiss, and then into Morgan's eyes, where tears gleamed. "What have you done?" he whispered. "You little fool."

Morgan stared at him, then brushed his fingers lightly over Loftus's cheek. "I? *I'm* the fool?" They kissed once more, and then they both turned to face Soulden.

"It was my fault, my lord," Morgan said, at the same time Loftus said precisely the same thing.

Soulden stared at them, brows raised.

"Truly, my lord," Loftus protested. "It was my fault."

"No, the fault was *mine*!"

Loftus opened his mouth to speak, but Morgan rushed on. "I could not help myself. Oh, Loftus, can you ever forgive me for leading you into temptation? For foisting upon you my...dark and restless hunger?"

That was a line straight out of *The Maiden Diaries* volume three, chapter four, and by Lord Soulden's snort, the viscount knew it too.

Loftus hesitated. Morgan was offering him a way out of this. A chance to blame this all on Morgan. But Loftus could not do it. He had never cared for anyone in his life as he cared for the man beside him. Suddenly, the enormity of what he had done crashed over him. However terrible he had been in the past, however selfish and unthinking, he had never done anything quite so deliberately awful. He was not sure he could live with himself if he admitted to having attempted it. But he was *certain* he could not live with himself if he lied about it.

So he addressed Soulden rather than Morgan, blood roaring in his head so loudly he could scarcely hear his own voice. "My lord, I came here seeking you."

Morgan jumped in again. "Because he had so admired your cravat earlier! What a bold choice to wear apricot when everyone else seems to be wearing white or cream."

Soulden regarded them, and there was not enough light for Loftus to see his expression. But the disapproval in his voice was clear. "Mr. Notley, my cravat is rose gold, not apricot, and I am certain you of all people would know the difference."

"I—the light is so poor—" Morgan stammered.

Loftus motioned him quiet, determined to take responsibility for his actions, but growing more nervous by the second. What would Soulden do to him? To Morgan? What if Soulden challenged him to a duel? Or at the very least planted him a facer? Loftus's sallow complexion would certainly not be helped by a yellowing bruise. "My lord, I am so very, very sorry. I have behaved unforgivably, and—"

"Loftus!" Morgan squeaked. "You do not have to do this."

"Morgan, I do!"

Before Loftus could force out the rest of his confession, Soulden stepped forward. "I agree. I do not need to hear any more. The two of you need to get back to the party at once."

But Morgan was already babbling. "Lord Soulden, please do not judge him harshly. He was not in his right mind. You see, his beastly father recently had the idea to marry Loftus off to a sheep farmer in New South Wales. You can imagine how ghastly that would be—" the lamb bleated as if on cue "—especially for a diamond of the first water like Loftus. He has been beside himself, and I beside him, and it is especially difficult because his parents treat him poorly, and I am only beginning to realise that my own parents are not so fond of me as I once thought. Loftus got it in his head simply to come *talk* to you, just *talk* to you alone in the maze and *see* if you might reconsider. But I am afraid I followed after, seeking to offer him a—a *comforting* embrace, and it rather...went...from there."

"You did not!" Loftus exclaimed. "My lord, nothing happened here! Between Mr. Notley and I, that is." He drew a deep breath and stepped away from Morgan.

Soulden's dark gaze darted from Morgan to Loftus, and then back to Morgan, and then back to Loftus again. "Oh, dear God," he said. "Were you trying to entrap me? Am I being entrapped?" He took a step backwards. "Because I can swear on my brother's grave, and I will, that I haven't laid a hand on either of you!"

"But aren't you a rake?" Loftus asked, his voice rising in desperation. "Why don't you want to ravish me?"

Soulden's jaw dropped. "Oh, dear God," he said again. He shook his head. "Boys—"

Loftus glared at him.

"*Gentlemen*," Soulden amended, "as I have endeavoured to explain to you both, on multiple occasions, I—"

At that moment a short, sharp *crack* filled the air.

~

Morgan leapt, startled, and then let out a breathless laugh. He wasn't aware Lady Grosvenor was having fireworks! He peered up at the sky, wondering if he would see any from inside the maze. Because he was peering up at the sky, he was rather startled when Loftus launched at him and tackled him behind the knees, bringing him to the ground with a painful thump.

"What the hell do you—" The rest of his indignant query was muffled by Soulden's hand over his mouth.

Morgan blinked at him. He was lying on the ground in Lord Soulden's embrace! It was like a scene out of *The Maiden Diaries*!

Except Loftus was pressing up against him from behind, and—no, actually, that was also like a scene from *The Maiden Diaries*. The presence of the lamb, wriggling somewhere near his knees, was a novelty, but Morgan was still only partway through volume four, so it was possible the livestock didn't enter the picture until later chapters.

"Please don't cry out," Soulden whispered. "Your very lives depend on it."

Their very *lives*? Morgan blinked at him. Were there... were there *not* fireworks after all?

Soulden very slowly removed his hand from Morgan's mouth. His other one, Morgan couldn't help but notice, was clutching Morgan's hip. So was one of Loftus's hands. It was terribly confusing.

"How often, my lord," Loftus hissed in a whisper, "are you shot at?"

Shot at? Morgan jolted, and barely had time to open his mouth before Soulden slapped his hand over it again.

"Oh, not often enough that I ever get used to it," Soulden whispered back to Loftus, his breath ruffling Morgan's hair, "but neither is it entirely an unexpected occurrence. Ballocks. I hope we're not rescued now, or who knows which one of you I shall have to marry?"

A startled laugh rose up in Morgan's throat, and was muffled by Soulden's hand. "'Oftus," he mumbled against Soulden's palm. "Oo shoo marry 'oftus."

"What we're going to do," Soulden whispered, "is get behind that statue. We shall have to crawl, and stay low to the ground. Come now, quickly."

Morgan grabbed the lamb, and they all scrambled into position behind the statue of Leda. The plinth was a good size, and large enough for the three of them to sit there with their backs pressed against the stone. Morgan hugged the lamb to his chest.

Soulden, on Morgan's right, leaned carefully around the plinth.

Crack!

"Why is someone shooting at us?" Morgan whispered.

"Oh," said Soulden airily, "I expect they have their reasons. Now the real question is, why don't you two get married?"

Morgan's jaw dropped. "*What?*"

"You clearly care for one another," Soulden said, flinching as another crack sounded, and a shower of dust exploded from the corner of the plinth. "Damn, he's a good shot, isn't he?"

Loftus, on Morgan's left, twisted around and peered out from his side of the plinth. Morgan's heart clenched, and he grabbed Loftus by the coat and pulled him back.

"No shot on this side," Loftus said. "I think he's on your side, my lord."

"I think you're right," Soulden said, a note of approval creeping into his tone.

"I'm the third son of a baron, to answer your other question," Loftus said. "I am expected to marry up."

"Well, this one's a viscount's son, isn't he?" Soulden asked, his handsome brow creasing. "That's still up."

Loftus's mouth turned down. "My father has gambled our family's fortune away. The Notleys are not wealthy enough to satisfy his tastes. And Morgan's family also expects him to marry up."

"Loftus!" Morgan whispered urgently. "You must not talk about such things in polite society!"

"We're being shot at, Morgan," Loftus whispered back. "That's not very polite."

"So money and rank are both your families' considerations," Soulden said, tugging a handkerchief out of his coat pocket. He raised his eyebrows. "What are *yours?*"

"Someone handsome," Morgan said, his chest tightening. "Who likes me."

Loftus nodded. "And someone who doesn't live in New South Wales."

"Ah," Soulden said. "Mr. Notley, can you reach that stick? There's a good chap."

Morgan grabbed the stick and passed it to him. Soulden tied his handkerchief to the end of it.

"My lord, are you surrendering?" Loftus asked.

"What? No!" Soulden studied the flag he had made. "Ah, now there's the difficulty. My handkerchief is actually ivory, not white, though the difference is hard to make out in the dark. No, I thought to wave this around a little at the edges of the plinth, and draw his shots in one direction while we make our escape in the other. It's either this, or..." His gaze fell on the lamb in Morgan's arms.

Morgan gasped, and clutched the lamb closer. "No!"

"Not the lamb," Loftus said, in a steely tone that made Morgan tingle and feel warm all over.

Soulden slumped against the plinth, and rolled his eyes.

"What of your companion?" Loftus asked suddenly. "Surely he is coming into the maze to meet you? Will he not be able to raise the alarm?"

"Yeeees," Soulden said, the word drawn out slowly. "Though there is somewhat of a chance, slim though it may be, that it is my companion who is shooting at us." He sucked air through his teeth and then hummed. "My life has got rather complicated of late, I fear."

Morgan stared at him, one hand holding the lamb close to his chest and the other—the other holding tightly to Lotfus's. When had that happened?

"Well, then," Soulden said at last. "It seems to have stopped, what?" Another sharp *crack* called him a liar, and he winced. "Perhaps not. Perhaps not."

Morgan gasped, and buried his face in the lamb's fleecy side.

"It will be alright," Loftus whispered to him, squeezing his hand tightly.

"Well," Soulden said, "here's the thing, gentlemen. I'm going to make a dash for it, which should draw away the fellow's fire, and you two are going to wait here behind this statue where you won't get shot. Yes?"

"Yes," Loftus said, although it sounded like a question.

Morgan nodded into the lamb's side, and regretted it. The little creature was very pretty, but its barnyard smell was becoming more apparent with every passing minute.

"When I get out, I'll raise the alarm," Soulden said. "I shall say you are lost in the maze. A search party calling out for you should flush out our would-be assassin. Say nothing of anything else that has passed in here tonight, if you would be so kind."

"My lord, what *has* passed in here tonight?" Morgan asked, wrinkling his nose.

"Yes, wonderful." Soulden patted him on the shoulder. "Exactly the spirit!"

"No, it was a que–"

"Come and find me at Bucknall's as soon as you can get away." Soulden rose onto his haunches as he prepared to spring into action. "And remember, when they find you, that wearing a scandal is rather the same as wearing next Season's frock coat. If you do it with confidence, you shall be envied, not pitied."

And then he winked at them, grinned, and vanished into the darkness.

Several minutes after that, a merry crowd carrying lanterns and hallooing discovered Mr. Morgan Notley and Mr. Loftus Rivingdon, their knees dirty, their clothes in disarray, both of them with necks bared and buttons missing from their coats. It was quite the most shocking and wonderful turn of events for all of Lady Grosvenor's guests.

Morgan prayed that, as the story spread through the city as fast as a flood tide, no doubt washing up against the front doors of both their families and drowning their mothers in despair, at least nobody would mention the lamb.

CHAPTER 15

"What do you think Lord Soulden could want to talk to us about?" Morgan asked as he and Loftus arrived at Bucknall's and surrendered their hats and gloves to the doorman. He was aware he had asked the question several times already, and that Loftus was no more likely to have a plausible theory now than he had been five minutes ago. But Morgan could not help asking.

"I do not know," Loftus whispered back. "Tonight was so very thrilling."

"*Very* thrilling!" Morgan echoed. "I cannot believe I held a lamb for so long. Warry would be envious. My arms are sore!"

"I cannot believe we were shot at."

"Oh, yes, that too."

Morgan was not sure where they would find Soulden. He made his way through to the Blue Room, and then into the Green. It was sometime after one a.m., and most of the club's patrons were too far in their cups to take much notice of Morgan and Loftus. Which seemed a bit unfair. If Morgan was to be at the centre of a scandal, he wanted it to be far more talked about than Warry's scandal. Yet they barely drew any whispers or stares at all. Suddenly Lord Soulden was beside them, saying, "Ah, excellent. You're here." He ushered them to a table and motioned for them to sit. He tossed the tails of his coat behind him with a flourish and sat as well.

Morgan waited, unsure whether he was nervous or thrilled. Would Soulden explain who had shot at them hours ago? Had he decided to marry Loftus after all? If so, then Morgan supposed himself jealous, and yet with that jealousy came an unexpected flare of joy. Loftus would be saved at last from a desolate life in New South Wales!

"Right then." Soulden tapped on the table with one finger. "I have arranged for a carriage to take you to Gretna Green."

"Gretna Green?" Morgan and Loftus exchanged glances "Where is that?"

"Oh!" Loftus exclaimed. "My brother Geoffrey thought he might have to go there once. With a companion of his from school."

"A companion," Soulden repeated slowly. "Yes, of course."

"It is in Scotland," Loftus told Morgan.

"Scotland!" That sounded to Morgan rather far away. "Are we being banished from England because of our scandal?" How thrilling! Warry had never been banished from England.

"You are being sent to Scotland for a week in order to *prevent* a scandal. Though it is probably a bit late for that."

Loftus and Morgan stared at him.

"It is very clear that neither of you ever loved me. You love each other."

Loftus and Morgan started to protest.

Soulden held up a hand. Looked at Loftus. "If he had been shot tonight—" Soulden gestured at Morgan.

"No!" Loftus cried immediately. "Do not even suggest it, my lord. If he had been shot, I should have asked the assassin to kill me too."

"You would not have had to ask, but yes, precisely my point."

Soulden turned to Morgan. "If he had been shipped off to New South Wales to live with that sheep farmer—" He motioned to Loftus.

Morgan gasped. "No! I told you earlier, I would do anything to prevent it. Anything."

"Why is that?"

Morgan spoke without thinking. "Because he is kind and wonderful, and as beautiful and rare as a beautiful rare flower. He has encouraged me in my artistic pursuits and has been a true friend to me, and he does not deserve a loveless marriage, nor to smell like sheep for the rest of his life. He deserves the sort of affection I would shower him with daily—hourly—if I could." He clapped a hand to his mouth. Glanced at Loftus, then looked back at Soulden.

"Good man." Soulden turned to Loftus. "And you wouldn't have wanted Mr. Notley shot to death because…?"

"Because he is the only person who makes me feel seen and treasured for who I am. He tries to find the good in bad situations, and he always comforts me when I am in low spirits. Anyone who looks at him can see that he is so beautiful that the sun itself would envy—Oh dear." He stopped, glancing at Morgan.

"Marriages have been founded on less," Soulden said.

"Marriages?" Morgan exclaimed.

"At Gretna Green, you will be handfasted."

Morgan was unsure what exactly that meant, but he was fairly sure Slyfeel had done it to at least six people in *The Maiden Diaries*.

"That is a marriage ceremony that requires neither the church, nor your mamas' permission."

Ah, then Morgan must have been thinking of something else.

"But what shall we tell our mamas?" he asked, realising at once that his question should be something to the effect of how could he be expected to marry Loftus Rivingdon? When Soulden had suggested it earlier as they hid behind the statue, Morgan's heart had leapt with hope. And when he'd found himself holding hands with Loftus as bullets ricocheted off the plinth, he'd realised he never wanted to let go. He hadn't wanted to let go of the lamb either, but on the whole, the prospect of letting go of Loftus had been more unbearable.

But *marriage*?

"If I were you, I would not tell your mamas until the deed is done. Mamas tend to loathe handfasting, and as your mothers seem particularly dreadful—no offence—I should seize this opportunity to do as *you* wish, in defiance of your parents' machinations. And to avoid utter ruination, of course. Send word to your mamas that you require a holiday while the rumour mill runs its course."

"But what will it cost?" Loftus asked, no doubt thinking of his family's debts. Morgan reached for his hand under the table and squeezed it lightly.

"It is taken care of," Soulden said. "Expect just over two days' travel time. You shall arrive in the afternoon of the third day. The carriage will take you to the Blacksmith's Shop for the ceremony, and then to a rather charming inn, where you may spend the night…however you choose. I have allowed for two more nights at the inn, since it seems a shame to go all the way to Scotland and not see a bit of the country. Then you will cross the border back into England as newlyweds. My congratulations in advance."

Loftus and Morgan exchanged another look. Morgan realised, to his astonishment, that he wished to say yes. That he was not afraid. That this was rather the most astonishing thing that had ever happened to him. Besides getting shot at in a hedge maze. And sucking Loftus's prick.

But what if Morgan said yes and Loftus then said no? That would be humiliating.

Yet sometimes, life required one to take risks. "Yes," Morgan said, gazing at Loftus. "I should like that."

Loftus regarded Morgan with those stunning deep green eyes.

"Yes. This seems a rather wonderful solution." He turned to Soulden. "Only…the carriage will take us straight to the ceremony site? We are to be married after spending two days in a carriage?"

"Oh dear!" Morgan whispered. "Will this blacksmith's shop have a bath?"

"And a place to change?"

Soulden sighed. "I assure you, it is not the sort of establishment where you will be expected to present well."

"Still, might we send word ahead that we will require a pitcher of water? Several perhaps?"

"I will see what I can do."

"Then we agree to this plan," Loftus declared, sounding as giddy as Morgan felt.

"Very good." Soulden checked his pocketwatch. "I gave myself fifteen minutes to convince you, but you were persuaded in ten. Splendid. The carriage should arrive shortly. When you return to England, I hope to have sorted a few of your other problems as well."

"My lord?" Loftus enquired, and Morgan, who had been pushing back his chair, stopped to listen. "Why are you doing this?"

Soulden leaned back in his seat. "I don't know. I often find myself doing favours for people. I am not always sure why. I suppose because I can, and I am very bored."

"Your life does not seem boring, my lord," Loftus said—which was precisely what Morgan had been thinking.

Soulden winked at Loftus—*winked*!

"I am sorry," Loftus said softly. "Truly. For the past few weeks. And for tonight, especially. You must think me an awful—"

Soulden made a dismissive gesture. "Life is far too short for regrets. I was your age once. I do not miss it. Except when I do." He stood. "I must be going. Safe journey, my friends. I'm rather glad we were not massacred tonight. I expect you will have many…*interesting* years together."

He was gone as quickly as he'd appeared, leaving Morgan and Loftus to await their carriage. Life was indeed too short for regrets. And Morgan was determined not to have any regrets at all about marrying Loftus Rivingdon.

Looking at Loftus, Morgan was certain he felt the same. Morgan's own delight was reflected in Loftus's green eyes, and Morgan should have liked to kiss him right there. But then Loftus's smile slipped, and horror replaced giddy anticipation in his eyes. "Morgan!" he whispered. "Our clothes! We are to leave London at once, for over a week, and we do not have any clothes!"

~

As it happened, Soulden had made arrangements for clothing too. Just as he had made arrangements for them to stop that first night at an inn that offered a large copper basin for bathing. Loftus had wondered if spending so many hours in a carriage with Morgan might grow dull, but it was quite the opposite. They talked endlessly, until Loftus's voice grew hoarse. They recounted several times the horrors they had experienced at Lady Grosvenor's garden party—each insisting his fear had been greater than the other's, but also that his confidence in Lord Soulden's ability to save them had been greater than his fear. Until something shifted that first night, and Loftus insisted that his fear *for Morgan* had been greater than Morgan's fear for him, and Morgan had insisted that no, his own fear for Loftus's life had been the greatest fear he—and indeed anyone—had ever known.

They speculated on the fate of the lamb, and how Morgan's brother and Mrs. Notley were faring with their new arrival. "I wonder if I shall ever see the baby?" Morgan said, sorrow flashing in his large eyes.

"Of course you will! We shall be back in England in just over a week."

"But what if Mama has cast me off? What if Cecil refuses to see me?"

A horrible, cold knot formed in the pit of Loftus's stomach. Hours ago, the idea of marrying Morgan Notley in defiance of his father had seemed such an appealing idea. He had not wished to think too hard on his mother's inevitable disappointment. But surely neither of their mothers would cast them off. When they returned to England, they would explain to their families that they had done as their hearts had instructed. His mother would weep, no doubt, but she would understand, as she herself had once married for love. And then he realised that perhaps it did not matter if his mother was disappointed. For she had disappointed him. No, it was more than disappointment. She had hurt him, more terribly than he had ever been hurt. She had stood by while his father said terrible things about him and arranged for him to marry Wilberforce. The love match she had made, though it no longer held any love at all, was still something she would choose over him.

The thought was rather like a hammer swung into his midsection, and he hunched as he stared out the window at the drizzle that fell over rolling green hills.

"If they think less of us for loving each other," he said with surprising assurance, "then perhaps they are not worthy of our concern."

"Well, yes," Morgan said. "I have thought of that. But I should still like my family's money." He paused. "And...I should like to see the baby. Truly. And Cecil. Was I very horrid to him when he wished me to leave the party with him and go to Harriet? I suppose I was. I was worried about you, though."

"I do believe you will see the baby, Morgan. Cecil seems a reasonable fellow in spite of his manners. And your mama is too afraid of losing a war against mine to urge your father to cast you off. And mine is also too afraid of losing that war to do the same with me. The difference is that my father cares not for their rivalry. He may well disown me."

"Oh," Morgan whispered. "Loftus, I am sorry. We could turn back?"

"No." Loftus shook his head, a strange calm settling over him. "I do not wish to turn back."

A moment later, he felt a weight on his shoulder as Morgan rested his head there. Fingers twined with his. He drew a deep breath and leaned his head against Morgan's.

"I will take care of you," Morgan said softly. "If your family will not. Assuming my own family does not disinherit me, that is. But even if they do, perhaps I could sell my buttons and support us?"

Loftus sighed into Morgan's dark hair. He did not know how much one could make selling buttons, but he suspected it was not very much—even though Morgan's buttons were beautiful. "I will take care of you too. We will do that for each other."

They sat in silence for several long moments. Morgan squeezed his hand, and Loftus squeezed back. Then turned his head and kissed Morgan's temple. "This week, I do not wish to think of our families, who seem rarely to have acted in our best interests. I wish to think of being married to you."

"Oh." Morgan's breath fluttered a lock of his hair. "I wish that too. Loftus…" He lifted his head and gazed at Loftus. "This week, I wish to be happy."

~

Loftus had thought he would recall every moment of the handfasting ceremony, but in truth, the details bled together. The two witnesses Soulden had provided accompanied Loftus and Morgan to The Blacksmith's Shop, where the blacksmith, who jokingly called himself a priest, bound their wrists together with ribbon as they stood beside an anvil. The ribbon was not of a colour that particularly went with either of their coats, but Loftus was so over-awed staring down at their bound hands that he did not care. Morgan's hand was soft and warm beneath his own. The blacksmith priest declared them legally bound, and then swung his hammer hard against the anvil, so that the sound rang out through all the village.

And just like that, Loftus was married.

It was hardly the lavish wedding he'd envisioned for himself. And he remained quite terrified of what his parents would say when he returned to England. Yet his heart soared with happiness, and a great deal of that happiness came from seeing the lightness in Morgan. In knowing that he and Morgan were friends, co-conspirators...and now husbands. Morgan would not allow the blacksmith to undo the ribbon, insisting they travel to the inn with their hands still bound. Once inside the carriage, Morgan twined his fingers with Loftus's and held fast.

The inn was small but cosy, and Loftus did not find himself wishing for more luxurious accommodations. Their room had cheerful yellow paper hangings and a stone fireplace. A bottle of wine sat on a cabinet beside a lamp. In one corner was a washstand with a pitcher painted with Scottish thistles. In another was a very small pink and gold tea table with matching chairs.

"Oh, this is lovely!" Morgan exclaimed. He nearly jerked Loftus's arm from its socket making his way to the tea table. With a sheepish laugh, he unbound their hands, and Loftus missed the feel of the ribbon holding them together. They removed each other's coats, and Morgan went around to every corner of the room declaring how lovely everything was. Presently, a servant brought up tea and cakes and opened the wine bottle, and Morgan announced that this was lovely as well and thanked the woman profusely. Loftus could not stop grinning as he watched him, and when Morgan finally turned to him, they both broke into laughter.

Loftus opened a drawer in the cabinet and found a small bottle of oil, which made him gulp and shut the drawer quickly. He was quite aware, thanks to *The Maiden Diaries*, of what uses oil might have in a bedchamber. He joined Morgan at the tea table. Morgan rushed to pull a chair out, saying, "Husband?" with a gesture of his hand.

"Thank you, husband," Loftus replied, sitting.

They drank the tea and ate every single cake. Eventually the maid returned to bring more hot water for the washstand and to take the serving tray.

"Ought we to have wine?" Morgan was biting his lip. At some point amid their laughter and joking, Morgan had grown quieter. Loftus wondered what was on his mind. Perhaps he, like Loftus, was wondering about the practicalities of their wedding night.

"Not just yet," Loftus suggested, lifting cake crumbs from the table with his finger in a most ungentlemanly fashion.

Morgan had already risen from his seat and was standing near the cabinet with the wine on it. "Ah, all right. Later then." But he did not return to the table, and his shoulders seemed tense.

Loftus rose. "Come." He tugged Morgan to him, sliding one arm around Morgan's waist and joining his free hand with Morgan's. He swept him around the small room in a dance, and Morgan relaxed, laughing once more.

"You do not lead so well as I," Morgan said.

"I never thought I would have to lead. I assumed someone very tall and strong, such as Lord Soulden, would always be leading me in the waltz."

Morgan stiffened again, and Loftus let him pull away, wondering what he had said wrong.

"Do you still wish you had married Soulden, then?" Morgan asked, staring at the white bed with its blush-coloured curtains.

"No," Loftus said, sincerely and immediately. "I do not." He meant it. And yet there was the tiniest pang as he recalled the life he'd imagined—a life where he married a peer and rescued his mother from her unhappiness. Where he was admired by all, but most especially by his very wealthy, handsome, and important spouse.

"I know I am not what you wanted," Morgan said.

"I did not know what I wanted. I knew only what Mother wanted for me."

"But Loftus…now that I am trying to think of other people and their feelings, I wonder what will become of her? Will your mother suffer greatly because of your father's debts? And his cruelty?"

"There are options for her. She could…divorce him."

Morgan shuddered visibly. "Do not say such things!"

"But think. There must be many such people trapped in marriages with cruel spouses. If they wish to escape such arrangements, oughtn't they to be able to do so without censure?"

"I do not know," Morgan whispered. "I do not know anything anymore." He paused. "But what you say makes sense. If my father was cruel to my mother, I would want her to be able to free herself from him. But divorce is so very gauche! Not to mention wicked."

"But if you think about it, there are many wicked practises that we do not question, such as killing elephants for ivory." Loftus saw Morgan wince. "And so it follows that there might be many practises we call wicked, but which do not actually hurt anyone and therefore are only wicked because saying makes it so."

"Oh, goodness. You are very clever, Loftus."

"You are what I want," Loftus said firmly. "I am sorry it took me so long to see it." He reached out and took gentle hold of Morgan's upper arms, smiling when Morgan's gaze met his.

Morgan offered him a tentative smile in return. "I am sorry too. I think I knew for a long time that I cared for you, but I did not say it." He hesitated, and Loftus did not speak, letting him gather himself. Eventually Morgan asked, "Do you love me?"

The question rather stunned Loftus, and so he did not answer right away. Morgan's large eyes held a sheen of disappointment, and Loftus wanted to declare that he felt for Morgan the sort of love that launched wars, inspired sonnets, transcended earthly existence. But he thought it important to be honest about this matter above all others. "I care for you a great deal."

"But you are not in love with me?"

"I do not know how one ought to feel in love. I know that I find you more beautiful than anyone I have ever seen—including Lord Soulden. I know that I want you—in every sense. That I should like to be someone you turn to when you are in need of company, or comfort, or…anything at all. But we do not know each other well. My mother was in love with my father when they married and now despises him. To be in love seems rather like a costume one might put on for an evening. While truly loving someone seems like one's own skin, that grows and changes with age but that is always a part of one." Loftus was not sure where these words were coming from. He had never been asked to express himself so fully and honestly. Also, it was quite upsetting to think of skin aging. He chafed Morgan's arms through his shirt. "You recall in volume three of *The Maiden Diaries*. When Lady Mary and Lord Stanhope at last realise their feelings for each other after they are each—" He searched for a polite word, and could only come up with one from the book, which he was not sure applied when done to ladies, or when done with vegetables "—backgammoned by Slyfeel, on separate occasions and with separate aubergines?"

"Yes," Morgan said. "They are rather one of my favourite pairings."

"Well, they marry, but it is only over the course of the third and fourth volumes that they become genuine partners, and that their mutual affection deepens to truest love. I think that love must be cultivated."

"Cultivated. That is beautiful, Loftus."

"Yes." Loftus rather thought so himself.

"I want to be good," Morgan said quietly, and with a great deal of sincerity. "I try to be. I can be, don't you think?" He looked at Loftus with naked vulnerability.

Loftus let go his arms and brushed his fingers over the smooth skin of Morgan's cheek, then cupped his face. "Of course you can be. You are."

Morgan shook his head, and Loftus let his hand return to his side. "I'm not. When I think of the things I have done and said to you, and how dismissive I have been of others' feelings. When I think how little I know of...of the world." He swallowed visibly. "How can anyone stand me? How could anyone love me?"

"I have just said—"

"That you do not love me *yet*. And what if you never do? I am not trying to convince you to declare anything you do not mean. I am only saying that I worry I have not—*will* not—ever earn your love, or anyone's."

Loftus drew him into an embrace and said into those dark, glossy curls, "I do love you. I may not know precisely what that love is just yet, but I have every certainty this feeling will strengthen with all the years we spend together."

"Yes." Morgan sounded choked.

"And I do believe your Mama loves you."

"I don't know."

"And your cousin Rebecca seems rather fond of you. She was most displeased with my efforts to break your foot."

Morgan gave a shaky laugh, adjusting his arms around Loftus, tightening the embrace for a few seconds. "She thinks I'm very stupid. And I am. I feel sometimes that I am only smart enough to know how stupid I am. That seems unfair, doesn't it?"

"You are not stupid."

"It is all right if I am. I only ever wanted to be beautiful, not intelligent."

Loftus laughed and drew back slightly to see Morgan's face. He was feeling something he never had before—a desire to protect, rather than be protected. To admire and worship, rather than be admired or be worshiped. How strange, the way he wished to *give* Morgan happiness, when so recently he would have thought happiness his to take. "I shall care for you now and always."

"Unless you come to despise me."

"I do not think that will happen. More likely it would be the other way around. But if any cold feelings develop between us one day, that is an issue for one day. Not for tonight."

Morgan exhaled. "I am very glad to hear you say that. For I also thought...well, what if we do not know each other well enough yet for true love? Yet I feel such affection for you, and I am certain we will cultivate genuine love, one day. I want to be here for you, through every good and bad thing, just as you said. I want you to turn to me."

"There now. You are good," Loftus assured him quietly. "Or else you would not even have such concerns about being good. Don't you see?"

Morgan snorted, not quite meeting his gaze, though his arms remained around Loftus. "I think I always tried to be. I just didn't realise what it meant. I thought it meant being...superior, I suppose. In society's eyes. But I should like to be good for the sake of it rather than for appearances."

Loftus drew him forward and kissed him. "We shall both vow to be better tomorrow than we are today, and we shall make the same vow each day. That is all we can do."

Morgan leaned against him, resting his chin on Loftus's shoulder. "I will try."

Loftus rubbed his back for several moments, aware of the stand he was now sporting, but unsure whether their conversation on serious matters was finished for the moment.

As if reading his thoughts, Morgan lifted his head and gazed at him. He kissed Loftus, a long, sweet kiss that had Loftus's heart quickening. After a moment, they parted to regain their breath. "Husband?" Morgan whispered. "Now that we are wed, does this mean we must attempt volume one, chapter eight?"

Loftus inhaled so sharply he nearly choked. "Well. There is nothing we *must* do. We shall do what pleases us." He hesitated.

"Yes. I have wanted to for ages. Do you?"

Loftus's throat was suddenly dry. "I do. I think."

"Which, um…in which configuration?"

Loftus considered the matter. "I should like to try both ways. Eventually."

"Yes! That is excellent, for I have been thinking the same."

A grin spread over Loftus's face. "We *do* have all night. And the next night. And the next."

"And a great many years after! We shall attempt a few experiments." Morgan draped his arms loosely around Loftus's neck.

They fell back against the wall, laughing between kisses. But Morgan soon grew serious again. "I should like…for you to spend inside me first. If that is all right with you?"

Loftus nearly spent right there in his drawers. "That would certainly be satisfactory."

"All right. I shall, um. Go to the washstand."

Loftus attempted to lean comfortably against the wall while Morgan refreshed himself, but the wall was not comfortable, and so Loftus sat at the tea table, gaze flicking from the table's patterned border to Morgan, and back. Morgan had removed his cravat and undone the three buttons of his lawn shirt, and was patting at his face and neck with a cloth.

"There is soap," Morgan said. "Isn't that lovely?"

"It is," Loftus said, growing increasingly nervous. He had read every volume of *The Maiden Diaries*, but the book, for all its numerous depictions of swiving, was not terribly instructive. How, precisely, did one go about backgammoning? In theory it seemed very simple. In the book it seemed very pleasurable. But in practise…would it not hurt? He went to the cabinet and poured them each a glass of wine. He drank his rather faster than he'd intended, and Morgan accepted his own with clear gratitude while Loftus went to the wash stand. "You have used all the warm water," Loftus accused.

"I certainly have not."

Loftus threw a smirk over his shoulder at him. "Liar." He

removed his waistcoat and unbuttoned his shirt so that he might slip the cloth under his arms. When he finished, Morgan was watching him. Or, more precisely, studying the V of skin exposed by Loftus's undone shirt. Loftus felt himself flush.

"What if I cannot do it?" Morgan asked, almost inaudibly.

Loftus put aside his own nerves on the subject, made his voice low and soothing. "Of course you can. But if you do not wish to, then naturally we will not do it."

"You will not be greatly disappointed?"

"Not at all," Loftus said honestly.

"And the marriage will still be consummated? Even if this effort is not successful?"

"We are married no matter what we do in bed."

Morgan paused, large eyes growing serious, his lips slightly parted. "You will go very slowly?"

"*Very* slowly."

"You will kiss me a lot?"

"I would not be able to resist."

"Well then." Morgan set one hand on his hip. "You may strip me. Carefully, for these pantaloons are my most expensive pair."

Loftus stepped forward, trying not to let his hands visibly shake. The combination of wine and arousal was dizzying. Morgan held perfectly still, as though Loftus were a surgeon about to make an important cut. Loftus first undid the buttons of Morgan's midnight-blue waistcoat. Morgan breathed out softly as Loftus slipped the garment off his shoulders. As he did, his hand brushed the back of Morgan's shirt and he paused.

"Morgan?"

"Yes?"

Loftus touched the back of his shirt again. "This is a bit damp."

"What?"

Loftus ran his hand over the fabric. "Not horribly so. But…I do believe you are sweating."

"Impossible!" Morgan drew away.

Loftus tried with little success to hide a grin.

"I do *not* sweat. I am a gentleman!"

"Even gentlemen sweat. Won't you come here?"

"Not if you are going to point out my *sweat*, Loftus."

"I promise not to mention it again."

"You swine. It is water that dripped when I was washing my face."

"Even Lord Soulden sweats. I could feel it the other night when we were being shot at. His hands were damp."

"Liar."

"Come here. Let me finish undressing you."

"Should I wash again?" Morgan's expression was agonised.

"No," Loftus said softly. "We are only nervous. My shirt feels the same."

Morgan sighed. "I wish to be perfect for you. To look and smell and…and behave perfectly. For you."

"You are absolutely perfect right now." Loftus assured him. "The only way you could look any better would be if all of your clothing was on the floor."

Morgan chewed his lip for a second. And then the corners of his mouth twitched up. He stepped toward Loftus. Their eyes met again as Loftus tugged Morgan's shirt over his head.

Loftus could not speak at first, as Morgan stood bare-chested before him. That sweet, lithe body was everything he could have imagined. Morgan was slender, but his pale, smooth shoulders were well-defined, and his arms had more muscle than Loftus would have guessed. Morgan crossed those arms over his chest, shivering. "I have never undressed in front of you."

Loftus felt his cheeks prick with warmth at the reminder that he himself had been half dressed in Morgan's presence before.

"You are simply stunning," Loftus whispered.

"Flatterer."

"No." Loftus took his arms gently and eased them to his sides. Kissed his cheek.

Morgan softened then, sighing as he angled himself so that Loftus could undo his pantaloons. When they pooled at his ankles, he stepped out of them as gracefully as a dancer. Underneath he wore silk drawers. Loftus almost laughed. Of course Morgan Notley had silk drawers. He almost wanted to leave them on, caress Morgan's stand through the silk. And so he did not remove them just yet. He moved around behind Morgan, running his fingertips along the line of the man's spine, his prick hardening at Morgan's sharp inhale.

He planted a feather-light kiss on the bare shoulder before him. "I will not hurt you," he whispered.

Morgan breathed out a shaky laugh. It quickly turned into a gasp as Loftus kissed the back of his neck. He bowed his head, allowing Loftus access. His dark, glossy curls parted to reveal the soft nape that Loftus suddenly wanted to kiss forever. He moaned very softly as Loftus's lips brushed a trail down between his shoulder blades. Shivered a little. "I don't know why I should be so nervous to do something I have imagined doing a thousand times. Dreamed of doing, even. Are you nervous?"

"Very," Loftus replied honestly.

"Why?"

"Because I want this to be so incredibly pleasurable for you that you are never afraid of it again. And I would like it to be pleasurable for me as well. I would like us to both be satisfied."

Morgan's breath hitched. "I want that too. I want you, Loftus."

Loftus had never heard such beautiful words in all his life. He led Morgan over to the bed and seated him on it, then knelt and rolled down one of Morgan's stockings. Ran his fingers over Morgan's shin, feeling the curls of dark hair layered over smooth skin. Morgan tipped his chin up, his spine arching, his stand clearly visible through his drawers. Loftus could have spent from that sight alone. Instead he leaned forward and pressed a kiss just below Morgan's knee.

Morgan's leg jerked, his foot catching Loftus fully in the chest, sending him sprawling backward.

"I'm sorry!" Morgan yelped. "Loftus, I am so sorry! I am very ticklish just there."

Loftus slowly picked himself up. He groaned.

"I'm sorry." Morgan reached to help him. "I did not mean to."

Loftus settled himself back on his knees, snickering.

"Loftus, are you crying? Did I damage you irreparably?"

Loftus shook his head and looked up at Morgan with a grin. "I thought I was being very seductive."

"You *were!*" Morgan sounded horrified. But an instant later, he began to laugh too. "Oh, I did not expect you would kiss me there. I am horribly ticklish–there and on my feet. As a child I injured two different doctors who wished only to ensure that a sprained ankle was healing properly."

Loftus laughed harder. "I shall have a bruise tomorrow."

"Don't say that!"

Loftus went to work on the other stocking, careful not to touch too lightly. When Morgan's stockings both lay in the corner with his other clothes, Loftus shuffled forward between Morgan's legs, set his hands on the other man's thighs, and looked up, meeting Morgan's gaze.

"Lie back," he instructed softly.

Morgan went back on his elbows, hips positioned awkwardly at the edge of the mattress.

"All the way," Loftus urged. "Get up on the bed." He hoped he did not sound as terrified as he felt. His prick was as hard as it had ever been, but his fear that the act would hurt Morgan was pervasive.

Morgan climbed fully onto the mattress and lay on his back. "Like this?"

"That is perfect."

"Doesn't Slyfeel often…ride from behind?"

"Is this all right?" Loftus began undressing himself. "So that I might see your face?"

"Yes. I think I will be less nervous if I can see you."

When Loftus was down to his linen drawers, he hesitated, then stripped them off and stood naked before the bed. Morgan lifted his head to study him. Loftus's bare skin prickled with self-consciousness. But Morgan smiled at him without a hint of mockery. "You don't know how many times, after that day we examined your stays, I have thought about seeing you without your clothes."

"Flatterer."

"No. Never." Morgan's smile had faded. "I meant it then, and I mean it now. You are beautiful."

Warmth spread through Loftus, and he found he was no longer quite so apprehensive. What he wanted now more than anything was to ensure that Morgan was not at all afraid. He knelt on the bed and untied Morgan's silk drawers. Tugged them off, careful not to snag them on Morgan's stand, which pointed straight upwards. "And you," Loftus whispered, "are a work of art."

"Slow," Morgan reminded him, a little breathlessly.

"I promise." Loftus leaned over him to kiss him, their stands brushing together, making them both squirm.

It took a few moments of arranging pillows underneath Morgan before they settled on what Loftus hoped was an ideal position for unspeakable acts. After a rather long interlude in which Loftus kissed Morgan until they were both panting, Morgan canted his hips invitingly. Loftus took the oil from the table and promptly spilled rather a lot of it on the bedclothes in his eagerness. He slicked his prick, and then, recalling several scenes from *The Maiden Diaries*, dripped a bit of it into the cleft of Morgan's arse.

Morgan remained very quiet and still as Loftus positioned himself.

"Is this still what you want?" Loftus asked.

Morgan nodded, but no sound came from his parted lips.

"You're gorgeous, Morgan. This is going to feel very good." Loftus prayed that was true.

Alas, once Loftus had the tip of his prick between Morgan's arse cheeks, he realised he was not entirely sure where, precisely, the entrance was. He tried pressing forward, but Morgan grunted and his fingers sank into the counterpane, and Loftus had a feeling he was in the wrong spot. He let go of his stand and used his hands instead to part Morgan's cheeks. Now he could see where he ought to aim, and he pushed his hips forward until the head of his prick nudged the small, dark hole. Morgan whimpered, but it was not an entirely pleasurable sound. "It is all right," Loftus soothed him. "I'll be careful."

"Yes," Morgan agreed softly.

Loftus began pushing in. Morgan immediately went rigid.

"Try to relax," Loftus whispered.

"Yes," Morgan repeated.

Loftus pushed forward again, and his prick slid up the cleft of Morgan's arse. "Ballocks."

Morgan laughed, a warm, genuine sound that made Loftus smile even as his face flamed with embarrassment.

"It is too slippery!" Loftus protested. "I cannot hold my stand in the right place *and* um, hold your—I mean, see what it is I'm doing—"

"Here." Morgan reached around his bent legs and held his arse cheeks parted. "Does this help?"

"Thank you," Loftus said, relieved. *"The Maiden Diaries* did not prepare me for this."

"You *are* nervous," Morgan observed.

"I don't want to hurt you! I suddenly feel I would rather die than do so."

"It is all right. I do not feel so worried anymore."

"Now that I have made a fool of myself?"

"You didn't! I mean, perhaps a little."

"We'll see how well you do with this bit later," Loftus leaned down to give him a quick kiss.

Morgan stuck out his tongue and made a most ungentlemanly sound that had them both laughing, until Loftus leaned in and kissed him more firmly. Morgan's expression grew hazy with lust. "Please? Try again?"

Loftus lined up his prick once more and frowned as he pushed in. He could feel Morgan watching him, and he raised his own gaze to meet the wide, dark eyes—the sight of which made everything much easier. He continued to push, stopping when Morgan's eyes squeezed shut and lines of tension appeared in his smooth forehead.

"Keep going," Morgan urged through his teeth. When Loftus remained frozen, he raised his voice. "Please, Loftus, just keep going! You won't break me."

A second later, Morgan's body yielded, and Loftus's prick slid deep into Morgan. Morgan gave a strangled yelp, and Loftus bit back a sound of shock at the sudden rush of pure pleasure. He concentrated on Morgan instead, rubbing his hip. "Is it all right? Does it hurt?"

Morgan's eyes darted about the ceiling, his fingers flexing against the counterpane. He was breathing harshly. "It feels… strange. It doesn't hurt. Well, only a little."

"A little?" Loftus cried in alarm.

"No, it is not bad. It is only what one might expect. And already it is fading. Oh God, Loftus. I can't believe we did it!"

Loftus flushed with delight. Now that he was not so worried about hurting Morgan, he could concentrate on how very, *very* good it felt to have his prick up Morgan's arse. The tightness and heat, the overwhelming sense of *closeness*…

There was a problem, however. And that was that if Loftus were to move at all, even a fraction of an inch backward or forward, he would spend. It was bad enough that Morgan's arse kept contracting around his prick. If he experienced any friction whatsoever, he feared losing any chance at giving Morgan a proper ride.

"Loftus? Are you all right?"

Loftus barely managed words. "You feel…very good…and I don't…know how to…to keep from…"

"Oh, don't you remember volume two, chapter seven? When Slyfeel says he will ride the Count of Ammonleigh for ten straight minutes straight, yet he is so attracted to the Count that to keep from spending he must think of his worst enemy? You must try that."

"My worst enemy until very recently was you," Loftus ground out.

"Ah, yes, I see how that could be a problem."

Loftus let out a breath, some of the urgency in his body subsiding. Yet he knew that if he looked into Morgan's gorgeous eyes, or let himself notice the becoming blush that was sure to lie on Morgan's cheeks, or—God help him—looked down at the place where his prick disappeared inside Morgan, he would lose his restraint.

"But Loftus, please, I am dying. I must know what it feels like to have you move in me. I know! Why don't you think of people who still wear knee breeches as daywear?"

Loftus tried, but all he could think about was the unbearably tight heat encasing his prick. He drew back a little, groaning, then thrust forward.

"Cravat pins that are lopsided," Morgan panted.

Loftus gave another tentative thrust.

"Mud-splattered Hessians."

Loftus was going to lose his stand altogether if Morgan took this too far.

"Pink and bronze ribbons worn in combination."

"All right! All right, I am fully in control of myself now."

"Phew. I was growing rather ill speaking of such atrocities."

Morgan gave a little groan that turned to a whimper as Loftus delivered a long, slow thrust.

Loftus recalled how Morgan had wanted to be kissed, and he risked shifting positions slightly, hoping he could lean down and press his lips to Morgan's.

"Oh God!" Morgan cried out, his arse gripping Loftus's prick.

"What?"

"Do that again," he cried.

Loftus was not sure what he had done. But he tried shifting once more, and Morgan yelped. "Wh—"

Suddenly Morgan's upper body was off the bed and he was clinging to Loftus, attempting to rock his hips. "There is something —some place in there, Loftus, when you drive in just right, it feels like the most indescribable pleasure and sickening torture all at once."

"Sickening torture?"

"Yes, but it is a good thing. I think? Please!"

Loftus shifted his hips again, then again, and soon Morgan was whimpering and moaning, grabbing fistfuls of the bedclothes.

"Please don't stop," he begged.

"You are so perfect," Loftus whispered through his ragged breaths. "How sweet you are, laid out like this for me." He was thrusting harder and faster now, and somehow they had both adjusted so that Loftus was nearly lying upon Morgan, leaning down to kiss Morgan's chest, his shoulders, loving how Morgan shuddered and clenched tighter around Loftus with each new touch. Morgan lifted his head, seeking Loftus's lips, but he jerked suddenly, spending onto Loftus's belly with a series of delightful little yelps that undid the last of Loftus's control. Loftus drove one final time into Morgan and spent with a stifled howl of pleasure.

His arms shook from holding himself up. He began to withdraw, but at Morgan's moan, he slowed the movement, easing himself out with care.

"Loftus," Morgan whispered

Loftus kissed him, careful and slow.

Morgan shivered, though his skin was hot. So hot, in fact, that Loftus found himself gently wiping beads of moisture from Morgan's forehead.

"You cannot deny you're sweating now," he teased.

"It must be your sweat that has fallen onto me."

"Little liar."

Morgan's laugh was soft and sweet. It soon faded. He gazed at Loftus, eyes catching the waning light outside. Loftus stroked his cheek, then got up and went to the washstand to clean himself. He returned to the bed and curled around Morgan, and they lay together until the room was twilit, and outside they could hear the stirring of night insects.

At last, Morgan said, "That would not have been anywhere near as satisfying with Lord Soulden."

Loftus gave a guffaw that echoed in the darkening room. "Soulden would not have been so proud of you either."

"*Proud* of me?" Morgan rolled onto his back. "You were proud of me?"

"Yes. It does not seem easy to do that for the first time. And you were good enough to trust me. You felt so wonderful when I was inside you—so tight and warm, and you moved so beautifully. I shall never forget how you felt."

Morgan swallowed, then turned his head, kissing lightly at Loftus's jaw. "It was good. But it felt quite uncomfortable at times. I would not have been able to take Soulden's girth, I don't think. Yours was much more manageable."

Loftus stiffened. "Thank you."

Morgan lifted his head from the pillow. "There I go again! I say these things, and I do not intend to be insulting—well, sometimes I do—but in this case, I did not. It is a good thing, you see. I do not want a stallion." He ran his fingers over Loftus's shoulder. "You are perfection."

"But you did like it?"

"Oh, yes! It was not what I expected. Slyfeel never seems to have trouble getting it in. His paramours sometimes feel a stretch, but then an instant later he is always seated inside them and they are crying his name with pleasure, but that is not how I felt at first. I felt pleasure," he added hastily. "Yet I was quite anxious, and I thought the part where you entered would never end and that the entire act would hurt as that first part did. If you had not spoken to me as you did, and kissed me, I would not have wanted to go on."

Loftus's fingers traced the line of Morgan's throat as Morgan swallowed again. He tilted his face slightly toward Loftus. "I liked what you said to me. Everyone always pays me compliments on such general things. You…you tell me what you really see."

"It is not difficult to find good things to say about you."

"I think you are the first person to ever be proud of me for anything other than my eyes or my manner of dress. And even you are merely proud of me for taking a prick up my arse."

"That is not the only reason. I am proud of you because you are working on your button designs even though your mama disapproves. Because you are trying to unlearn what you have been taught and learn instead to treat people kindly. You have made me want to learn that as well."

Now Morgan turned and buried his face in Loftus's chest. Loftus stroked his hair. "I am proud of you too," Morgan murmured. "You have finally made a decision that is for you and not your parents. Your father is cruel, but you do not wish to be like him. You are kind to me when I am unsure of myself. You could wear yellow every day, and I would still love you just as I do now."

Loftus kissed him. "Perhaps we ought to have a dinner tray brought up?"

"Not just yet. Lie with me a while longer, please?"

Loftus was happy to oblige.

At last Morgan asked, "Would Soulden split me apart, do you think?"

"Do not think of him now!"

"I'm sorry, but surely you must have thought it too, at some point during all this."

Loftus hesitated, considering the matter. "It would take a *lot* of practise to accommodate him."

"But what if he is the one who likes to be ridden? He did not specify."

"Do you think he would be satisfied with either of our girths? Or do you think—say you had him on all fours—would he call back over his shoulder that he can barely feel that?"

Morgan snickered. "Stop!" He swatted Loftus's shoulder lightly. "It is very wrong of us to talk like this. And besides, would you not want to bed him face to face, as you did me, so that you might see that strong jaw the whole time? And kiss those wonderful lips?"

"I would be afraid to see the disappointment in his eyes if I did not satisfy him!"

"You would satisfy him. You satisfied me." He nestled a bit closer to Loftus.

Loftus absently stroked Morgan's hair. "But if he does not want a gentle ride—it might be easier to ride him roughly from behind. Do you know what I mean? Perhaps he does not want tender kisses and gazing into each other's eyes."

"Not *tender* kisses, no. But perhaps he would want his lips bitten, and his throat."

Loftus glanced at him. "Would *you* want that?"

Morgan's breathing was shallow. His gaze darted up to Loftus's. "Yes. Yes, I think I would. But not too hard."

Loftus propped himself on an elbow, leaned down, and kissed Morgan's cheek.

Morgan closed his eyes and sighed.

Loftus kissed the corner of his mouth. Then flicked his tongue against pressed-tight lips. Morgan yielded, lips parting, his eyes still shut. Loftus slipped his hands beneath Morgan's back, digging his fingers into Morgan's shoulders. "Loftus." Morgan's parted lips curved up. "Even if we practise until I can take a stallion," he whispered. "I will still only want you."

"Thank you. I shall take whatever scrap of a compliment I can find in that."

Morgan laughed too. "If you are kissing me, I cannot accidentally say insulting things."

That, Loftus realised, was very true. And so he went to work making sure the only word Morgan remembered by the end of the night was Loftus's name.

And then, tomorrow, they would start learning how to be in love for the rest of their lives.

CHAPTER 16

Two weeks later.

The house in Westminster was delightful. In fact, since returning from Scotland, everything had been delightful. Oh, Mama had wept into a large pink handkerchief when Morgan had gone around to visit her and to collect his belongings, but Morgan was satisfied that she would soon be her old self. Or perhaps, like him, she might even be a better version of her old self. Though he was not holding his breath on that account; when he'd mentioned his intention to study portraiture under Mr. Buck, she'd brought the servants running with her wailing. A *job*? And he would ruin his beautiful eyes! But Morgan was determined to paint. He wanted a portrait of Loftus to hang in the hallway, because he looked so dashing in his Royal Dragoons uniform. Lord Soulden had paid for his commission, just as he was paying for Morgan's art lessons with Mr. Buck, and had sworn them both to secrecy. Morgan's father had unhappily paid the rent on the house in Westminster. It felt thrilling to be an independent gentleman, though when Morgan had voiced his opinion aloud, his father had gone into a paroxysm of coughing and had to be revived by having a glass of port waved under his nose.

The house was not as lovely as the one he had shared with his parents in Curzon Street, and it only had six servants, but Morgan was a changed man these days, humbled by thoughts of elephants and love, and he didn't mind terribly much. He and Loftus were forging their own path, and it was wonderful.

He only wished things were quite as wonderful for Loftus.

"There now. Just seal the envelope and send it," Morgan urged, standing over Loftus's writing desk, his hand on Loftus's back.

"What if she turns it down? Or worse, what if she never acknowledges it at all?"

"She will," Morgan insisted with more certainty than he felt. Loftus's mama had not dealt with the news of their marriage nearly so well as Morgan's. And last week, Loftus had received a letter from his father that had caused him to storm up the stairs and shut himself in the bedroom. When Morgan had knocked on the door, Loftus had called out angrily that he wished to be alone. However, Morgan heard his footsteps approach the door, and then the door opened just a crack, and then came the sound of retreating footsteps and of Loftus hurling himself onto the bed as he called again, *"Did you* hear *me? I wish to be* alone!*"* So Morgan had entered the room and discovered that Loftus did not truly wish to be alone at all. This marriage business was not so difficult as he had feared.

Loftus sighed. "Perhaps I should change the wording here…"

Morgan set his hand firmly on Loftus's before Loftus could pick up the quill again. "Enough. The wording is just fine."

They sent Lady Rivingdon the invitation to tea. Loftus fretted for the next hour, until Morgan suggested an early bedtime and Loftus replied that did not sound fun at all, and then Morgan undid his pantaloons and Loftus at last took his meaning.

~

*I*f Loftus could have frozen one moment in time and held onto it forever, it would have been Morgan's expression when he first laid eyes on his niece.

"Little Morgana!" Morgan kept repeating, gazing down at the bundle he held in his arms. He looked up at Mrs. Notley, and then at Cecil. "I cannot believe you named her for me!"

"Yeah, well," Cecil said gruffly. "If she turns out anything like you, I may regret the choice."

"Cecil! What an awful thing to say."

"Don't be thick, Morgan. Though I suspect that's a bit like telling the sky not to be blue, isn't it? I've only been hanging around Curzon Street for ages, enduring our mother's company, trying to get her to tell me where you live now so that I might visit you and we can talk. Two bloody weeks, it's taken!"

"But why would you want to talk to me? You hate it when I talk about anything."

Cecil shifted uncomfortably, his hands deep in his pockets—where Loftus thought he must have stuffed them to keep from reflexively reaching out every time Morgan shifted and nearly forgot to support the baby's head. But Morgan always remembered the baby's head before it flopped too much. Loftus was rather proud of him. "About wanting you to be a part of her growing up, is all."

Morgan stared at him again. "You...what?"

Cecil shrugged. "I thought maybe we ought to start spending more time together. So that you could really be an uncle to her, you know? Although now that you're the biggest scandal of the Season, I am wondering whether it's best to pretend I don't know you at all."

Morgan beamed at Loftus, bouncing the baby slightly. "Yes, we are the talk of London at last!"

Loftus studied the floor, his throat tight. He had received no response from his mother to his invitation. It was now ten past the hour and there was no sign of her. He supposed he ought to put her from his mind and concentrate on being a good host to Cecil and Mrs. Notley, and little Morgana. But he couldn't quite push the hurt away.

"What the hell were you doing in Scotland for a whole *week*, anyway?" Cecil asked his brother.

"I was getting handfasted," Morgan said primly.

"I'll just bet you were," Cecil muttered.

Lady Notley arrived late for tea, but Morgan had already explained that her tardinesss should be expected; it was not so much a fault of character as it was a test in patience for those receiving her.

"Ballocks," Cecil said. "It's because she likes to feel important by making others wait."

"Cecil, you say such dreadful things!" Morgan exclaimed, looking both fond and appalled. "Mrs. Notley, how do you put up with him?"

"Now that's a dreadful thing to say," Cecil grumbled, but he flushed and smiled when Mrs. Notley patted his arm as she went and took a seat on the chaise longue.

"I am very lucky to have married my dear Cecil," she said, and looked as though she meant it too.

Lady Notley arrived in a cloud of feathers, lace and perfume. She was pinched and a little sharp of tone—dare Loftus think shrill?— as she bid them all a good day, and the smile she wore was as false as the delicate blush on her still-smooth cheeks. She set her reticule on the floor, and her little dog leapt out of it and scuttled away.

"Morgan, you must show me your house!" she said imperiously.

And before Loftus knew it, he had an armful of little Morgana, and Morgan was sweeping Lady Notley away.

"Oh," said Loftus, looking to both Mrs. Notley and Cecil, but neither of them seemed inclined to relieve him of his burden. Morgana really was a pretty baby—she took after her mother, not her father, thank God in all His mercy. "Hello, there."

The footman appeared suddenly in the doorway. "Sir," he said. "Lady Rivingdon."

Loftus somehow managed to keep his hold on the baby as his mother glided into the room. "Mother!"

She inclined her head.

She was—she was clearly deeply unhappy. Her mouth was pursed in disapproval and her eyes narrowed, and yet she was *here*. She could have cut him, and yet she was here. Loftus didn't know what that meant, and he hated the flutter of hope that rose in his chest and threatened to catch in his throat, because he did not trust his mother not to crush it.

"Loftus," she said at last.

Mrs. Notley moved forward to take the baby. "Shall we sit?" she asked brightly. "And shall we ring for tea now?"

"Y-yes," Loftus said, grateful for the distraction. "Tea and cakes, yes."

"I suppose you are not watching your waist, now that you are married," Mother said, arranging the fall of her dark blue dress as she sat. The fabric was dark enough that it almost looked black, as though she was in mourning, and Loftus did not doubt she was making a point.

Cecil thumped down, the couch under him creaking. "And a good thing too, eh? Besides, nothing like a little bit of flesh to hold onto and keep you warm at night. That's what I tell Harriet whenever I have a second piece of cake."

He probably did too, Loftus thought, but again, he was grateful for the distractions the Notleys were providing.

"Um, Mother, this is Mr. Cecil Notley," he said. "And Mrs. Harriet Notley. Mr. and Mrs. Notley, Lady Rivingdon, my mother."

Mrs. Notley, bless her, immediately launched into a dull but polite conversation about the weather, forcing Mother to respond. Mother kept casting suspicious glances at Morgana, and Loftus supposed it was terribly gauche to take an infant visiting for tea, but Morgan had been quite interested in meeting her. That interest had turned to slavish devotion the moment Cecil had announced her name, and Loftus was sure that Morgan would be a fine uncle. He jolted a little as the thought occurred to him—*he* could be a fine uncle to Morgana too! Morgan could teach her how to draw, and Loftus could dress in his uniform and play hobby horses with her. If he couldn't have his own family, he could have Morgan's! Well, perhaps not his mother—but his brother and sister-in-law were definitely an improvement on anything the Rivingdons had produced.

Loftus rang for tea and cakes.

When the door opened, it was not the maid. It was Morgan and Lady Notley. Loftus fought the urge to flinch as the mothers caught sight of one another.

"Lady Rivingdon," said Lady Notley.

Mother's mouth puckered like the rear end of a cat. "Lady Notley."

For a moment Loftus thought there would be fireworks, but he realised, with a dawning sense of astonishment, that not only did the rules of polite society forbid them from screeching at each other, but also neither of their mothers could express their obvious disapproval of the marriage without it reflecting badly on themselves. To save their pride, and their mothers were nothing but prideful, both ladies had to pretend that they were satisfied with the match, or else risk being taken to task for raising a boy with terrible morals. Because Loftus and Morgan were equally to blame, and had proclaimed as much when they'd been discovered in the maze. Their mothers were, quite simply, stymied.

Morgan came to sit beside him, and they exchanged a disbelieving look. Loftus ducked his face to hide a smile, and reached out and took his hand.

Both their mothers glared at their linked fingers, but said nothing.

"Well," Cecil said happily when the tea and cakes arrived, beaming around at everyone, "isn't this *nice?*"

And Loftus supposed that in a ridiculous way, it was.

∼

"*L*oftus," Morgan chided that night, "you are supposed to be looking at the embroidery! Are you looking at the embroidery?" He jutted himself forward, lifting his chin, and knowing full well that his husband was not looking at the embroidery on the collar of his nightshirt, but rather at the way the neckline slipped and displayed his clavicle.

"Embroidery," Loftus echoed, raising his hand to run his fingertip along Morgan's collarbone.

Morgan shivered at the touch. "Yes, is it not lovely?"

"Oh." Loftus's gaze met his, and dropped again to his throat. His beautiful mouth curled. "Yes, it is indeed lovely. Such delicate craftsmanship."

Morgan twirled, breaking their contact but making his nightshirt balloon around him for a moment. "Warry bought it for me, which is very nice of him, for I do not know when we will have the means to shop at M. Verreau's again, alas! It is alright for you, in your dashing uniform, but what about me? My clothes will not be so fashionable next Season!"

"Lucky you have already caught a husband then," Loftus teased.

Morgan laughed, and reeled him in to peck him on the lips. "Yes, it is lucky indeed."

"You ought not to have spent so much on my gift. Beautiful though it is." He glanced toward the wardrobe, where he'd propped the new olive wood stick Morgan had given him.

"I needed to, Loftus. Believe me."

Loftus was already dressed for bed, in a nightshirt that was not as lovely as Morgan's, although he refused to admit it. But at least he had mostly stopped wearing yellow. The currant coat Morgan had given him was quite his favourite, and Morgan showed his approval in very enthusiastic ways when he was dressing himself. Dressing together was the best part of the day, because it usually led to undressing together, and then some other wonderful things happening before they could even think of clothing again. The servants were accustomed to them coming late to breakfast.

Loftus lifted Morgan's hand and kissed it, and threw him a smile as he headed for bed.

The fact they shared a bed was also a scandal, Morgan supposed, for Mama had gasped on her tour of the house, but Morgan didn't want to get cold feet by traversing the hallway in the middle of the night whenever he wished to visit his husband for matrimonial relations. At their current rate, it would entail at least three visits a night, and how could they cuddle together afterwards and gaze into one another's eyes if they were in separate bedrooms?

He watched as Loftus checked the curtains were properly closed to keep the sunlight out in the morning, and then climbed into bed.

Morgan picked up his candlestick and joined him. He set the candlestick down on the table on his side of the bed, and blew the candle out. The light from Loftus's was enough to read by.

Agnes gave a sleepy bleat from her basket.

Morgan climbed under the covers and curled against Loftus's side. He put his head on Loftus's shoulder and splayed his fingers over his chest so that he could feel his heartbeat. "Tea today with our mothers wasn't terrible."

Loftus gave him a look as though he'd suggested pairing a green hat with orange ribbons, or something equally ghastly.

"Well, they didn't murder one another, at least."

"Or us."

"Or us," Morgan agreed. He tapped his fingers on Loftus's chest. "Now, what chapter were we up to? Eight?"

"Eight," Loftus agreed, and reached for the book. He opened it to the correct page, and began to read. "'Slyfeel let out a wicked laugh as he entered the nunnery.' Oh, this will be a good one!"

Morgan laughed in delighted anticipation, and together they began to read.

AFTERWORD

Thank you so much for reading *A Rival for Rivingdon*! We hope that you enjoyed it. We would very much appreciate it if you could take a few moments to leave a review on Amazon or Goodreads, or on your social media platform of choice.

ABOUT J.A. ROCK

J.A. Rock is an author of LGBTQ romance and suspense novels, as well as an audiobook narrator under the name Jill Smith. When not writing or narrating, J.A. enjoys reading, collecting historical costumes, and failing miserably at gardening. J.A. lives in the Ohio wilds with an extremely judgmental dog, Professor Anne Studebaker.

You can find J.A.'s website at https://jarockauthor.com.

ABOUT LISA HENRY

Lisa likes to tell stories, mostly with hot guys and happily ever afters.

Lisa lives in tropical North Queensland, Australia. She doesn't know why, because she hates the heat, but she suspects she's too lazy to move. She spends half her time slaving away as a government minion, and the other half plotting her escape.

She attended university at sixteen, not because she was a child prodigy or anything, but because of a mix-up between international school systems early in life. She studied History and English, neither of them very thoroughly.

Lisa has been published since 2012, and was a LAMBDA finalist for her quirky, awkward coming-of-age romance *Adulting 101*, and a Rainbow Awards finalist for 2019's *Anhaga*.

You can join Lisa's Facebook reader group at Lisa Henry's Hangout, and find her website at lisahenryonline.com.

ALSO BY J.A. ROCK AND LISA HENRY

When All the World Sleeps

Another Man's Treasure

Fall on Your Knees

The Preacher's Son

Mark Cooper versus America (Prescott College #1)

Brandon Mills versus the V-Card (Prescott College #2)

The Good Boy (The Boy #1)

The Boy Who Belonged (The Boy #2)

The Playing the Fool Series

The Two Gentlemen of Altona

The Merchant of Death

Tempest

The Lords of Bucknall Club Series

A Husband for Hartwell

A Case for Christmas

A Rival for Rivingdon

A Sanctuary for Soulden

An Affair for Aumont

ALSO BY J.A. ROCK

By His Rules

Wacky Wednesday (Wacky Wednesday #1)

The Brat-tastic Jayk Parker (Wacky Wednesday #2)

Calling the Show

Take the Long Way Home

The Grand Ballast

Minotaur

The Silvers

The Subs Club (The Subs Club #1)

Pain Slut (The Subs Club #2)

Manties in a Twist (The Subs Club #3)

24/7 (The Subs Club #4)

Sub Hunt (The Subs Club #5)

"Beauties" (All in Fear anthology)

"Stranger Than Stars" (Take a Chance Anthology)

Sight Unseen: A Collection of Five Anonymous Novellas

Touch Up: A Rose & Thorns Novel, with Katey Hawthorne

ALSO BY LISA HENRY

The Parable of the Mustard Seed

Naked Ambition

Dauntless

Anhaga

Two Man Station (Emergency Services #1)

Lights and Sirens (Emergency Services #2)

The California Dashwoods

Adulting 101

Sweetwater

He Is Worthy

The Island

Tribute

One Perfect Night

Fallout, with M. Caspian

Dark Space (Dark Space #1)

Darker Space (Dark Space #2)

Starlight (Dark Space #3)

With Tia Fielding

Family Recipe

Recipe for Two

A Desperate Man

With Sarah Honey

Red Heir

<u>Elf Defence</u>

Socially Orcward

Writing as Cari Waites

<u>Stealing Innocents</u>

Manufactured by Amazon.ca
Acheson, AB

15619495R00133